WAYNE STINNETT

APALACH
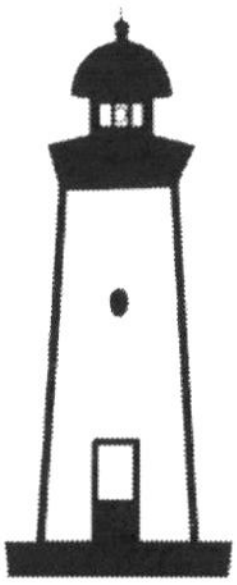

AFFAIR

A JESSE MCDERMITT NOVEL

CARIBBEAN ADVENTURE SERIES, VOLUME 28

DOWN ISLAND PRESS

Published by DOWN ISLAND PRESS, LLC, 2024
Beaufort, SC

Library of Congress cataloging-in-publication Data
Stinnett, Wayne
Apalach Affair/Wayne Stinnett
p. cm. - (A Jesse McDermitt Novel)

ISBN: 978-1-956026-87-0 (print)

If you'd like to receive my newsletter, please sign up on my website.
WWW.WAYNESTINNETT.COM.
Once or twice a month, I'll bring you insights into my private life and writing habits, with updates on what I'm working on, special deals I hear about, and new books by other authors that I'm reading.

THE GASPAR'S REVENGE SHIP'S STORE IS OPEN 24/7.

There, you can purchase all kinds of swag
related to my books, and even my books themselves,
in whatever format you choose.
You can find it at
WWW.GASPARS-REVENGE.COM

ALSO BY WAYNE STINNETT

The Jerry Snyder Caribbean Mystery Series

Wayward Sons
Vodou Child
Friends of the Devil

The Charity Styles Caribbean Thriller Series

Merciless Charity
Ruthless Charity
Reckless Charity
Enduring Charity
Vigilant Charity
Lost Charity
Elusive Charity
Liable Charty

The Young Jesse McDermitt Tropical Adventure Series

A Seller's Market
Bad Blood

The Jesse McDermitt Caribbean Adventure Series

Fallen Out
Fallen Palm
Fallen Hunter
Fallen Pride
Fallen Mangrove
Fallen King
Fallen Honor
Fallen Tide
Fallen Angel
Fallen Hero
Rising Storm
Rising Fury
Rising Force
Rising Charity
Rising Water
Rising Spirit
Rising Thunder
Rising Warrior
Rising Moon
Rising Tide
Steady as She Goes
All Ahead Full
Man Overboard
Cast Off
Fish On!
Weigh Anchor
Swift and Silent
Apalach Affair
Dominica Blue

Rainbow of Collars Motivational Series

Blue Collar to No Collar
No Collar to Tank Top

Dedicated to Dawn Lee McKenna,
her family, and her fans.

"You never know when you are doing something
that is affecting someone."
—Martin Sheen

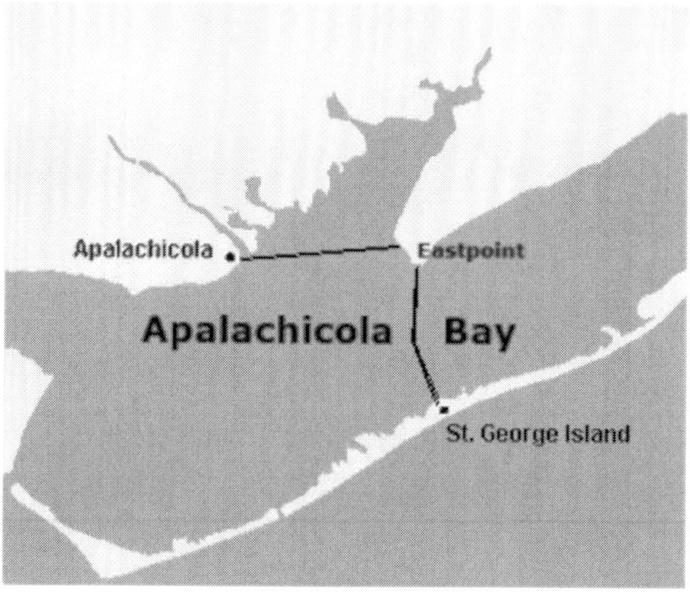

Apalachicola Bay, Florida

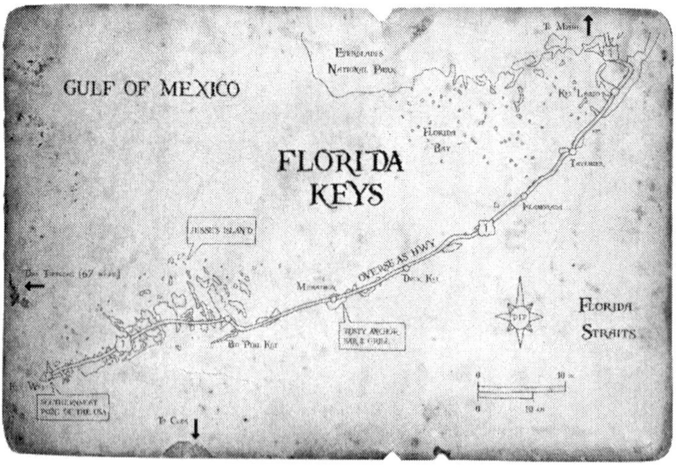

The Florida Keys

CHAPTER ONE

Apalachicola National Forest
Wednesday, August 21

Deep in the backwoods of central Franklin County, the natural beauty of the dry sandhills, tall pines, and scattered scrub had been sullied. You could see evidence of it in the leaves of myrtles, live oaks, and saw palmetto fronds that hung forlornly, as if giving in to defeat against the dense, seasonal sea fog that covered the low-lying areas.

Needles from hundred-year-old sand pines littered the forest floor, which was typical, and was what made the pine forest so quiet and peaceful. But usually, the needles were brown with age. Now, newly fallen green and yellow pine needles covered the old in many areas.

There were no birds chirping in the scrub either, no cry from a red-tailed hawk, watching for movement on the forest floor. There was no rustle of mice under the pine bed, no six-lined racers scurrying after insects, and no gopher tortoises burrowing into the soft sand.

But it wasn't the fog that was distressing the flora and fauna.

Some nights, there was a heavy, chemical scent in the air.

The odor was pungent and smelled like a dozen raw eggs wrapped in a urine-soaked towel and left in a closed container for weeks in the blazing Gulf Coast summer sun.

The air in the pine forest was so still, the sea fog from miles downstream followed the contour of the land, filling the low-lying areas first. The stench seemed to have settled on and blanketed everything.

Determining exactly which direction the disgusting meth lab odor was coming from was virtually impossible.

It was confined to a few limited areas, but where it was located, it touched everything, and seemed omnipresent.

There were no traffic sounds that far out in the woods. The nearest road was miles away, and people were also absent so deep in that part of the forest. The particular areas where the chemical odors were evident were nearly surrounded by inhospitable wetlands and swamps.

There were no distant voices from hikers on one of the many rustic trails, either. They were also too far away and across the wetlands.

It was exactly that last factor that had prompted Leo Bishop to choose such a remote area.

The labs' locations were a forty-five-minute drive from his trailer in Eastpoint, just across the bridge from Apalach, then a good thirty- or forty-minute hike, way off the marked trails, deep into the boundary area between Tate's Hell State Forest and the larger Apalachicola National Forest.

The smell from each meth lab stayed confined to a relatively small and totally isolated part of the forest, as remote a location as you could find in Franklin County.

Leo and a few of his friends had built several mini labs, each capable of cranking out up to two hundred grams of ice in a single cook. They used a different lab for each batch, and only cooked once a week, in the middle of the week, when there were fewer tourists hiking the trails through the woodland.

The tiny labs were underground, a mile from any marked trails, and so far, they'd proven to be impossible for the cops to locate, though the police had sent out teams of deputies at least twice.

On one of those occasions, Leo had been manning one of the labs in preparation for the night's cook. He'd had to pull the solar panel down inside and hide out till the searchers passed.

Leo and three others had dug the holes at night, taking several weeks to complete each lab. While setting them up, they always took a different route through the woods. Each lab had a GPS location they could find on foot and known only to the four of them.

All four were built at the top of low sandhills to minimize rainwater intrusion into the lab. They'd carefully cleared a large area of pine straw and twigs to be used later, then began digging the holes.

The top layer of soil had been loose sand and would cascade into the hole as they dug. Deeper, it became more densely packed brown dirt.

So, they'd cleared the loose sand from around the holes to make room for the roof, which would extend two feet beyond the sides of the main holes.

Building each roof had been the really hard part. They'd each had to lug three ten-foot-long boards to each site, to be used for the frame, plus four sheets of corrugated metal for the top. That alone had taken three nights.

But Leo knew his idea would work, and he knew they could do it, and kept urging his friends on when they got tired.

Once the holes were excavated, they brought five large, wooden pallets to each site— again, lugging them through the forest under cover of darkness. The pallets were screwed together to make walls and a floor to hold back the dirt and allow any water that did find its way in, to leach into the soil below the floor.

The roof was simple two-by-four frame construction, covered with corrugated panels of galvanized metal, with a small hatch on one side, where they could climb down using boards nailed to the underside of one of the pallets.

The roofs fit neatly over the holes, slanted slightly downhill, and sat below the loose top layer of dirt. Then the whole thing was covered with the sand, and the remaining dirt was scattered around the area they'd cleared.

Once finished, the ground level looked normal, and then they raked the pine straw back into place and smoothed everything out.

When finished, each lab was five feet square, and the corrugated metal roof extending another two-and-a-half feet beyond the walls would keep rainwater from seeping back into the holes by allowing it to run off below the loose sand and pine needles and seep into the ground on the downhill side.

Each lab was equipped with a propane camp stove, a battery- powered blower on the end of a long tube, which could be attached to an overhanging tree branch while cooking, then stashed inside during the day. The battery for the fan and an LED light was kept charged by a small solar panel.

The only outwardly visible sign of the lab was a small string tangled on a nearby palmetto frond or scrub oak branch to mark the spot. At first, the other end had been tied to the handle on the hatch, but after a few visits, they didn't need it anymore.

The day before a cook, someone had to go out and spend the whole day just sitting there watching the solar panel and shifting it out of the shade as the sun moved across the sky. They couldn't leave it out unattended in case some lost hiker came along.

Or in case of something like what had happened the fifth week of operation, when the cops had sent a search party out.

Leo had been at lab number two when he heard them coming long before they were within sight, and he'd wasted no time getting below ground with the solar panel.

He'd sat huddled in the bottom of the hole, listening and hoping they wouldn't notice the disturbed area at the hatch. He'd heard several voices, and they made lots of noise, which meant they'd been very close.

After a few tense minutes, the voices and sounds faded and Leo had been so sure of himself afterward that he'd climbed out and continued charging the battery.

All four labs were situated three or four hundred feet apart, each one on the opposite side of a low hill from a small stream about fifty yards away.

Each cook produced a little over 200 grams of meth, less than half a pound. What was left was about two or three ounces of unusable waste, which they just dumped in the little stream when they cleaned all the equipment.

Leo had scouted all around the sandhill area and knew that the stream wound back and forth for over a mile before it flowed into a small lake next to a horse farm, and then emptied into the Apalachicola River after another mile. So there wasn't much chance of anyone smelling it.

For a good ten miles after that, there wasn't anything or anyone downstream, so there was little chance of anyone noticing anything they did so far back in the forest.

Out of each batch they cooked, the first sixty grams were distributed to the four people involved, fifteen grams each for their own use.

After that, what was left, which was always more than a hundred grams, was sold on the streets of Carrabelle, Eastpoint, and Apalach, but mostly in the rural areas and trailer parks, where people came out of unlit homes when Leo's Mustang pulled up, cash in one hand and a bubbler in the other.

At a hundred bucks a gram, they were raking it in, but more than half of the ten grand they brought in every week went to supplies for the next cook.

The four of them split the rest of the money equally, each man pocketing about a thousand bucks for the week.

It was a lot of work on the front end with no pay, but now that everything was operational, the bulk of their time on the project was spent getting the ingredients for the next cook.

And they could blow all the clouds they wanted on top of the thousand bucks.

None of them were heavy users. They had it under control. And each of them worked part-time day jobs.

Through the rest of the week, each of the four of them were tasked with gathering the needed supplies for the next cook—ephedrine cold medicine, acetone, red phosphorus, hydriodic acid, and a number of other ingredients, none of which was easy to find, and, if bought together or in large batches, raised red flags. So, they gathered ingredients for days, spreading the purchases out over a wide area, even all the way to Panama City and Tallahassee, which were larger and had more sources.

Scrounging all the stuff needed was equal to another part-time job for each man.

They followed the exact same recipe and procedure for every cook, never deviating from it in the slightest. Leo and his friends knew a good product when they smoked it and had come up with exactly the ice they wanted for themselves. They had the process down pat after a couple of months, and the cops had no idea.

Well...they had an *idea*. They just didn't know the backwoods, *way* out past where the blacktop ends.

CHAPTER TWO

Gulf of Mexico, south of Apalachicola Bay
Sunday, September 1

The sun blazed white-hot in the midday sky, reflecting off the water with nearly blinding intensity. The dog days of summer had passed, but it seemed someone had forgotten to tell Sirius, also called the Dog Star, to turn off the furnace.

From early July until late August, Sirius, the brightest star in the *winter* sky, would rise after dawn, and for those "dog days," it wasn't visible from Earth. Early man learned that as the rise of Sirius came closer and closer to sunrise, the hottest days would soon be upon them. In ancient times, the disappearance of the Dog Star was the harbinger of hot, muggy weather, heavy rains, and flooding. It still is today, but now we know why.

Summers are hot. And in the little latitudes, hot and sticky.

But if I had to choose between extremes, I'd take temperatures and humidity, both in the nineties, over boots and heavy coats any day of the week and twice on Sunday.

I was born and raised in Southwest Florida and spent a lot of my youth outdoors and on the water. I don't remember ever having air conditioning in our house until I went to live with my grandparents when I was eight. Even then, Pap didn't have it installed until two years later, when Mam insisted, during a particularly hot and humid summer.

As far as my eyes could see, the water was flat calm, not the slightest ripple marring the surface. Well, except astern.

We were motoring almost due north at four knots, running solely on the stored energy of the sun. The triple ripples *Taranis* left in her wake provided the only texture to a perfectly smooth mirror of blue water. Our trail could be seen all the way to the horizon.

I sat at the flybridge helm, shirtless, with my bare feet up on the console. The only wind was four knots over the bow, and that was only because of our forward movement through the still, heavy air. I had the sunroof closed to the tormenting sun and was fairly comfortable, but again, I like hot and humid weather, so I was alone on the flybridge.

Over the past six months, we'd stayed fairly close to home, taking weekly trips on *Taranis* out into Florida Bay, up along Cape Sable and the Ten Thousand Islands, and even as far north as Naples.

Our outings before this one had been short two- to three-day trips, completely unplugged and off the grid, getting used to our new floating home.

And that's exactly what *Taranis* was—a home away from home. As far as living space went, she had more than our one-thousand-square-foot stilt-house in the Content Keys, and she had twice as many bedrooms.

These last six months were also spent getting to know our new family member, and for Tank to get used to life on a boat. Some dogs just aren't cut out for life afloat, but Tank had really taken to it. Which was good, because there was no second option.

Until recently, he'd had to remain inside while we were underway, and watched closely while on deck at anchor. Growing puppies are clumsy, but Tank was now a little over eight months old, full of curiosity and far less ungainly, perhaps because he now had more weight holding him to the deck. He was a very good swimmer and well trained... at least as far as basic commands went, anyway.

Since his initial obedience training with Warren Kennedy, a retired Miami-Dade police lieutenant-turned-police-canine trainer, he'd come to live with us, and learn more about his role in our family.

Tank was a fast learner and had quickly picked up many more simple commands, like "fetch" and "catch." He also knew the words "swim" and "boat ride" very well.

At times, he even seemed to anticipate what was coming next. I could tell from the start that he was a highly intelligent dog, and next month, he'd be going back to Warren's training facility for four weeks of protection training. Then he and Warren would fly over and join us in the Med and there would be several more weeks of onboard training that Savannah, Alberto, and I would also be a part of.

Warren had predicted that the second phase would be the most difficult. Tank's father was a Tibet mountain dog, or more correctly, a Tibetan mastiff, one of the least aggressive canines on the planet due to their size. A large male could outweigh me, and I'm two-twenty. Because they're so big, they have nothing to be afraid *of*, so are naturally non-aggressive.

However, they're an extremely protective breed, and Warren had told us that Tank would probably see us as his "flock," to be protected at all costs. But getting a non-aggressive dog to overcome that trait on command would be difficult.

Few people meeting Tank in the last couple of months thought he was a puppy. At eight-and-a-half months, he was bigger than most adult dogs, already tipping the scales at ninety pounds. Warren had told us he'd be close to one-twenty by the time he was full grown. Huge for a Lab, which was what his mother was, but on the smallish size for a male Tibet mountain dog.

He looked like a large adult black Lab in almost every way, from his webbed toes and dense black coat to his powerful tail.

Except his head.

Tank's forehead was higher and more pronounced, with a large skull and heavy jowls, like his mountain dog father. His neck was nearly as big as my thigh and his chest was a full hand width between his front legs. His shoulders, back, and legs were beginning to develop larger muscles, and with the shorter Lab-like coat, easily seen flexing as he walked.

We were going to have one very powerful dog on our hands soon.

Alberto had been taking him out to the shallows on the west side of our island in front of Jimmy and Naomi's house almost every day we were home for "boogie board training."

We'd bought a harness for Tank and Alberto would ride a kneeboard while the playful puppy pulled him at a trot in the shallows.

A trot for Tank was a dead run for Alberto, who'd watched a bunch of sled dog videos on YouTube and thought it might be good exercise for Tank.

Just like any repetitive exercise, it was. Tank's pulling power was freakish and he was still gaining two pounds every week. I doubted there was a man alive who could hold him back if he wanted to move. He obediently followed commands to stop or heel, but if you didn't give them, he could drag two men through the palmettos chasing a squirrel.

During our short cruises around Southwest Florida's coast, we often traveled late into the night, and a few times, Savannah had stayed up with me and we'd talked at length about the events of last spring, and of other problems over the years.

She'd made the point to me during one of those heart-to-hearts that Tank wasn't the only "freak of nature" in her life, because she also had me to deal with. I possessed an unusual amount of righteous indignation at the suffering of others and that, coupled with good genetics, dogged determination, and years of hard training, made me more dangerous than most.

She'd told me that she wanted to help and support me in any way she could any time I saw a wrong that needed to be righted. But she insisted on always being privy to everything going on, and she'd demanded equal veto rights.

And I'd agreed, not that it mattered. Where *Taranis* could take us, it was unlikely trouble would follow.

We had become very familiar with all of *Taranis's* systems and capabilities through the spring and summer and we'd finally cast off the lines three days ago for a three-week cruise around the eastern half of the Gulf of Mexico, starting with a direct course, skirting the Southwest Florida coast, then continuing to Apalachicola Bay and arriving by the first of September.

The crossing would be a final test of full-time passage-making speed and energy consumption. We'd carefully monitored our power usage and had become accustomed to doing all the things that required energy during daylight, like cooking, communications, and bathing, while the solar panels provided more energy than the electric motors used.

During the day, with good sunlight, we could power all the systems *and* the two electric motors, while still supplying enough to slowly recharge the huge battery banks in the mechanical room that everything drew power from.

The first day, we'd motored at just three knots and the following morning, when the sun began recharging the batteries, we still had thirty percent. Since then, we'd been cruising constantly at four knots and had crossed the Gulf of Mexico using no fuel at all.

Taranis's whole flybridge roof, except the retractable sunroof, was covered with solar panels, as was the brow over the lower helm's windshield, and they produced more energy than we used to motor at that speed, keeping us moving, while recharging the batteries.

At night, the stored energy in the batteries slowly dropped as the motors drained them, and by dawn they were almost depleted and waiting for the sun to start again.

Taranis had been designed to be able to motor continuously at 3.5 knots without using any fuel, so I was really happy with the extra half-knot during the crossing.

Of course, that couldn't always be expected. We'd been motoring northward, and the panels were exposed to the sun all day as it passed across us. Going east or west, the brow panels would be shaded by the flybridge for part of the day. But unlike those on the flat roof, they were angled more toward the sun when heading east in the morning or west in the evening, so they produced more than lying flat for those few hours.

There was a switch and a button on the dash, and Alberto had painted the button red, with a gold lightning bolt, and dubbed it the "Thunder Button" in honor of the lightning bolts the Celtic god Taranis could hurl.

Taranis could cross any ocean on electric power, but if we needed more speed, with the flip of the ignition switch and a press of the Thunder Button, the 650-horsepower Caterpillar diesel two decks below would awaken, and we could easily outrun any storm.

At night, we kept energy usage to a minimum, conserving battery power for the electric motors in the amas. If needed, we could run at about eight knots, but even with the dedicated fifty-kilowatt generator kicking on, our range was limited to about five hours, or roughly forty nautical miles, and then we'd be running on generator power with the motors running at half speed. But at three or four knots, we could cross the Pacific without using a drop of fuel.

Savannah and Alberto were down in the salon, playing a board game with Maddy, who had decided to accompany us and help out. Alberto adored her, and at twelve, probably had the beginnings of an adolescent crush on the young woman. Maddy was almost twenty-five, but she had an innocent, child-like way about her, especially when she was around kids.

Also with us on the trip were Savannah's and my daughter Florence, and her husband David Stone, both recently graduated from University of Florida. Though Flo had started a year behind him, she'd just finished her degree over the summer, and had walked across the stage two weeks ago, just three months after he did.

David had graduated last spring and he'd asked me if they could come along as sort of a graduation present for her.

They'd both worked hard and deserved a late summer escape.

Hearing footsteps behind me on the stairs leading down to the cockpit, I turned and saw David coming up, with Tank bounding ahead of him and then coming to my side. For the past two weeks, he'd been allowed to be off his leash while on deck, unless we had to move quickly to outrun a storm. So far, the weather had been perfect.

"Hey, Tank," I said softly, when he put his big head on my knee for me to stroke. "How you doin', boy?"

He lifted his head and looked over the dash, his nose twitching as he tested the air.

"He hates being cooped up," David said, taking a seat at the port- side lounge and looking around. "But there's not much to see up here either, is there?"

"I saw a dolphin about an hour back," I replied. "And a loggerhead surfaced off to port a few minutes ago. He can smell and hear things we can't."

Tank barked, his voice deep and jowls flapping, as his dark brown eyes locked on something ahead of us and above the horizon.

"Good boy, Tank," I said, stroking his head again, then turning to my son-in-law. "Never assume there's nothing there, just because you can't see anything."

"What's he see?"

I shrugged, then scoured the area with a pair of binoculars in the direction Tank was looking. After a moment, I saw it. Or at least, saw motion.

"First sign of land," I replied. "A flock of seagulls."

David looked ahead, squinting against the bright sunlight. "What are they doing?"

"Probably diving on a school of baitfish," I replied, glancing at the chart plotter and noting that we were still almost forty miles from the entrance to Apalachicola Bay.

"Can I ask you something?" David asked.

"You just did," I replied. "But what's on your mind?"

"Why are you *really* going to Apalachicola?"

David was a technical contractor for Armstrong Research, an organization I'd once worked for. Jack Armstrong and his head of security, Colonel Travis Stockwell, fielded a small army of covert operators, doing things governments couldn't dirty their hands with.

David knew a few of the operators, but mostly by code names, as he'd worked as an analyst for a while. So, he was naturally curious if I was actually retired or still connected, and our trip was some deep cover mission.

It was an easy assumption for him to make. Most of Armstrong's operatives didn't even know one *another*.

I glanced over at him and grinned before replying, "Oysters."

"Harvesting has been shut down for a few years," David said. "Won't reopen until the end of next year."

"Sustainable aquaculture hasn't," I replied. "An old friend of mine started raising oysters there in the bay about eight years ago. He used to be a shrimper in Key West and helped me set up the first aquaculture tank on the island."

David gave me a serious look. "You're really going four hundred miles at a crawl to eat oysters you could have shipped overnight?"

"Not just eat," I replied. "I'm curious to see what Carl's been up to lately. Did you know there used to be an extensive oyster bed in Chokoloskee Bay, and some say there were once huge oyster beds in Florida Bay."

David shook his head. "But crossing the Gulf of Mexico in late summer? You're not worried about storms?"

"Worried and uninformed are two different things," I replied. "Sure, it's a confined space, but the Gulf's still pretty big, and if a storm forms, we'll know about it." I pointed upward. "We might be unplugged from shore, but we're still connected to the internet, and *Taranis* can reach any point in the Gulf of Mexico from any other point faster than most hurricanes move."

"What about the ones that move faster?"

For all his learning, training, and intelligence, David sometimes overlooked the obvious.

"We wouldn't run in the same direction the storm's going, Son. We'd crash on the shore with a hurricane bearing down behind us."

"So, this is just a fun cruise?" he asked, still sounding a bit skeptical.

"Almost all fun," I replied. "For the last three days, we haven't used a drop of fuel, and we now know we can motor about ninety to a hundred miles a day unless we go farther north, where there's less sun. Anywhere in the tropics to somewhere else in the tropics, non-stop, zero fuel burn."

I let that sink in for a minute, then added, "Besides, September is traditionally the start of oyster season—the months with an R in them."

Tank barked again, then stood on his hind legs with his front paws on the forward bulkhead, continuing to look ahead.

I stood and trained the binos on the gulls. There was something moving on or just below the water's surface.

"What is it?" David asked, rising and standing beside me.

"Something floating in the water," I replied.

I used the autopilot control and adjusted our course a few degrees to pass closer.

I handed him the binoculars. "Have a look."

He gazed through the field glasses for a moment, then handed them back. "Something dead, and the gulls are feeding on it?"

"More likely the gulls are picking up scraps," I replied, spotting the first fin. "Sharks are feeding on something big from below."

It wasn't uncommon to see sharks feeding in the open ocean. Usually, it was a dead whale or dolphin, or even another shark.

As we got closer, I could see the sharks moving around the carcass, which was brown and wide, and barely floating. The sharks moved in slowly, in a leisurely fashion, taking bites in non-frenzied feeding. There were at least five of them.

"What is it?" David asked, as bare feet could be heard on the steps.

I handed him the binos again, as I turned to see Savannah coming up, her golden hair bouncing in the light breeze. "You changed course?"

"Something in the water," David said, raising the binos again. "Tank spotted the gulls from two miles away."

She stepped up beside Tank and hugged his neck, ruffling the thick fur on his chest. "Good boy, Tank. You have some sharp eyes. Gulls are a good sign." Then she stood and looked over the bow. "What is it?"

"Sharks feeding on a carcass of some kind," I replied. "The gulls are picking up the scraps."

"It's a... horse," David said, incredulously.

"A *horse*?" I pressed, glancing over at him. "How does a horse get all the way out here?"

CHAPTER THREE

It'd been brought up a couple of times in the last few weeks that they should consider ramping up production to make the operation a real money-maker, but Leo had explained that to do it right, they'd have to save up to make bigger inventory purchases ahead of time.

They were already putting in a lot of hours getting the needed supplies for just *one* cook a week, and they'd agreed buying more at one spot would raise suspicion. That meant even more time spent driving to more places, if they wanted to continue buying ingredients in small quantities.

Doubling production meant running two labs once a week instead of one, and needing twice the ingredients. Two labs twice a week would be a big upfront cost, but would make them rich in a hurry. If the cops stayed away. Running all four labs nightly for a week would set them up for several years. Doing all four for just a month, and they could all retire. But it had to be done right.

The amount of supplies that'd need to be purchased to do that boggled Leo's mind. Ramping up production meant they'd need to increase the workload exponentially and was another reason to keep unspent cash in reserve.

But the way the zombies came out of the trailers each time he drove up a certain road told Leo they could never make enough.

He slowed, then turned off Highway 98 on a side road in Eastpoint, headed north into the boonies. A mile up the road, he turned into a mobile home park, then turned left on the first street he came to.

Watching his mirrors carefully, as well as both windows and ahead, he crept down the street slowly, a loaded .38 sitting on the console in plain sight beside him.

The deep rumble of the Mustang's engine was like a wild bird call to the tweakers, and Leo was unworried about a lawman patrolling the trailer park. He thought his cover job was super smart and it allowed him to meet all kinds of people.

It'd taken him a year, but he'd managed to get his juvenile record expunged when he was eighteen and had avoided any trouble with the law since then, so he could be a registered rideshare driver. The sticker on the Mustang's windshield could explain why his car was moving slowly through a neighborhood at night.

He only logged on to the rideshare app a couple of times a week to pick up a few fares, just to keep up appearances. Besides, driving tourists around was just fun.

A girl came running out of a trailer behind him on his left, and he stopped. As she approached the Mustang's driver's side, Leo put one hand on the gun, watching her as well as the surrounding trailers closely.

She was skinny, not slim, and Leo recognized her when she stepped into the light from a neighbor's porch.

He'd known Candy most of his life. She was just a couple years older than him and had been a very pretty and popular girl all through school.

Now she was just another tweaker who couldn't get enough and would do anything to get it.

"Hey, Leo," she said, standing beside the car, one hand on her hip.

Three years ago, the pose would have made any guy's jaw drop, but now it was just sad. At twenty-four, she looked decades older, with stained teeth, frizzy hair, bony hips, and ribs showing below a deflated tube top.

"Whatcha need, Candy?" he asked warily.

It'd be just like these trailer park tweakers to try to distract him, then rob him. He no longer found Candy distracting.

"I got fifty," she replied, holding out a wad of cash, mostly ones.

He reached into his shirt pocket, where he kept the smallest rocks in tiny little zippered plastic bags.

"Fifty's half a G," he said, holding it up for her to see the weight—0.51 grams, written on the little bag with a marker.

Her eyes widened, and she stepped closer. "That's all?" she asked, attempting a seductive pout. "I'll throw in a blowjob for a whole gram."

"Not for fifty," Leo replied, moving the bag back to his shirt pocket.

"Okay, okay," Candy responded, thrusting the money toward him.

Leo took it and handed her the tiny bag. Then she took off running back toward her trailer as a man approached from the opposite direction.

It took ten minutes and three more stops in the trailer park, but Leo sold the last of the twenty-five grams he was responsible for, and then tore out of the trailer park like he'd stolen the Mustang.

When he reached 98, he hung a right and hit the gas again. But he quickly slowed as he saw blue lights ahead on the highway's shoulder. A Franklin County sheriff's deputy had two cars pulled over, a Jeep Cherokee and a Chevy pickup.

As he rolled slowly past, preparing to turn left just beyond the flashing blue lights, Leo realized he had it backward. It wasn't one cop with two speeders.

The black Cherokee had a blue light flashing on the dash.

Out of the corner of his eye, Leo spotted a short woman with dark hair, wearing a black windbreaker that had FCSO on the back.

"Good goin' there, Dep-uh-dee *Dogs*," Leo said, looking back at them in the mirror. "That guy must be some kinda *des-per-ah-do*."

Turning left, Leo drove a quarter mile farther to the stop sign at old US-98, now called the Big Bend Scenic Byway Coastal Trail. A big name for a narrow little backroad.

He crossed over old 98 to his own street and parked in front of his trailer. Kenny's truck was there, and Marc was with him, both sitting by Leo's fire pit, drinking beers from a small cooler on the ground between them.

"How'd it go?" Kenny asked.

"All gone," Leo replied. "You?"

"We both sold out in ten minutes, man," Marc replied. "We gotta figure out a way to make more."

Leo looked around. "Where's Lucas?"

Kenny waggled his new smart phone. "Just got a text from him. He should be here any minute."

"Then let's go inside," Leo said. "Two cops got someone pulled over out on the highway. I think one of 'em was that lady cop."

Kenny's head came up in alarm. He didn't like cops, and especially didn't like the woman detective and her friend who'd rousted him and Lucas a few years earlier. The friend had punched his lights out after distracting both of them with an upskirt flash.

Leo led the way up the steps and into the trailer. The living room was dominated by a giant 65" plasma TV and gaming console, with a couch and two chairs clustered in front of it.

The squeak of brakes could be heard outside, and as Leo parted the blinds to look, the other two slumped into the new recliner chairs.

"He's here," Leo said, moving to the couch and sitting down.

A moment later, Lucas opened the door and came in. "Cops out on the highway, man."

Leo nodded. "Yeah, I saw 'em a few minutes ago. How'd you do?"

"So-o-old out," Lucas said, pulling a wad of cash from his pocket and taking the last seat.

The others did likewise, and each man started counting his own take.

"Dammit," Leo said, shaking his head. "Only nineteen-ninety-six. I bet that Candy bitch shorted me. She paid mostly in ones, just before Ray-Ray walked up."

"There's a tweaker who makes me nervous, man," Marc said. "Don't worry about it. Give her a smaller cookie next time."

"Two thousand," Kenny said, placing the last bill on his stack.

"Same here," Lucas said.

Marc nodded. "Me too."

"Switch," Leo said, pushing his pile of bills across the coffee table to Lucas, sitting next to him.

Each of them did the same, counting again.

They came up with the same numbers, a haul of $7,996, which was almost double what they'd need to buy the supplies for the next cook.

After setting aside four grand to buy the stuff for the next cook, Leo counted out a thousand to each of them, leaving himself with a stack that was four bucks short.

"Last night's batch was really good, Kenny," he said, handing his friend his cut.

"You already tried it?"

Leo shrugged. "Ray-Ray."

Ray Sprocket was as paranoid as they came. And he was big. Not fat, just all over big. Adding those issues to being a tweaker with a heavy habit made him extremely unpredictable. He always wanted to see Leo take a hit himself to prove he wasn't with the cops.

"It's Wednesday," Lucas said. "Last time we went shoppin' was a week before last Monday, and we only spent twenty-four hundred for the ingredients."

"And the week before that, we spent over four grand," Leo replied, knowing what was coming. "Last week's extra is in reserve, man. We all agreed on a thousand a week."

"What happens if we keep the price down?"

"If it piles up to be more than what it'd cost for a week's supply," Leo said with a shrug, "then we'll all get a bonus. Call it a dividend."

"We all got our stops wrote down," Marc said. "So I say let's switch notebooks and go to the same places we did last week."

"Solid," Leo agreed, nodding. "Knowing what and where *would* save a lot of time, and the prices were good."

There was a light knock on the door.

"Shit!" Leo exclaimed in a low voice, snatching up the stacks of cash and lifting the middle of the tabletop.

There was a magazine drawer beneath it, so he stuck the cash inside with his personal stash, digital scale, and a box of the little bags they used and closed it again.

The knock came again, slightly more urgent.

"Did anyone follow you?" Leo asked Lucas in a hushed tone.

Lucas shook his head, looking nervous.

"Stay cool," Leo whispered, rising and moving toward the door.

He looked through the peephole and saw a man on the porch wearing a pastel peach shirt, his back to the door, and another tall, bald man just beyond him.

Leo gulped and opened the door.

The man on the porch turned slowly as his very large friend moved a hand to the inside of his jacket at his waist.

The movement was intended to send a signal and Leo got it, loud and clear.

The visitor with the peach shirt was older, sandy hair going gray, with fine lines at the corners of his brown eyes. He was smallish but looked fit for his age.

He looked up at Leo and smiled as he absently scratched one eyebrow. "Good evening, Mr. Bishop."

"Um... hi."

The man's smile turned downward. "I understand you've been selling drugs in my town."

CHAPTER FOUR

The animal had been long dead, probably more than a week, with its abdominal cavity bare and little but bone left on the ribs and extremities dangling below what was left of the horse's back.

The sharks were just picking at it, and it wouldn't be long before it sank, so we left them to their grisly task.

I'd heard of livestock being taken down by saltwater crocs before, and in the past there had been incidents of cattle being swept off cargo ships.

The sharks had been smallish and none of the bones seemed to have been missing. That ruled out a croc—they'd grab a leg or head and start rolling until whatever they had hold of came off. I could almost eliminate the horse being in the surf zone with a large shark as a cause for its demise for the same reason. Big sharks rip off large chunks, including bones, but this skeleton had been intact.

The seas had been very calm for days, even weeks, which probably reduced the chance of a livestock transport accident to almost zero as well. Just by how much flesh was removed from the lower legs, I knew it'd been in shallow water at some point, where crabs feed.

The coastline in that area was an estuary of marsh and wetland, so the horse might have gotten bogged in the mud and died, or drowned near shore after falling in the water. Then the carcass might've drifted out to sea, as all manner of crabs, worms, fish, and sharks feasted.

Florence had been sleeping when David and Savannah had joined me topside. She and David had split the midwatch, so by the time she came up to the flybridge an hour later, the grim scene was far astern, and the weather was cooling.

"How does a horse end up in the middle of the ocean?" she asked, puzzled at our explanation.

"Not to split hairs," Savannah said, "but it's a gulf. And none of us has a clue."

"It either fell in the water," I began, "maybe from a bridge, or just waded too deep, and drowned. But I'm sure it came from shore and didn't fall off a livestock transport."

Alberto looked at the chart plotter. "Thirty-six miles from shore?"

"Think you can pull up the currents for this area?" I asked him, knowing he could, and wanting to get his mind off what he'd seen as we'd passed by.

"Don't have to," he said with a slight smirk. "Where Apalachicola is, along with the bay and the whole area it spans, is part of a big river delta. So, it could have drifted down from there."

He got to work on his tablet, which was actually his second one in a year. Not that he broke them; he just needed more power and resources.

"Even this far out," he said, looking up at me, "the current is from the Apalachicola River. It's a big watershed, starting up near *Atlanta*." He looked back down at his tablet and read more. "It discharges nine *million* gallons a minute into the gulf, through Apalachicola Bay."

"That's farmland and forest north of there," Savannah said. "Charity told me about the area. So, maybe it fell in the river somewhere."

I nodded, not that it made any difference to the horse. "That'd be the most likely—"

"*Sécurité, sécurité, sécurité,*" the VHF crackled on channel sixteen, the international hailing and distress frequency. "*This is Coast Guard Sector Mobile, Coast Guard Sector Mobile, Coast Guard Sector Mobile. For a weather advisory in the vicinity of Apalachicola Bay, switch to channel two-two-alpha.*"

David was standing, so he reached up and switched the radio frequency.

"*...adjacent waters up to ten miles offshore. Break... A special weather statement has been issued to all mariners in the vicinity of Apalachicola Bay. A Dense Sea Fog advisory will go into effect from 5PM Sunday until noon on Monday. A dense fog will be moving into the Apalachicola Bay area by late afternoon. Expect close to zero visibility in some areas. This statement covers Bay County, Gulf County, Franklin County, and adjacent waters up to ten miles offshore. Break... A special weather statement—*"

"That's not good," Savannah said, as the message looped and started over. She switched the radio back to channel sixteen. "I don't like unfamiliar waters in the fog at night."

"I'm not a fan of combining any *two* of those."

Alberto and I looked at one another. I scratched at my three-day stubble. "Hm... sounds like bad weather is approaching, Son."

He grinned enthusiastically. "The Thunder Button?"

We both looked at Savannah.

"Can we at least get to an anchorage in the bay before the fog?" she asked. "That friend of Charity's she told us about? If it's going to be dark *and* foggy, I'd rather anchor than go to a marina."

Alberto nodded. "Yeah, easy. And the batteries will be fully charged for the night."

"As much as I've enjoyed the last few days of peace and quiet..." she said, trailing off. Then she looked down at Alberto, "Have I mentioned that I really don't like fog?"

"What's a thunder button?" Florence asked.

I nodded at Alberto. "Show your sister the power of the Celtic god of lightning, Son."

When I stepped away from the helm, Alberto took my place, then flipped the main engine's ignition switch on, and pressed the start button.

The tach on the instrument display came on, showing the big diesel was idling at 625 rpm. Other than that, you could just barely hear the exhaust, more of a low whine from the turbo than anything. Down in the wheelhouse, it'd still be silent.

With the main engine disengaged and warming up, Alberto pushed the twin power controls for the electric motors slowly forward and *Taranis* began to accelerate.

When we reached her top speed of eight knots, running just on the twin electric motors in the amas, Florence got up from the lounge and joined us at the helm.

"That's it?" she asked. "That wasn't so thunderous."

I nodded at Alberto. "Give me twenty-five knots, Son. Slow increase."

His tongue came out of the corner of his mouth as he moved the main engine control into gear, then brought the speed up slowly, and at the same time, toggled the electric motors off, so the shafts would fold up into the hull, lessening the drag.

At eighteen knots, the hull rose imperceptibly, but enough to decrease friction even more with the amas barely touching the water. The surge of speed could be felt.

"Twenty knots, speed over ground," Alberto announced, pulling back a little on the main throttle. He glanced down again, adjusting it a little more. "Twenty-five."

Florence looked around at the calm waters fifteen feet below us. It was impossible to judge speed due to the lack of any fixed reference point, but the wind through her hair was a good indication.

Then she looked back and saw the triple wakes crashing against one another, then morphing into one.

"Twenty-five knots in a boat this big?" she asked rhetorically. "I never would have thought it."

"And we're not at full speed either," Alberto added, then looked up at me. "Can I turn the autopilot off?"

"Otto can't see the water ahead," I replied. "But you can. Drive it like you stole it, Son."

He checked the magnetic compass, then looked at the shadow of the roof supports falling across the dash, as I'd taught him. With no clouds to use as a visual bearing, keeping a shadow in the same place in your peripheral vision for a short time was easier than focusing on the compass.

"You should call the Haverstocks," I said to Savannah. "We might not make it all the way to downtown. Ask them if it's okay for us to lay up for the night in the bay near them. Charity anchored there, so I know it's deep and has good hold."

"I'll send a group text to them and Charity, to let her know we arrived."

Alberto mounted his tablet on the console and plugged it into the communications port, which automatically connected to the modem, and then a StarLink satellite. He pecked at the screen as he steered, glancing over and scrolling.

"What are you looking for, Son?" I asked, as Savannah moved to the lounge to sit down out of the wind.

He tapped the screen and scrolled a bit. "It's a weather statement from St. George Island Airport. It says fog will arrive there at sixteen-thirty and the area will be completely socked in by seventeen hundred."

"Can they be that precise?"

He shrugged. "You're the pilot."

I grinned. Fog *was* a bigger problem for pilots than boaters, especially for those flying under visual flight rules. The airport on St. George Island was just a small strip and most flights in and out were likely VFR.

I glanced at the chart plotter.

"We'll get there after the fog," Alberto said.

I put one hand on the wheel. "Better let me take over, Son. But I want you right here, helping me watch."

He stepped to the side, and I pushed the engine throttle to the stop, feeling a fresh flood of power as *Taranis* accelerated.

"Speed over ground is thirty-one knots," Alberto advised, looking ahead with a big smile.

I couldn't help but grin. I don't know if he picked up his passion for speed from me or it came naturally, but he liked going fast.

Savannah slid off the lounge and stood next to me, holding her phone to her chest. "The Haverstocks have invited us for an oyster roast," she said over the wind. "They have several friends coming and she said there's plenty of room for all of us."

I smiled and nodded. "Charity *did* say the people here were really friendly."

She put the phone back to her ear. "We'd love to attend, Heather. It's very kind of you to offer."

She listened for a moment then looked at the chart plotter. "We should be anchored by four o'clock, so five will be perfect."

After listening a few more seconds she said, "No, that's alright. Our dinghy holds everyone. See you soon."

Savannah ended the call and looked up at me. "I like her. Don't ask me why; I've never met the woman. But Charity spoke so highly of her, and she has a nice voice."

"So did Ted Bundy," I said.

She elbowed my ribs. "If the Haverstocks were serial killers, Charity would have known it and done..." She glanced down at Alberto. "...something. Will we get there before the fog now?"

"We'll beat it by half an hour," Alberto replied. "But no way we'll get all the way to the marina."

For the next hour, *Taranis* gobbled up the miles, with everyone aboard keeping their eyes peeled for any floating debris. Even Tank seemed to understand the immediacy of the situation, if nothing else, and was alert.

I wasn't sure if my boat's insurance policy covered a collision at sea with a horse and if there was more than one, I didn't want to find out.

"There!" Alberto shouted, looking through the binos and pointing off to the left of our course. "I see the lighthouse."

"East Pass is about thirteen miles to the right," I said. "We probably won't see it for another ten minutes or so."

Fifteen minutes later, we moved through the pass at fifteen knots with beachgoers gawking from both sides. Once we cleared the jetty, I turned southwest, brought the speed down to six knots, and shut down the main engine. If the forecast was accurate, we had time to spare and there was too much of a chance of encountering small boats.

"I take back any doubts I had about storms," David said, as everyone relaxed and sat down.

"Jesse designed her to do all we would ever need her to do," Savannah said. "And in trawler comfort and style."

We were in the well-marked main channel, which ran perfectly straight to the high arch of the bridge and beyond. But we could run outside it if we wanted—the surrounding bay was mostly six to seven feet deep, and anywhere there were shoal waters, they were clearly marked as well. Apalachicola was a working bay and there were crab trap floats everywhere outside the channel. Besides, we had to go under the high arch, so there was no reason to leave the channel.

With battery power to spare, I kept the speed at six knots all the way to the bridge, and an hour later, as we were approaching the waypoint near where I guessed the Haverstocks lived, I could see a small gathering of people on shore, several of them moving around backyard tables with white tablecloths.

Two men and a woman separated from the group and walked out onto a dock, the woman waving. When they reached the gazebo at the end of the dock, an amplified voice called out, "You found us."

I tapped the powerful airhorn twice.

"This is Rudy," he said over the PA system. "If you draw less than five feet, you can just tie up to the dock instead of anchoring. We have shore power available, and the expected fog won't lift until noon tomorrow."

"I've seen fog so thick," Savannah said, looking up at me, "that finding the boat in a dinghy wasn't as easy as you'd think."

"So you *want* to tie up to a dock?" I asked.

She ticked off a finger. "Unfamiliar waters." She ticked another. "Inclement weather." Then a third. "It's a moonless night. That's three strikes. Time to tie the lines to *something*."

I switched on the loudspeaker and keyed the mic. "Thanks, Rudy. That'd be nice. We haven't seen land in three days."

"Still think they're serial killers?" Savannah asked.

"You never know," I replied, switching the controls over to the joystick. "Take over, Son. You can practice your docking skills."

"Fi...!" He caught himself. "Um, yeah!"

"Just like on the docking simulator," I told him, stepping aside. "You've done it hundreds of times. There's almost no current, the water's flat calm, and there's no wind at all."

The builder had created several computer apps to practice different tasks, like using the docking station controller, or joystick. A laptop, or in Alberto's case, his tablet, could be plugged directly into the helm and would display very realistic settings. It used the boat's actual joystick control to move the boat on the simulator, and it even worked with the wireless remote.

I turned to David. "Give me a hand with the fenders?"

Savannah's phone beeped and she looked down at it. "Charity responded." She looked up at me. "She says her car's in the Haverstock's garage if we need it."

That surprised me. "Charity owns a car?"

She shrugged. "First I've heard."

"Tell her thanks, and we might take her up on it if we need to make a grocery run."

David and I went down to the side deck and put three fenders out on the port side as Alberto maneuvered *Taranis* toward the dock. As we read-ied two dock lines, *Taranis* skidded to the right, then began crabbing side-ways toward the dock, where Rudy and the other man stood ready to take our lines.

The Haverstocks looked to be mid-thirties, fit, and successful. Both were tanned and dressed comfortably for a cookout. She was blond and wore white shorts and a pale pink sleeveless blouse. His hair was a shade darker, and he was dressed as if he'd just stepped off his yacht.

The other man was dark-skinned, with black hair turning gray at the temples. He wore a tunic of some kind; either Indian or Pakistani, if I had to guess.

"Jojo?" Savannah called out from behind me.

The dark-skinned man smiled and waved. "It is so exciting to see you again, Savannah."

CHAPTER FIVE

Alberto put *Taranis* against the dock very smoothly, though one fender made contact slightly before the other. Once we had her tied down and the boarding ladder extended from the cockpit, we welcomed the Haverstocks aboard, along with their friend, Jojo.

"Jesse, this is Jyotira...ditya Laghari," Savannah said, struggling only slightly with the pronunciation.

He seemed surprised and delighted that she remembered.

"Jojo, this is my husband Jesse, our daughter, Flo, and her husband, David, our friend, Maddy, and up at the helm, our son, Alberto."

He extended his hand to me. "Please, all my friends just call me Jojo."

I shook his hand and then Jojo swept his other hand toward our hosts. "Allow me to introduce my good friends, Rudy and Heather Haverstock."

There were more handshakes all around before I said to Rudy, "We greatly appreciate your hospitality."

"Nonsense," he said, clapping my shoulder, then pointing northward across the bay. "Look."

The sun was only halfway to the western horizon but when I turned, I saw it shining on a wall of dense fog no more than two miles out, when it'd been clear just a few minutes earlier.

"It's another seven miles into Apalach," Rudy said. "You wouldn't have made it. Say, what kind of boat is this, anyway?"

"One off, custom," I replied. "Except for the last thirty or so miles, we've motored all the way from the Keys on solar power alone."

"And the last thirty miles?" Jojo asked.

"We used the Thunder Button," Alberto said, jumping off the second step, with Tank hesitantly following.

Rudy looked up at the flybridge. "Were you the one docking this beautiful yacht?"

"Yes, sir," Alberto replied, smiling. "I'm First Mate Alberto."

Rudy turned to me. "You're to be commended, Captain. A fine vessel *and* crew."

Tank sat beside Heather and lifted her hand with his big head.

"And who's this?" she asked, rubbing his neck.

"Tank's our puppy," Alberto said, crossing his arms. "He's eight-and-a-half months old."

Alberto had been getting a kick out of watching people's reactions when he told them Tank's age.

Rudy glanced up at me, a doubtful look on his face. "Really?"

I nodded. "His trainer says he'll be about one-twenty when he's full-grown. And he eats like it."

"What is he?" Heather asked. "He looks so regal and beautiful."

"His mom was a black Lab," Alberto replied. "A police dog trained to find drugs. And his dad was a Tibetan mastiff, or mountain dog, one of the biggest dogs in the whole world."

"That explains it," Rudy said.

"The other guests will be arriving in less than an hour," Heather said to

Savannah. “The fog is never as thick out here on the islands, and usually the bridges and houses are above it, as well. Today is our annual oyster roast and we have plenty, so please don’t think you’re putting us out in the least. Your arrival is perfect. Any friends of Charity’s are friends of ours.”

“How is she?” Jojo asked.

“She’s doing quite well,” Savannah replied, then turned to me. “Charity and I met Jojo during the, uh... Yucatan affair. He was very helpful in how things turned out.”

“Then you will remember our oyster roast as the ‘*Apalach* affair,’” Heather said. “We’ll leave you now. Just come up to the yard whenever you’re ready.”

We saw them off the boat, promising we wouldn’t be long, then we all went into the salon.

“The Yucatan affair?” I asked Savannah, walking forward to our stateroom. “You write mystery novels now?”

“Well, I wasn’t expecting to see him here.” She stopped and looked through the wide windows on the port side as the others came in. “But Charity knew him from here, so I guess I shouldn’t be that surprised.”

David stopped at the forward ladderwell to the lower deck with Florence. “What was the Yucatan—”

“Mom and Charity helped a girl and her mother there,” Florence interrupted. “I told you all about it. Remember?”

Alberto paused beside the port side ladderwell. “What she means is, you’re not supposed to talk about *some* things in front of me.”

Florence giggled as he turned and descended the steps.

Maddy shrugged. “I won’t even ask,” she said, and followed Alberto down to the two staterooms in the port ama.

"Jojo was with a couple of U.S. Fish and Wildlife agents," Savannah explained to David, then looked up at me. "That little redhead, Poppy McVie, and her boyfriend, Dalton. Jojo was acting as arbitrator between the kidnappers and the girl's father, who was a federal judge."

I turned to check the side hatch and looked out the window. "Holy crap!"

The others turned, looking past me, just as the edge of the mist enveloped the boat.

I glanced up at the clock overhead. It was 1629. "The weather guy was a *little bit* off."

The fog became thicker and within seconds, water droplets started to bead on the glass as the warm moist air from the Gulf collided with an expected cold front. But I'd never seen fog form so quickly. Looking forward, I could barely see the pulpit.

I turned to Tank and tested his new training. "Watch the boat, Tank."

He jumped onto the lounge seat on the port side, which had a commanding view of the dock and gazebo, or as much as the fog allowed.

"Good boy," I told him, as Savannah opened the hatch into our stateroom, and I followed her in.

In the large tubular enclosure in the forward part of the head that we called a shower stall, and which took up the full width of the ama, we showered together. Mostly because we were in a hurry, and it was so large that we could do so without bumping into one another.

But we had. A few times.

Toweling off afterward, I put on a pair of skivvies and khaki shorts, then went up to our stateroom and sat down bare-chested at the auxiliary navigation desk, where I pulled up the local weather report.

Over my shoulder, I could see Savannah open her wardrobe, wearing just bra and panties.

"It says here that heavy fog is typical around here in spring and fall," I called down to her, then read some more. "And this one has enveloped the entire cape and inland wetland areas, but it's densest over the warm water of the shallow bay."

"That makes sense," she said, stepping into a pair of navy shorts and wiggling them over her hips.

She opened my hanging locker and came up the steps with a shirt, which she laid on the bed for me.

I turned and watched her go back down, admiring the long, taut muscles on either side of her spine. She sat at the vanity and turned on the blow dryer, then turned her head and looked up through the open hatch at me.

"This area is unusual in many ways," she said loudly, her hair flying about in the hot wind.

"Yeah, it is," I agreed, raising my voice over the noise. "And it's just like Alberto said. The whole wetland area is some kind of inland river delta, and I bet these barrier islands were probably built up naturally from silt carried down during floods."

I glanced at the shirt she'd laid out. Not my choice for comfort, but I'd long since given up function over form whenever she insisted. And her laying the shirt on the bed, subtle and rare though it may have been, was her way of insisting.

So, I shrugged and pulled the blue-and-white-striped "Yachty McYachtface" shirt over my head.

Savannah dressed quickly, adding a light-blue sleeveless blouse, going for a similar style to what Heather had been wearing, but a different color.

"It might be a little chilly," she said, leaning toward the mirror and applying just a little makeup to her lashes. "That light-weight blue blazer would go well."

"So would a blue denim work—"

Her eyes clicked to mine in the mirror, and I gave up once more.

Savannah was stylish, even when she was in cutoffs and bare feet, and not even trying to be. She always had been.

Though she'd skippered a shrimp boat in her younger years, she was still a product of the upbringing she'd rebelled against, and that was of the Old South—where folks were "gentrified."

What did I know? I was just a dumb grunt. So, I went down to the head, got the blazer from my hanging locker, and put it on. Shrugging it into place, I looked at myself in the mirror.

"Should I have shaved?"

"No," she replied. "We just came off a three-day passage with an hour to get ready for this *soiree.* You look good with a stubble."

We met Florence and the others in the salon a few minutes later and I realized I must not have gotten the memo. They were all dressed nautically comfortable. Apparently, Savvy's sense of style had rubbed off on Florence, who'd "insisted" to David. With all those years they'd spent alone on *Sea Biscuit*, it was no wonder. Powerful women raise powerful daughters.

"Should we bring Tank?" Savannah asked.

I glanced over at the big black dog on the lounge seat. He was in the corner, his side against the backrest, where he could see all around just by turning his head. Of course, he couldn't see outboard—the master stateroom blocked that—but it was very doubtful any threat would come from the water in this pea soup.

"I think he wants to stay aboard and keep *watch*," I said, reaching over and patting his shoulder.

Tank gave a low chuff, as if agreeing.

We went aft, then out into the cockpit. If anything, the fog was thicker as I led the way to the boarding ladder. I stepped over onto the dock, then took Savannah's hand as she stepped down.

"Be careful," I cautioned. "We don't have our land legs yet."

"I've never seen or even heard of fog like this," David said.

"We'd get a heavy sea fog up in Beaufort sometimes," Savannah said. "But I don't remember it ever being like this. You can't even see the other side of the gazebo."

We passed through the covered area and walked toward the foot of the pier, still out of sight, but I could hear voices. After a good fifty yards, we arrived at a set of steps up to the lawn.

As soon as we ascended and started up the yard, the fog dissipated.

I glanced back and realized we'd only risen above the heaviest part. All I could see was the gazebo's roof and *Taranis's* flybridge.

"Welcome!" Rudy said, stepping away from another couple and approaching us. "Like Heather said, it's not nearly so bad up here. We won't let it *dampen* things any more than necessary."

There were two long tables set up, along with a large gas grill on wheels. Several people in white jackets and heavy rubber gloves were moving oysters from the grill into several large tubs. Around the tables, people mingled, mostly couples, it seemed.

"Do you like oysters?" Heather asked Savannah.

"It's a tradition where I come from as well—the South Carolina Lowcountry."

"You must try ours then," Heather said, taking her elbow and guiding her toward the table. "Apalach oysters are the best in the world."

I went along, wanting to try what Apalachicola Bay was most famous for and maybe find out where the servers obtained them.

Several other guests were busy with oyster knives—short, thick-bladed knives with wooden handles. More knives and towels were presented, and Savannah showed Alberto how to roll the towel and loop it over her thumb. Then she put an oyster in her toweled hand, showing him the hinge.

"You simply work the tip in the other end," she said, demonstrating. "Get it in good and deep, then twist like this."

The oyster opened slightly, and she moved her blade. "Work it down the side and twist some more."

Finally, she gripped the shell with her manicured fingers, and opened it fully. "The muscle has to be cut here and here," she said, moving her knife deftly.

Then she dabbed a little hot sauce on it from a bottle on the table, put it to her lips and swallowed. "Mmm."

I had to admit, they were very good.

"Where do you harvest?" I casually asked one of the servers, playing dumb as I opened another. "Just anywhere in the bay?"

"No, sir," he replied. "Wild harvesting is on hold until after next year. Our supplier is Trent Seafood, and they've been raising oysters for about ten years, I think."

"Carl Trent?" I asked, a bit surprised.

He nodded. "Yes, sir."

"You know him?" Jojo asked, from across the table.

"He used to work for me," I replied. "We built an aquaculture system on my island to raise Louisiana crawfish. Seeing his operation was one of the reasons for our visit."

"You own an island?" he asked, as a couple of other people looked over, curious.

"It's not like it sounds," Savannah replied. "Our island is barely two acres. And that's only at low tide."

The woman next to Jojo laughed.

"Charity left her car with us," Heather said. "I'm sure she wouldn't mind if you used it to go see your friend."

"Yes," Savannah said, placing an oyster on a cracker, then dabbing hot sauce on. "She's already suggested we could."

"Perhaps you should *see* her car before deciding," Jojo said, putting down his oyster knife. "Come, I will show you."

CHAPTER SIX

Being curious about what kind of car Charity would drive, I followed Jojo toward the corner of the house. And Alberto, being an even more curious twelve-year-old, followed me.

My guess would be a fairly new German import—a Mercedes sedan, or maybe a BMW. But knowing Charity, it was just as likely to be an antique farm truck.

We walked around the side of the house, which was built on massive concrete pilings with a "blow-out" area below. Glancing at the houses next door and across the street, I noticed they were all built similarly, the main floors of each being at least ten feet above the ground, which was only eight or ten feet above sea level. The area below each home was used for storage, an enclosed garage, or just open, gravel parking.

In the event of a hurricane with a high storm surge, the island itself wouldn't be much of an obstacle and would be inundated, just as mine had been during Hurricane Irma. These homes, built above the possible storm surge, stood a better chance.

The yard was built up in one area toward the front, and there was a large box, mounted just off the ground, with pipes coming out that extended below ground.

"What's that?" I asked Jojo.

He looked where I was pointing and replied, "That is the Haverstocks' water treatment system. Every home on the island has a similar septic system that treats the wastewater before injecting it deep underground."

He opened a side door to a semi-enclosed garage, and I followed him inside. "I am afraid Miss Charity's auto will not fit all of you," he said, turning on the lights.

"A Miata?" I asked, observing the low-slung, light-blue convertible.

"Actually, it is a '*Fi*ata,'" he replied with a light chuckle. "It is a Fiat 124 Spider Abarth."

"Wait... what?" I asked, moving closer.

"It is built on the Japanese Miata platform," he explained. "But the drivetrain and suspension, as well as a few body and interior upgrades, are purely of Italian design."

"What's a-bart mean?" Alberto asked, walking around the little car.

"Abarth is an Italian racing- and road-car manufacturer. It is spelled with a T-H, but the H is silent. They also have a performance division, supplying other automakers with racing parts. In the case of the 124, Abarth supplied the drivetrain, suspension, and other modifications over the Japanese design." He smiled. "I am a bit of an aficionado."

Savannah walked in with Heather, who said, "You'll probably need a scarf."

"A sports car?" Savannah asked, as she approached us. "I never would have guessed *that*."

"Me either," I agreed, walking around the front of the car.

On the leading edge of the hood was a red and yellow disk with a black scorpion and the word "Abarth" at the top. I noticed a few other styling modifications I thought were different from the Miata, including the hood, which bulged in the center.

"To hear Charity tell it," Rudy said, coming in behind the women, "she could paint a number on the side and compete on road courses, just as the car sits."

"Maybe Carl will have a bigger car and can come pick us up," I suggested to Savannah, having noted that the only other car in the garage was a Cadillac sedan that seated five, which I assumed belonged to the Haverstocks.

"In the meantime," Heather said, "there's a key to the garage in a conch shell beside the door, should you need to go anywhere. We have almost no crime out here on St. George."

"We'll be heading to the marina as soon as the fog lifts," I said to Rudy. "Your hospitality is appreciated."

"Which one?" he asked. "We keep our Hylas at Battery Park Marina, just this side of the low bridge. The mast is too high to go under."

I arched an eyebrow at the mention of the high-end sailing yacht. "A Hylas?"

"Do you sail?" Heather asked.

"We have," I replied. "A Formosa ketch."

It was Rudy's turn to look surprised. "Now that's a ship! They don't make boats like that anymore."

"We have a slip reserved in the same marina," I said, answering his question. "Our air draft isn't much under the bridge height, and Marines aren't patient waiting for tides."

Jojo turned toward Savannah, then looked up at me. "Yes, I seem to remember Savannah telling me you used to be a Marine."

What all had she told this man? I wondered.

What happened in the Yucatan had hardened Savannah. I knew that she'd done things and met people I had no idea about.

"Yes, I'm a Marine," I replied, not correcting his use of the past tense. "I retired from the Corps many years ago, though."

"I have a client in town," he went on. "I am a financial advisor, and this client was also in the Marines. Gray Redmond is his name. He's lived here all his life, and I think you might like him."

My head came up quickly. "Did you say Gray Redmond? Big man? Mid-sixties?"

"You know him?" Savannah asked, always surprised at how small the Corps really was.

"I served with a Gray Redmond," I replied, as we headed back out of the garage. "I knew he was from the Panhandle, but don't remember what part. He was a sergeant and about to get out when I arrived at Camp Lejeune in late 1979."

Jojo nodded. "He never speaks of his military service, so I wouldn't know. But I do remember his daughter saying he was once a sergeant."

Gray Redmond? I hadn't even thought of him in years.

A couple of months after my friend, Rusty Thurman, and I finished infantry school, we were offered a week's leave for the New Year. It was our first year in the Corps and came about when a couple of Sergeant Redmond's guys, who were senior to us, got themselves into trouble and had *their* leaves canceled. Just the month before that, he'd brought both his wife and their little girl to the birthday ball. He decided to get out shortly after we returned from Fort Drum when his enlistment was up.

I could never understand why a Marine, after reaching sergeant in four years, would give up the early retirement opportunity a higher rank would provide.

"Is he about my height?" I asked. "Probably close to the same weight, too, if I remember correctly."

"He is tall," Jojo replied, strolling back toward the tables. "At least as tall as you, yes. But Gray had lung cancer many years ago and had to have part of a lung removed. That was long before we met. He is quite thin."

Cancer? I remember him being a powerfully built man, smart, and quick-thinking.

"I'd love to talk to him while we're here," I said, shucking another oyster while watching Savannah and Heather talking to another woman out on the lawn. Their clothes and faces were the only color against a hazy gray background.

"Say no more," Jojo said, then wiped his hands on a fresh towel.

He pulled his cell phone out of his pocket, tapped the screen a few times, then held it to his ear.

"Yes, Gray, it is me. How are you?" He listened for a moment, then said, "I am at the Haverstocks, over on St. George. Do you know them?"

He paused. "Yes, the Hylas. I just met a man here who thinks he may know you from your time in the military."

Another short pause. "Yes, in the Marines. I'll let him tell you." Jojo extended his phone toward me.

I took it and put it to my ear. "Sergeant Redmond?"

"Nobody has called me that in a *very* long time," the voice on the other end said.

"First Battalion, Eighth Marines?" I asked. "Seventy-nine?"

"Ooh-rah!" he grunted, and I heard the familiar sound of a recliner closing. "Do we know one another?"

There was a spark of excitement in his voice.

"I was a lance corporal then," I replied. "Jesse McDermitt."

"Too Tall!" he nearly shouted. "Seriously?"

The moniker had been hung on me when the battalion deployed to Fort Drum in Upstate New York for cold weather survival training. When we returned, I lost it just as quickly, when a six-five Marine transferred in from Okinawa.

"And nobody's called *me* that since Fort Drum," I responded. "How are you, Gray?"

"Old," he answered. "Thank God for that. How about you? You're here in town?"

"I'm doing well, thanks," I replied, catching a questioning look from Savannah. "We're cruising and will be at Battery Park Marina tomorrow afternoon to spend a few days. It'd be great to catch up."

"Do you remember Corporal Cowboy?" Gray asked. "He lives here in Franklin County, as well."

I searched my memory. Everyone in the Corps had a nickname at one time or another. There was a guy who was on his way out the week I arrived at First Battalion. He'd been called Cowboy for his music choice and clothing. He listened to country and western and always wore a Stetson and cowboy boots when off duty.

"First name's... Wayne?" I asked, trying to remember his last name.

"That's him," Gray said. "I'll give him a ring and see if he's busy tomorrow. The oyster beds are shut down, so he's been helping me out at the boatyard."

That piqued my curiosity instantly. "Boatyard?"

"That's right!" he exclaimed. "Your dad was a boat builder, right?"

"My grandfather," I corrected him. "Dad too, but he was killed during the Tet Offensive."

There was a moment of silence, as often happens when that subject came up.

"I remember that too," he said softly. "First beer's on me. Have Jojo give you my number and call me when you get close. We don't live far from the marina."

I agreed, ended the call, entered the number on Jojo's screen into my phone, then handed it back to him.

"It is a small world," Jojo said, a bright twinkle in his dark eyes. "A chance meeting in Mexico leading to a decades-long reunion of old friends. It is Karma, my friend."

I'd only just met Jojo Laghari, but I'd quickly sensed a completely non-threatening person of kindness. And exuberance. He seemed to relish everything life had to offer—the boat, the oysters, the car, and just meeting new people and finding things in common.

As the evening went on, he'd told me he was born in Bangladesh, but his family had immigrated to California when he was young. He'd grown up surfing along the beaches of Southern California, and at times he seemed to have as much of a West Coast accent as a Hindi one.

He and our host, Rudy, had several things in common, besides the obvious wealth. The three of us talked about many things, but there was no discussion of politics or religion, which I found refreshing. Especially considering the current political climate and looming election.

I wasn't opposed to either, but I knew from experience that the political and religious views of different people were often at odds and so engrained in each of us that you could never change a person's mind about either. Yet people often seemed to try, and quite often very fervently.

"Where will you be going from here?" Rudy asked.

"Back to the Keys," I replied. "This is our final shakedown before we cross the Caribbean to Dominica later this year. Maddy will fly back from here on Tuesday with a friend of mine, but Florence and David will spend a week with us as we drift around the Big Bend. We plan to drop them in Cedar Key, where their boat is—they just graduated from UF and have to close down their apartment in Gainesville. After that, Savannah, Alberto, and I will spend the rest of the month in the Ten Thousand Islands and Cape Sable, my home waters."

"You will be totally off the grid?" Jojo asked. "I noticed the solar panels below the flybridge."

I nodded. "They cover most of the roof, as well. We were making almost eighty kilowatts per hour at the peak of the day, while using fifty. And we have internet just about anywhere with StarLink. But other than that, we can be completely untethered from shore for months at a time."

"Your son is a very bright young man," Jojo said. "Do you homeschool or is Maddy his tutor?"

"She's a friend of the family," I replied. "Or family of a friend, depending on which way you look at it. But yes, we homeschool him for now. But he's just about to the limits of what we can do. By the way, if he offers to play chess for money, be smart and decline."

Jojo glanced over to where Alberto and another slightly older boy were sitting on a blanket with Maddy and another young woman.

"He is that good?" Jojo asked.

I arched an eyebrow. "Or it could be that my friends and I just aren't much of a challenge for him."

"Jojo is a candidate master," Rudy said. "It would hardly be a fair match."

"Still..." I grinned. "I wouldn't bet on it."

CHAPTER SEVEN

Jojo strode over to where the kids were talking on the blanket and knelt beside the two girls, chatting and smiling. After a moment, I saw Alberto's eyes snap toward Jojo's.

He smells chum in the water, I thought.

Alberto said something, and when Jojo replied, the boy grinned.

Fish on!

"Your boat intrigues me," Rudy commented. "How fast will she go again?"

I knew where he was headed. For decades, the debate had been diesel or sail—one was fast, the other economical. Now the argument is over which economical boat is faster, electric or sail.

"Depends on if we're in a hurry or taking our time," I replied with a shrug. "Full-time electric cruising is possible at four knots, all day and all night, and only moderately affected by wind speed or direction."

"And the 'thunder button' your son mentioned?"

"The 650-horse main diesel engine," I replied. "Wide-open throttle and with both electric folded into recesses in the hull, *Taranis* can make better than twenty-five knots." I guessed at the length of his Hylas and its possible hull speed, then grinned. "Or cruise at eight knots with the generators kicking on a few times, especially at night, burning ten or fifteen gallons a day."

"That sounds very versatile," he said. "Will she be capable of ocean passages?"

I nodded. "At the right time of year, with careful planning before and during, *Taranis* can cross from the Panama Canal to Melbourne, Australia without using a drop of fuel."

He tried to hide the smirk but failed. "And how long would that take?"

Hylas yachts were luxury performance boats, and I knew that with a good skipper and moderate wind, even a small one would leave *Taranis,* running just on electric, far behind.

I grinned at him. "Not as long as you'd think. She's equipped with a kite sail."

"Oh, ho-*ho*!" Rudy exclaimed, obviously thrilled. "Now you're just teasing."

"At the *right time of year*, she could make the ten-thousand-mile passage in about forty days, non-stop." I winked. "But the fun is in stopping along the way, right?"

He raised his glass. "Bora Bora!"

"It's on my bucket list," I replied, tapping his glass with my own.

Just then, my phone vibrated and chirped in my pocket. When I glanced at it, I saw it was Carl Trent calling. "Excuse me. It's my friend Carl."

He nodded and took my glass, then headed to the bar.

I stabbed the *Accept* button and put the phone to my ear. "Hey, Carl."

"Have you made it in yet?"

"Just before the fog," I replied, noticing Savannah approaching. "We couldn't get to the marina, so we're tied up to a friend's dock on St. George Island, enjoying your oysters, as a matter of fact."

"Is that Carl?" Savannah asked, as Rudy returned with a fresh drink.

I nodded at her, accepted the rum from Rudy, and set it on the table.

"You're at the Haverstocks'?" Carl asked.

"The fog beat us in," I replied. "We have a mutual cruising friend, and Rudy was nice enough to invite us to tie up at his dock for the night until it lifts."

"Most of the people there are about as interesting as watching paint dry," Carl said. "But Rudy, Heather, and Jojo are good folks. There might be one or two more. Mark my words, though, when the caterer starts packing it up at six, most of 'em'll disappear within minutes. Rudy's been wanting to see the farm. Have him drive you over."

I cut my eyes to Rudy's. "Carl wants to know if you'd like to see his oyster farm. After your party."

"Yes, I would," he replied, as Jojo joined us with the kids.

"Would what?" Jojo asked.

"Would you care to go on an after-hours tour of the Trent Seafood farm?" Rudy asked him.

Jojo shook his head. "Young Alberto and I were going to borrow your chess set in the study," he replied.

"Y'all can go on ahead," Maddy insisted. "I'll stay here with Alberto and Jojo. I'm still getting used to the Keys, and saltwater fish, so an oyster farm sounds yucky."

"We'd love to see it," David added, as he and Florence joined us. "If that's okay."

Rudy nodded. "It's settled then. You two can ride with me and Heather, and Jesse and Savannah can drive Charity's car." He turned to me. "You *can* drive a stick shift, I presume."

I nodded. "If it has wheels, wings, rotors, tracks, or a hull, I can drive it." Then I put the phone back to my ear. "Can you text me the address, Carl?"

"No need," Rudy said. "I know where it is."

"Done," Carl replied. "See you about seven?"

"Looking forward to it," I replied, then ended the call.

For the next hour, Savannah and I mingled with the other guests, an activity I'm just not into, especially as it became painfully obvious that what Carl had said was true. I'd been more entertained a time or two waiting for paint to dry.

Soon, the trays of steaming oysters were empty, the caterers started to pack up their equipment, and just as Carl had predicted, the guests began leaving.

"Will you need to gather anything before we leave?" Rudy asked, rescuing me from a conversation on equity trading.

"I'll need to take Tank for a walk," I replied.

"Your son and one of the other children have that in hand," he said, nodding past my shoulder.

I turned and looked. Tank was playing fetch with Alberto and another boy in the fog, with Florence, David, Jojo and Maddy looking on.

"Then I guess not," I said, nodding to the two men Savannah and I were being bored to death by. "Nice to meet you."

"I'll run and tell them we're leaving," Savannah added, anxious to get away. "And gather up David and Flo."

She returned a moment later with the older kids in tow, and Rudy extended a key on a small ring. "It's turbocharged. You'll probably want to let it warm up for a minute or so."

Heather joined us as we walked toward the side entrance of the garage. "Did you tell him?" she asked her husband.

"Tell me what?" I asked, assuming she meant me.

"Jojo won the first game," she replied. "But your son won the second, so they're going to play a deciding game after the last guests leave."

"You're okay leaving before your guests?" Savannah asked. "Sorry, that didn't come out right."

Rudy smiled as he opened the door, then leaned toward her conspiratorially. "They're leeches, but it brings in business. Jojo will make sure they don't steal the silverware."

I opened the passenger door of the blue sports car for Savannah, then went around and opened the driver's door. Feeling around under the front of the seat, I found the handle and pushed the seat all the way back before sliding into the car.

It felt like my butt was an inch above the deck, and it probably was.

The engine started easily, and I detected a very slight turbo-whine. I tapped the accelerator pedal a couple of times and the choke disengaged, letting the engine settle into a burbling idle.

"Are you sure you can drive a small car like this?" Savannah asked, a sparkle in her blue eyes. "It could fit in the back of *The Beast*."

I grinned at her as the Caddy beside us started up and the garage doors began to open. "You can drive on the way back."

I let Rudy back out first, then, once he was turned around, I put the shifter in reverse. When I eased the clutch out, the transmission whined quite loudly.

"Is that okay?" Savannah asked.

"True sports cars don't have synchronized reverse gears," I replied, turning the wheel, then stopping and moving the shifter to first gear.

I pulled out behind Rudy and the turbo-charged engine belched softly as I shifted to second, and again when I went to third.

"I wish it wasn't so foggy," I said. "I bet this thing's a blast on the backroads."

When we reached the main road, I followed the Caddy to the left, shifting up through the gears smoothly with a little more throttle. The exhaust barked playfully with each shift.

Rudy turned left onto the causeway, and I followed, accelerating easily as the road rose and went out over the water. I let them get farther ahead, but not so far that I lost them in the fog.

"It's incredible the difference just the height of the bridge makes," Savannah said, as if reading my mind.

It seemed almost like we were driving on a road through the clouds. I could see patches of blue above and visibility ahead, on the bridge, was a good half mile, but over the sides, nothing but fog.

"Kinda creepy in a way," I said, reaching sixth gear, with the engine barely loping, cruising at fifty miles per hour.

A Jeep Cherokee went past going the other direction, and brake lights came on. When I glanced back again, it was turning around in the middle of the bridge.

"What the hell's he doing?" I asked rhetorically.

"Who?" Savannah asked.

A blue light on the Jeep's dash began flashing and I cut my eyes to the speedometer—I was driving a little under the speed limit.

"There's a cop behind us," I said.

Savannah turned in her seat and looked back through the little back window. "How fast were you going?"

"Under the speed limit," I replied, as the Cherokee got closer.

There was nothing coming ahead, so I eased over in my lane slightly, to allow the cop to see ahead and pass us.

"Do not stop on the bridge!" an amplified woman's voice ordered. "There is a road on the right after the foot of the bridge, just past the one-eighty to the fishing pier."

"Oh, great," I grumbled, continuing at the same speed. The flashing blue light filled the rearview mirror. "What do they want?"

For the longest three minutes of my life, I continued on, the unmarked police car behind me, lights constantly flashing.

The fishing pier came into view on the right. It looked like it could probably have been the remnants of what was an older causeway. I remembered when we passed under the bridge, I'd seen parts of an older bridge on the east side of the one we were driving on.

I slowed, seeing a turnoff ahead. Rudy had also slowed, but drove past the road as I downshifted, then made the turn.

Pulling over onto the grassy shoulder, I shut off the engine and dug my wallet out of my hip pocket. The Cherokee parked behind us, partially blocking the lane and angled toward the center of the road, to provide cover for the cop if it was needed.

I rolled the window down, then pulled my driver's license out and held it in my left hand before putting both hands on the wheel.

Cops didn't like it when people started digging around for their things as they waited beside the car.

The SUV's door opened and a woman with thick, dark hair got out. She was wearing black slacks and a white blouse with a windbreaker over it.

After pushing the jacket back over her sidearm, she unsnapped the holster and approached slowly, her hand on the butt of the weapon.

Not good.

"License, registration, and proof of insurance," she said, staying well back from the Fiat's door.

I slowly extended my left hand with the license. "This isn't my car, officer, and I don't know where the owner keeps her papers. My wife can look if you like."

"I know it's not your car," the cop answered, taking my license. "That's why I stopped you... Mr. McDermitt, is it?"

"Yes," I replied. "The car belongs to a friend, but we have her permiss—"

"Please step out of the car, sir."

Very slowly, I moved my right hand to the handle and opened the door, keeping my left extended. Then, with both hands out the window, I stepped out and made sure to keep my hands away from my sides.

The first thing I noticed was that the cop was small. Not much over five feet tall, and slim, probably half my weight.

"This is all just a misunderstanding, officer," I said, smiling, and trying to appear as nonthreatening as I could at twice her size.

"Captain," she corrected me, being very cautious about maintaining her distance. "Captain Hamilton, Chief Investigator, Franklin County Sheriff's Office. Please step over there on the other side of the car, sir."

A police captain? I thought. *Making a* traffic stop?

I walked past her as she backed away, eyes locked on mine and her palm resting assuredly on the pistol's grip.

When I reached the other side, I put both hands on the low fender and extended my legs back, spreading my feet wide.

"I see you're no stranger to procedure," the cop said, standing behind me. "Whose car are you driving?"

She made no attempt to frisk me. Probably waiting on backup.

"Her name is Charity Styles," I replied. "She keeps the car at Rudy and Heather Haverstock's house when she's away." I heard a car stop back at the intersection and looked. "That's them in the Cadillac, along with our daughter and son-in-law."

"Should I get out?" Savannah asked from the passenger seat.

"No, ma'am," Hamilton answered. "Please stay in the car."

I heard a couple of beeps behind me, then the captain said, "Yes, it's me. Did you loan your car to someone?"

She knew Charity.

CHAPTER EIGHT

A marked patrol car turned off the highway, its blue lights joining those of the Jeep in illuminating the fog amidst the dense pines with an eerie glow.

"No. No trouble," Hamilton answered to an inaudible question behind me, obviously talking on a cell phone with Charity. "I saw it and stopped him because there have been some car thefts lately." She paused for a second, then started laughing. "Yes, on the causeway. But the other end this time."

"Can I stand up?" I asked, as the other police car pulled up behind the Jeep.

"Okay, bye," Hamilton said. "Yes, you can stand up now, Mr. McDermitt."

"Everything okay, Mags?" a deputy asked, getting out of the patrol car.

"All fine, Dudley," she answered, as I slowly turned to face her.

He waved a hand. "Okey-doke."

"I apologize, Mr. McDermitt," the captain said, extending my license. "I know Ms. Styles is away and there *have* been a rash of car thefts recently. Meth addicts, usually."

"No problem, Captain Hamilton," I replied, taking my license from her hand. "A simple misunderstanding. I'm glad Charity has friends here to watch her back. Is methamphetamine a big problem in Apalachicola?"

"Apalach," she corrected me. "Unless you *want* everyone to mark you as a tourist, that is. Charity said she would, and *has*, trusted you with her life."

The captain was clearly curious.

"She exaggerates sometimes," I said, deflecting the question. "We're both prior military."

She tilted her head slightly, appraising me. "Somehow I get the feeling she was barely scratching the surface." Then she shrugged her shoulder. "In-home meth labs pop up like whack-a-moles," she answered, turning toward her Jeep. "Be careful driving in the fog."

"Thanks," I replied. "You, too."

Walking back around the car, I got in as Hamilton began turning around. She blocked the road with her emergency lights still on, allowing me to pull out, even though there hadn't been but three cars pass on the highway and none on the side road.

I started the car and made a quick three-point turn, then Hamilton turned her blue light off and moved on up to the stop sign, where she turned left, heading toward St. George Island again.

Savannah was busy on her phone when I'd gotten in the car, but finally put it away. "I texted Flo; they turned around again and are waiting on the shoulder. What was that all about?"

"I'm sure you heard as much as I did," I replied, making a right and spotting the Caddy ahead, just pulling off the shoulder. "Meth monsters stealing cars to support their habits. You would think in a small town like this, they'd be easy to spot."

"And just what does a tweaker look like?" she asked, with just a hint of what I called snarcasm.

"Point taken," I said. "But I wouldn't think we'd fit the profile."

We continued another mile or so, then turned left on US-98 and crossed another bridge over the mouth of Apalachicola River that was at least as long as the causeway to St. George Island.

Nearing the other side, I could see the bridge curving to the right, descending into downtown Apalachicola.

I downshifted, revving the engine between shifts and listening to the little turbocharged four-cylinder wind down as it slowed the car going into the curve.

Following Rudy through town, we ended up at a small warehouse on the water. The sign over the door read, *Trent Seafood Company*. And below that was a smaller sign that read, *Hatchery*.

As I struggled to get out of the low-slung sports car, the door below the sign opened and Carl Trent stepped out along with his wife, Charley.

"I think you need a bigger car," he said, coming toward me with his hand extended. "Good to see you again, Jesse."

I shook his hand. "Glad to *be* seen," I replied. "You're looking fit as ever." Then I turned to his wife. "And I don't think you've changed a bit, Charley."

She gave me a hug as Savannah came around the car, the others right behind her.

"Carl, Charley, I'd like you to meet my wife, Savannah."

The two women hugged, and Savannah turned to the kids. "And this is our daughter, Flo, and her husband David."

"We met once before," Carl said, shaking Flo's hand. "You were quite a bit younger then."

"I knew I'd seen your face before," Savannah said. "At the Rusty Anchor. You were with Jesse when my sister was killed."

He nodded somberly, no doubt remembering trying to pull Charlotte Richmond out of the water, only to have her snatched away by a shark.

Charley took the lead. "Y'all come on in out of the heat." She swept her hand toward the door. "A rack is about to spawn."

We followed them inside, through a small foyer, then down a hall with doors on either side. "These are our offices," Carl said, stopping at a heavy, insulated door at the end of the corridor. "But through here is where everything starts."

He opened the door, and we stepped through into a brightly lit warehouse that was cooler, almost cold. I guessed it was in the low sixties, quite a feat considering the size of the warehouse to be cooled and the current late summer Florida heat.

The exterior walls were covered with a white, expanding-foam-type material, creating a thick, wavy insulation blanket with a sort of bubbled texture that completely enveloped the large steel support columns. The ceiling was low, just ten feet, and no doubt had thick insulation above.

I detected ozone in the air, and the sound of water moving could be heard all around. Ahead, the warehouse was divided into two sections, the smaller left side taking up a third and consisting of two rows of long, low, rectangular fiberglass tanks, much like what we had on the island, except about twenty times as many.

On the right side of the building were three rows of round tanks, also low, to allow workers to look down inside. There were half a dozen people working in the warehouse, moving around the tanks, checking instruments, testing water, and carrying small trays.

"How many oysters can you harvest?" Florence asked.

Charley turned to her and smiled. "Last year we harvested over thirty million," she replied, then pointed toward the rectangular tanks. "But here, we hatch over a billion baby oysters every year."

We all moved toward the tanks.

"Do you lose that many?" I asked. "That's a ninety-seven-percent mortality rate."

"Oh, no," Carl said. "We lose less than two percent. But when they reach a quarter inch in size, they're moved over there to those round upweller tanks. Then, when they reach a half inch, we sell the stock we can't handle to other farms. We're one of the largest oyster hatcheries on the Gulf Coast."

"What we *do* keep," Charley continued, "are all hand picked, and go into cages that are put out in the bay. It takes about two years to mature to market size."

I counted the spawning tanks. There were two rows of ten, which meant each tank could produce fifty million oysters a year.

"How many times a year does spawning happen?" I asked.

"Each of these tanks spawns about once a quarter," Carl replied, taking a large oyster from the tank. "But never from the same batch, though. These just came out of the bay and have been prepped for spawning for the last two days, so your timing is perfect. A week after spawning, these oysters will go to market, leaving room and more nutrients for the little oysters to grow before they're moved over there to the upweller tanks to make room for the next batch coming out of the bay. So, roughly four times a year, we'll induce spawning."

The math in my head told me that'd be over ten million oysters per tank per quarter. It was mind-boggling.

"What if someone were to replicate this on a smaller scale?" Savannah asked. "That's a lot of oysters."

Carl looked over the tank at us. "If you add one more tank to your system, the same size as we did originally, then set the cages out in the flats north of your island, I'd bet you could raise enough to satisfy the demand from Marathon to Key West. And charge more than wild- caught."

I looked up and arched an eyebrow. "Really?"

"Right now, wild oyster harvesting in Florida is closed," Charley began. "The price for wild-caught oysters from other states is about thirty cents each, plus shipping, and it's a long way from Alabama down to the Keys in a refrigerated truck. We charge forty cents and can't harvest them fast enough to meet demand. We're only limited by our water lease on the bay, and that's controlled by DNR."

"I wasn't thinking about doing it on the island," I said. "I know it's been a while, but can you think of an area near me that might be better?"

He grinned. "That's good. 'Cause that basin is only so-so. The reason Apalachicola oysters are considered some of the best is the Bay and the surrounding barrier islands. There's a lot of outflow from the river and wetlands, but it's spread real wide, ya see. The barrier islands act as a sort of gate valve, holding back the seawater and creating a salinity that's perfect for oysters." He thought for a moment. "The Ten Thousand Islands would be good. Outflow from the Glades is rich in nutrients. So is Whitewater Bay behind Cape Sable, Hell's Bay, and most of the northern part of Florida Bay—anywhere you find constant freshwater flow over a wide area of brackish water."

Florence looked up from the bubbling water. "It isn't hard to figure out, Dad. Kim and Marty want to build a house in the Keys, but they need a flexible closing on their old one in Flamingo while the new one's being built. Jimmy and Naomi want to buy a house, *and* they want to start their own business. And lastly, you want to leave the chartering business behind and give Jimmy a nice wedding gift. Am I missing something?"

"Yes," Savannah said with a smile. "All of those things are looming in the *very* near future."

Florence wasn't wrong. The idea ticked all the boxes, and both she and Kim had already said they wanted to do something special for Jimmy and Naomi. Even Eve, who barely knew Jimmy, wanted to be part of it.

"Do you think they'd go for it?" I asked her.

Florence nodded. "I think so. It's not like it's a move across the country. It's just thirty miles in a fast boat."

"He doesn't take such good care of the fish and gardens because you *pay* him," Savannah added. "I swear, I've heard him cooing to those crawdads more than once."

"What are you thinking of doing?" Carl asked.

"Dad wants to offer Jimmy a stake," Florence said. "As a wedding gift. A water lease in Florida Bay to raise half a million oysters a year."

Carl and Charley looked at one another, each thinking independently, but, as I knew from my long and close association with them, thinking also as one.

Carl looked back at me. "He'll need one of these spawning tanks and three upwellers, then a good eight or ten cages on a half-acre of water near, but not too close, to an outflow source. Plus, all the pumps and monitoring equipment.... You're looking at a fifty grand startup cost, with two years before the first harvest, and working all day, seven days a week till then."

"Can you help me out on getting all the equipment?" I asked.

"What kinda timeline?"

"They're looking now," Savannah replied. "And getting married in the spring."

"I can spec out all the equipment easy enough," he replied, rubbing the back of his neck in thought. "Probably take a month to get it all together and shipped, though."

"It'd take that long to add a smaller version of this building on the back of Kim and Marty's property."

"Plan ahead," Carl said. "Go big with the building. He can store stuff in it until he grows his business."

"Jimmy's a good man," Charley said. "When it's set up, we'll give him three cages full of oysters, about ten thousand a cage, each at different growth stages with one that's ready-to-harvest adults to start spawning with. Learning the spawning techniques we use real early on will set them up for success." She looked down at the water, which had suddenly become clouded, smiling and spreading her arms. "Because *this* is where everything starts."

David stepped closer. "They're spawning now?"

"By the tens of thousands," Charley replied. "The eggs are too small to see with the naked eye."

Carl nodded. "Once his upwellers are full, he can sell the adults to live on, pull a second cage and start spawning again while the next batch reaches maturity. By the time they pull the third cage, they'll have two full cages to harvest and start over again."

"It's hard work," Charley added. "But he can easily produce ten thousand market-sized oysters a month and pocket about five or six thousand in cash after expenses. Doubling that by adding a second spawning tank and three more upwellers, he'd have to hire someone to help."

Carl nodded. "It is *definitely* a shit-ton of work, getting started and through the first harvest. But Jimmy ain't afraid of hard work. What's his girlfriend like?"

I grinned. "You'd like her. She's from your neck of the bayou and not afraid of work either."

"Then they could probably triple that in a year," Charley said, "and only have to hire one person."

A car started outside, and I heard the low whine of a turbo, then the grinding of gears.

Sprinting back toward the door we'd come through, I dashed outside to find someone in Charity's car.

I'd left the damned keys in the ignition.

The guy was trying to grind the transmission into gear without using the clutch.

Just as I reached the driver's side, he must have figured it out but dumped the clutch, killing the engine and chirping the rear tires on the pavement.

I yanked the door open and grabbed the man by the left wrist, pulling him out and twisting hard, forcing him to the ground, flat on his belly. He was surprisingly lightweight.

There was a screech of tires and when I looked up, I saw a car on the side of the road roaring off with a deep, throaty exhaust.

"What in the hell's goin' on?" Carl shouted, bursting through the door and running toward me.

I held the would-be car thief on the ground, one arm twisted to the point of dislocating the shoulder. "This guy was trying to steal Charity's car," I snarled, applying just a little more pressure.

"Lemme go, man!" the kid shouted in a nasally voice. "You're 'bout to break my shoulder!"

"He's just a boy!" Florence exclaimed.

I could see peach fuzz on the kid's chin. I eased up on his twisted arm and knelt lower. "If I let you up, remember this. If you try to run, I'll take you down... harder."

"Fuck you, old man!" the kid hissed in agony. "I'm seventeen and you'll go to jail."

"Seventeen-year-old shoulders break just as easy," I growled, applying pressure again. "I've been in a *Singapore* jail, kid. An American prison would be like a *vacation* by comparison, and your body cast won't even be hard by the time I get out."

Grand theft auto was a serious offense. The kid was seventeen and could be tried as an adult and end up in an adult prison with inmates who'd committed far more heinous crimes.

He stopped resisting. "Okay, okay!" he yelled in pain.

I released his arm. "Get up. And remember what I said. If you run, I *will* chase you down and tackle you, hard. Then we'll start this whole thing all over again."

The kid rose slowly, clutching his left shoulder, and looking around at the others, probably estimating his chance of escape. He had longish dark hair, stood about five-six, and couldn't have weighed one-thirty if he was soaking wet.

"I've seen you around," Carl said. "What's your name?"

"You're not a cop!" he hissed. "I don't have to tell you nothin'."

"You're right," Savannah said, taking her phone out and tapping the screen. "Nine... one..." She looked up at the kid with her finger poised over the screen. "You can tell him or tell the police."

"Lee," the kid replied, casting his eyes to the ground.

"What's your last name, Lee?" Savannah asked softly.

"Valdi," he replied. "I live over near Eastpoint."

He had no accent, unless you counted trailer-park, but I knew the last name was a fairly common name in Iran, and a bit less common throughout the Middle East.

"Who was driving the car?" I asked.

Lee looked up, then his eyes kept going until they met mine. "I dunno what you're talkin' about, Mr. Big Man."

I narrowed my eyes. I didn't like it when people lied to me. "You mean you weren't a passenger in that blue '64 Impala SS, tag number HLB-174 with two other punks in it? There are worse things than going to jail, kid. Lying to me is one of them."

Lee's face contorted with rage. "Fuck you, old—"

"One," Savannah said, tapping her phone's screen and putting it to her ear. "Yes, I'd like to report an attempted car theft."

CHAPTER NINE

We didn't have to wait long before a Franklin County Sheriff's cruiser pulled into the parking lot. The first cop on the scene was the same deputy who'd assisted Captain Hamilton, the man she'd called Dudley.

"Twice in less than an hour," he said, obviously recognizing me as he began walking toward us.

A second patrol car pulled in with Apalachicola Police markings on the door.

The deputy's name tag read "D. Schultz," and the chevrons on his sleeve told me he was a sergeant. My mind jumped instantly to the character in *Hogan's Heroes*, and I swore to myself I wouldn't call him Sergeant Schultz.

"I caught this kid trying to steal a friend's car," I replied. "His name's—"

"Reginald Lee Valdi," Schultz answered, glancing over at the boy, who was looking forlornly at the ground. "He's no stranger to us. Tell me what you observed, Mr. McDermitt."

The fact that he knew my name was a surprise but not a shock. He might've overheard the captain say it, or she might have told him more over the radio after they'd left us on the causeway.

I explained everything I'd heard and seen, from the starting of the sports car's engine, to the approaching sirens, adding nothing, and not leaving anything out.

Just the facts, the way cops liked.

He took notes on an electronic tablet.

"What's going to happen to him?" Rudy asked, standing off to the side with Heather.

Schultz glanced over at the city cop. "Cuff him and Mirandize him, Jim. Then take him to the station and book him on a 504 and an attempted 503. I'll be along once I finish taking witness statements."

As the other cop took the kid into custody, Schultz turned back to face us.

"He'll be charged with tampering with a vehicle and attempted auto theft," he answered, then faced me. "He also has an outstanding warrant. Did you know he was a minor?"

"I didn't ask for his ID as he was trying to steal the car, if that's what you mean," I replied. "Stealing a car's a pretty grown-up decision. But just as soon as he told me his age, I released him."

"And he didn't run?"

"Jesse might be a little old, Dwight," Carl said to the sergeant, "but trust me on this, there's no way the kid coulda outrun him."

Dwight? Hadn't Captain Hamilton called him Dudley?

"He'll be eighteen inside of two months," Schultz said. "Odds are, he'll be booked and held over for arraignment tomorrow. This is his third major arrest, so it's likely he'll be tried as an adult."

"He's not much younger than me," Florence said with a sigh. "How do kids go that far astray?"

Schultz looked over at Florence with a tired expression. "Drugs, ma'am; the kids *and* their parents."

The other car pulled out, with Valdi slumped in the backseat. I'd given Schultz a description of the other two youths who were in the classic muscle car, as well as the tag number.

"We know the car you described, too, sir," Schultz said. "It belongs to his brother, a local gang leader."

"Gangs?" I asked. "Meth heads and a rash of car thefts? Seems odd in such a friendly little town."

"I use the term 'gang' loosely, sir," Schultz answered. "A small group of local wannabe gangsters, mostly teens who live out in the sticks, and are usually high on this or drunk on that. Meth use among kids aged thirteen to sixteen is one of the biggest problems in rural America these days, and Franklin County is about as rural as they come."

"Thirteen?" Florence said, clearly surprised.. "Where are the parents?"

The man's eyes glistened in the soft, fog-filtered glow of receding daylight. "Mostly absent, ma'am," he replied, obviously affected. "It's something we see a lot of."

I looked off toward the water, blanketed in gray mist. "Does that boy have family here?"

"I went to school with his mother," Schultz answered. "He's the youngest of three, all with different fathers, who are all currently serving time."

"Such a beautiful little town," Savannah lamented. "What a shame."

"Yes, well, uh..." Schultz stammered uncomfortably. "I think I have everything I need."

"Will we have to come to the station?" Savannah asked. "Or appear in court?"

"No ma'am," he replied. "That is, not unless he pleads innocent. But since Covid, the judge does a lot of online depositions."

He turned and headed to his car.

"One thing, Sergeant," I called after him, my curiosity getting the better of me.

He stopped at the door and turned around. "Yes, sir?"

"Is it Dudley or Dwight?"

He grinned. "Both, I guess. Maggie's called me Dudley Do-Right since I joined up."

Maggie? Mags! That's what he'd called Captain Hamilton.

Captain *Maggie* Hamilton.

I grinned back at him, having been called the same thing a time or ten. "Be careful, Sergeant."

Once he got in his patrol car and backed out, Savannah and I turned to head back inside. The Haverstocks stood by the door, waiting.

"Such a terrible shame," Heather said.

"Yeah, it sure is," I agreed, walking past them and through the door, shaking my head in disbelief. "A seventeen-year-old who can't drive a stick?"

"I think she meant the boy's age," Rudy said.

I paused and turned to face him. "In some parts of the world I've seen, a seventeen-year-old *man* would be an honest, hard-working father and husband, providing for his young family, not out stealing cars for drug money."

Later that night, as I sat alone on the flybridge with my thoughts, watching several elongated pools of light move slowly through the fog, I added one more reason for giving up and leaving the human race behind.

Single moms raising children alone, when they were children themselves. Becoming addicted to drugs and easy prey for other men who used them, often physically abusive, and leaving them with another mouth to feed.

What I'd seen with my own two eyes was bad enough. But I've never been the brunt of crude or downright vulgar comments or actions from random jerks on the street, like my wife, daughters, and most women are on a daily basis.

It wasn't that way everywhere. But like in Apalachicola, it was seeping in.

The glowing ovals in the fog were from cars on the causeway. They seemed to slowly appear out of the north, far in the distance, like some kind of ghostly apparition or something. They became more pronounced as the cars neared the island, where occasional red glows could be seen from taillights that were quickly swallowed by the mist.

It was kind of surreal and beautiful, the fog masking the sounds of the cars. A sharp juxtaposition to how ugly the world had become, just in my lifetime.

I remembered Pap often telling me about his boyhood, growing up on the banks of the Caloosahatchee River. He'd played outside with friends until dusk, throwing a ball or playing tag, and fishing in the river and around Pine Island Sound.

My dad, and then I, had grown up the same way.

In many ways, Pap's childhood in the 1920s hadn't been much different from my own, almost fifty years later. And now we had teenage girls prostituting themselves for drug money and giving birth to unwanted children.

Alberto and Maddy came up to join me, both appearing silently out of the fog at the aft part of the flybridge.

"Whoa," Maddy said quietly. "You can see a lot better up here."

"Mom told us what happened," Alberto said, plopping himself down on the lounge seat to my left.

"Will that boy really go to an adult prison?" Maddy asked.

I glanced over at them and nodded. "It's possible. Drug use makes people do stupid stuff. Especially young people who haven't experienced much good in life."

"I've been offered meth a few times," Maddy said. "But I don't even like alcohol."

"Me, too," Alberto said, quietly.

My mouth fell open for a second. "You've been offered drugs?" I asked incredulously.

He looked over at me, his dark eyes glistening a little. "Drugs killed my real mom. You don't have to worry. I'll never touch them."

Alberto's biological mother had been an addict and prostitute in Fort Myers. She and several others were murdered as a statement to a rival gang over territoriality.

I looked out toward the bridge again as two glowing orbs headed toward one another, one gaining intensity and the other diminishing. "I think people turn to drugs when they think they don't have anything to live for anymore."

"Have you ever done drugs, Jesse?" Maddy asked.

I turned my head to find them both staring expectantly.

I'd done things in the past I wasn't proud of, and that was one of them. But I wasn't sure if I was ready to divulge to Alberto the series of bad decisions I'd made years ago.

Fortunately, Savannah chose that precise time to announce over the intercom, "The sandwiches are ready."

"Let's go," I said, rising quickly. "I'm starved."

The oyster roast had been early, we'd eaten lightly, and it'd been several hours since then. Plus, we were used to four meals a day, every six hours around the clock during our three-day passage. So, when we'd returned to the boat, Alberto had insisted once more on fried baloney and cheese sandwiches.

"It's clear up there," Maddy announced as we entered the salon.

"Everyone grab a plate, then," Savannah said. "As big as *Taranis* is, I feel claustrophobic in this fog. We can eat upstairs."

We carried our plates up, along with two tubes of stackable chips, and sat around the aft lounge area. The talk quickly turned to the oyster farm and whether Jimmy and Naomi would go for the idea.

The fog completely surrounded *Taranis*, with only the gazebo and the houses on shore rising above it. The pier connecting us to shore was completely invisible. Even the ama's bows couldn't be seen, so it seemed as if the flybridge was floating on a cloud.

Lights from the gazebo illuminated the fog, which, from our vantage point, resembled a slow-moving glacier of ice. It collected on the low windshield, where rivulets of condensation rolled down.

Yet, to the west, a thin sliver of a crescent moon could be seen, chasing the sun like a giant sail on a snow-covered plain.

Above, oddly enough, the thinner fog parted now and then to reveal many of the major stars. I guessed that above thirty or forty feet, the sky was clear.

"What time is the fog supposed to lift?" David asked. He and Florence were sitting on the sun pad, their backs against the aft rail and Tank lying in front of them.

"The airport still says noon," Alberto replied.

"We can head out before then," I assured them. "It's another eight miles to the marina—a couple of hours on electric—and with the sun up, we should be able to see well enough from here on the flybridge, and we'll just follow the chart plotter."

"Cast off around nine, then?" Savannah asked. "That'll put us there close to noon, with better visibility for docking."

I nodded as I swallowed the last bite of my sandwich. "Because of our beam, we can't fit between any of their finger piers, so they're giving us a slip on the seawall near the marina's entrance."

"And your friend is going to stop by in the afternoon?" Savannah asked.

"Two of them," I replied. "More like acquaintances than friends, though. Cowboy did four years and got out the same week I reported to One-Eight after infantry school, and Sergeant Redmond got out a few months after that. It's been since then that I've had any contact with either."

"And this Sergeant Redmond has a boatyard?" she asked, a look of mischief in her eyes.

I didn't see many of the guys I served with, except Rusty and Tom Broderick, who was once my commanding officer and now worked for me and Deuce. So, I was somewhat curious how their lives had turned out after the Corps.

Alberto looked up. "He owns a boatyard?"

"It could be he's building a rowboat in the left half of a two-car garage," I replied. "But yeah, he mentioned a boatyard."

Alberto looked over at Savannah. "Can I go?"

"Not this time," Savannah replied, smiling at me. "Dad and his Marine friends will be drinking beer and telling their 'sea stories,' which will probably be too grown up for you. Besides, I need you to help me carry bags. We're going to stroll every inch of this beach town and look for bargains to help dress up the inside of *Taranis.*"

"I think we'll do the same," Florence announced. "Just looking around in general, that is. We're here for a few days."

"I'll go with you," Maddy told Savannah. "I'd like to find some souvenirs and a T-shirt or two. I even brought an empty carry-on for the flight home."

CHAPTER TEN

We'd said our goodbyes to the Haverstocks an hour earlier than planned. When Alberto checked the local airstrip's forecast as soon as he got up, he'd found that the fog would be lifting earlier than we'd expected.

By 0800, we'd cast off the lines and pointed *Taranis* northwest, toward the marina seven miles away. I set a waypoint in the main channel just outside the marina and turned on the autopilot. It would steer a rhumb line on the chart plotter straight to our destination.

Away from shore, Apalachicola Bay had a consistent depth, but there were numerous shoals and oyster beds closer to the mainland.

There were marked channels for larger boats, but with a draft of less than four feet, I was unconcerned about running aground in the bay. The waypoint I'd set was half a mile from the coast.

We'd all awakened shortly after dawn and had breakfast before getting underway. But two hours after leaving I was already looking forward to lunch.

We were less than a mile from the entrance to the marina when the sky began to brighten. The sun's warmth was slowly "burning off the fog," as Mam used to say.

"I see trees!" Alberto said excitedly, standing at the forward rail on the flybridge.

Tank barked and looked up at him, probably already identifying the sounds and smells of dry land and wondering why Alberto had taken so long.

I plucked the VHF microphone from its holder, pressed the button on the side, and spoke into it. "Battery Park Marina, this is *Taranis*, hailing on one-six."

When I released the mic button, a woman's voice came instantly over the speaker. "*Taranis*, this is Battery Park Marina. Please switch and answer one-seven, Captain. Channel seventeen."

I switched channels and keyed the mic again. "Battery Park Marina, this is *Taranis*. We're one mile out, requesting slip assignment. We have a reservation."

"Will you be needing fuel, Captain?"

"Negative, Battery Park Marina," I replied. "We only used about ten gallons coming up from the Florida Keys."

"Roger that, Captain. We have you on the end of the west dock, where the fairway is widest. Or, if you can handle a little maneuvering, there's a ninety-foot spot available on the same side, halfway up the fairway."

I told her we'd take the ninety-foot slip.

Close maneuvering around the docks was what *Taranis* had been built for. Among other things. We'd want some extra room to launch and retrieve the dinghy if we wanted to use it, but the dinghy garage in the aft part of the main hull would likely be far enough from the dock that only a catamaran or another trimaran might block it.

It was doubtful they'd put anything in the ten to fifteen feet I planned to leave to our stern.

I looked over at Savannah. "You want to handle the docking this time?"

"That sounds pretty tight," she said.

"Twenty-four feet more than we need," I replied. "Forty-six, if you're only looking at the starboard ama. You can spin her around at the opening of the fairway where it's widest, then back in using the joystick."

"Okay," she said, a bit uncertain. "But I've only played with that simulator thing a few times."

"Piece of pie, Mom," Alberto said.

She scowled at him. "You're mixing metaphors, just like your dad."

"David, you and I will be fore and aft with boathooks to fend away if we need to. Alberto, what's the current and—"

"Low tide's in twenty minutes," he replied, looking at the clock in the overhead. "I already checked."

"Perfect," I said. "We'll get there in fifteen and it'll be slack tide as we maneuver to the dock."

"Maddy and I can jump off and tie the dock lines," Florence added, then ruffled Alberto's thick mop of black hair. "And you stay here in case Mom needs you."

He smiled at her. "She won't. I've seen her park her boat in a really bad storm all by herself."

He meant Savannah's fifty-foot Grand Banks trawler, which I'd also seen her maneuver quite well.

"Both helms are directly amidship," I told her. "Just find the center of where you want to put her and use the joystick to bring *you* to that spot."

Shortly, more of the downtown waterfront became visible and we could see the jetties and fishing piers on either side of the fairway opening. The channel was clearly marked, so I turned off the autopilot and turned the wheel slightly, lining up the jetties.

"She's all yours," I said, stepping aside so Savannah could take the helm.

As soon as we moved between the fishing piers, Savannah stopped *Taranis* right in the middle. Then, she slowly turned her around, using the joystick that controlled both ama motors, as well as the bow and stern thrusters in the main hull.

I stood in the pulpit, ready to fend us off the jetties, if need be, but the opening was at least twice as wide as *Taranis* was long and we had plenty of room.

Several people watched from the pier as *Taranis* turned completely around within her own length, then began backing into the fairway.

It's a maneuver we could have made farther in and without stopping, but if anything happened—a gust of wind or equipment malfunction—it was better to bang into shore or a pier than somebody else's boat.

I moved from the main hull's pulpit over to the bow of the starboard hull, and David did the same at the stern. I was in a better position to call out a course correction, and he could see any floating debris in the fairway that might foul a prop.

Taranis inched backward, and I saw the spot the dockmaster had indicated. It was between a thirty-foot center console, rigged for offshore fishing, and a Chris-Craft motor yacht that was probably fifty feet, and most likely older than me.

Perfect. We'd have no trouble at all getting the dinghy out. The center console was no wider than our starboard ama.

A woman stood on the dock near our spot with three old men, all looking our way. And a few fishermen on the pier had put down their rods and were following us on the jetty. It was quickly becoming routine.

"There's the slip, just aft that Chris-Craft," I called up to Savannah.

"Got it," she yelled over her shoulder.

I got the bowline ready as Savannah backed *Taranis* down the fairway. Maddy and Florence were at the boarding gate, prepared to jump down and grab the lines when we bumped the dock.

But as Savannah started crabbing *Taranis* sideways toward the slip, it appeared as if the onlookers were going to help.

The taller of the four moved away from the others, watching me. A tuft of sandy-brown hair hung over his forehead and there was a good bit of silver on the sides.

Another older man moved right, watching David. He was shorter, and sported a snowy-white, well-trimmed beard, but was completely bald on top. Like the taller man, he seemed fit, and both moved on the dock as if it were a second home.

I looked at the taller man again and he smiled.

Gray Redmond?

He was thinner than I remembered, not quite gaunt, but not far from it. He moved with the ease of a man who'd worked around boats all his life and was comfortable in his own skin.

"Forty-four years," he called out to me, "seven months, and maybe ten or twelve days. The last time I saw you, McDermitt, you didn't even own a car!" He spread his arms wide. "And now this?"

The sound of the thrusters ceased, and we drifted closer to the dock.

"Grey?" I asked, ready to hand the bowline down to him.

"We heard you on the VHF," he answered, as the bow thruster engaged for a second, straightening the boat with the dock. "So we walked over."

We were perfectly square to the dock when the fenders lightly bumped it, and I heard Savannah squeal and clap her hands.

I handed the line to Gray. "It's been a helluva long time, Gray. You look great."

As he bent to snub the line to a cleat, I put a hand on a stanchion, then vaulted the rail, dropping four feet to the dock and landing lightly with my knees bent. Gray straightened as I did, and I extended my hand.

He took it and pumped it vigorously. His grip was every bit as strong as I remember.

"It's really good to see you again," he said, then turned as the others approached. "You remember my wife, Georgia," Gray said. "You met her at the birthday ball before I got out."

I smiled and shook her hand. "You look just as beautiful as then, Georgia."

"Bet you don't remember me," the bald man said with a strong Gulf Coast accent.

"Cowboy?"

"In the flesh," he answered, pumping my hand. "That was some fancy dockin', right there."

"And this is another local Marine," Gray said. "Jesse, meet Jim Thibeault. Jim, this is my old friend, Jesse McDermitt."

He was older than us, probably near eighty, but his eyes were clear and bright.

"Jim's a Nam vet," Gray said. "Old Corps, back when Christ was a corporal. Cowboy and I worked one of his boats when we were teenagers and again when we got out of the Corps."

"That didn't last long," Jim said with a bit of a cackle, shaking my hand with what I decided was a typical oysterman's grip. "These two up and went out on their own as soon as they sucked all the intel they could outta me. Semper fi, son."

"Semper fi," I replied as David and the girls joined us.

Alberto and Savannah came down from the flybridge and more introductions were made, and then Jim nodded aft with a quizzical expression.

Tank stood on the starboard swim platform and when I looked his way, he barked.

"What's the leash laws?" I asked Gray.

"He's fine if he'll stay close to you," Gray answered. "Most folks around town accept dogs. He's a fine-looking Lab."

"*Herunter kommen,* Tank," I ordered. "*Bleib nah!*"

I'd been using the simple English commands Tank was already familiar with—come, stay, down, and so on—along with a few German translations, which I knew he'd be learning soon enough when he started protection training after the first of the year.

I hadn't been surprised when he picked them up easily and I could use either German or English. I just couldn't figure out how to teach him that when I give those German commands, he's to not only obey the order, but be on the alert while doing so.

Aggression was no part of his ancestry in his father's lineage; these dogs were simply too big to take anything as a threat. And with his mother being a black Lab, also a normally non-aggressive breed, by what means Warren planned to train him *when* and *how* to be aggressive, I didn't know.

Tank leapt to the dock and trotted toward a nearby pier post, where he hiked his leg.

"Ya teach your dog German, do ya?" Jim asked. "That meant come down and stay close."

"Sometimes," I replied. "For certain things."

"I didn't hear no motor," he said, nodding toward the stern again.

"It's electric," Alberto replied. "But we have a diesel for when we need to go fast."

"Electric, huh?" Jim asked with a doubtful tone. "How far ya get on a charge with a boat this big?"

Alberto grinned. "All the way around the world."

Jim's eyes widened. "Ya don't say."

"And then turn around and do it the other way," Alberto added, warming to the older man's attitude. "You know—when the first way gets boring."

Jim laughed. "Well, that sounds like a lot of fun for a young man."

"How long will you be with us?" Georgia asked Savannah.

"Maddy's leaving us in the morning," she replied. "She's flying home from here, but the rest of us are staying for a few days. So, we're taking her souvenir shopping to fill up an empty carry-on she brought."

Georgia turned to her husband. "I'm going shopping, Gray. Why don't you boys go do whatever it is you do."

"Mostly talk about you women," he replied with a wink. Then he turned to me. "You want to come with us to the boatyard?"

"Can you bring me back in a couple of hours?" I asked, as Savannah and Georgia talked.

Savannah and Georgia? I thought, grinning.

Savannah's maiden name was Richmond. Her sister's name had been Charlotte, and her parents were Jackson and Madison. And now our daughter, Florence. All cities in the Southeast, like Savannah, Georgia, not far from where Savvy grew up in the South Carolina Lowcountry.

"It's just a few blocks," Gray answered. "A ten-minute walk."

"I'll get Tank's leash and lock up," I said, then started toward the stern.

CHAPTER ELEVEN

Gray's boatyard was exactly that, a large, mostly gravel yard with scattered boating detritus lying around, including a lot of used lumber of varying lengths and curves. But unlike in most boatyards, the parts were all sorted, arranged, and on pallets.

A large grapefruit tree stood in the middle of the fenced yard, and there was a single small building beyond it that faced a short canal that was cut into the creek bank. The siding appeared to be faded wood planks beneath a flat metal roof sloped toward the back. There were two windows in the front that were too grimy to see inside, and altogether, there was an old and weathered feel to the place.

As we crossed the yard, I noticed the fruit on the tree was well past ripe. August and early September were usually when grapefruit were harvested in Southwest Florida and probably earlier up here. The overripe fruit had a pungent, citrusy smell that permeated the whole yard.

"Is there a reason for not picking the grapefruit?" I asked, thinking it an eyesore.

"Cuz I hate skeeters," Cowboy replied. "That smell is natural citronella. Ain't no skeeters 'round here."

When Gray opened the door and I followed him inside, I was a bit surprised. The interior didn't match the exterior.

And it was air-conditioned.

He flicked a switch on the wall and fluorescent lights flickered and hummed, illuminating the interior of a clean and very well-organized workshop with a number of boat hulls turned upside down and resting on blocks.

Gray turned and brushed a lock of hair from his forehead. "What do you think?"

"Amazing," I said, looking around at a lot of familiar tools and equipment.

Against the back wall was a long steamer box for making hull planks and ribs more flexible. There was a large table with hundreds of holes in it, where dowels were placed to bend the wood into an approximate shape. Hanging on the wall to the right were various-sized vises and clamps to hold boards in place, and a vast assortment of *real* hand tools, not battery- or electric-powered tools you *held* in your hand.

There was even a large, double-handled manual drill that took at least two men to operate, with one holding the top and guiding the auger tip, and another man— or two men— working the double-offset handles. I'd never seen one so big, though, and couldn't help but wonder what it'd be used for, since it looked like they were working on smaller boats.

The lights and AC seemed to be the only electrical devices in the shop, until I turned and saw a flat-screen TV and stereo in one corner with a well-worn leather couch in front of them.

Tank found a spot on a large rug in front of the sofa, did two turns, then lay down facing us, watching.

It was a wooden boat builder's man cave. Right down to the faithful water dog.

My attention was drawn to the three overturned hulls, each twenty to twenty-four feet long, flat-bottomed and very beamy, at least nine or ten feet.

"What kind of boats are these?" I asked.

"Oyster skiffs," Jim replied, moving toward the nearest. "This'un here belongs to the grandson of a friend of mine. Old Jack built this boat with his own two hands, back in fifty-six." He slapped the bottom of the hull with his palm with a solid thwack. "She's made from Franklin County cypress, and back when I was fourteen, Jack showed me how to work the tongs, my feet standin' right on these very planks."

"You're restoring them?" I asked. "That's what all the lumber and parts are for outside?"

"Yep," Cowboy said. "Gray's son-in-law got us a federal grant to get the fleet ready for limited operation when the ban is lifted."

"The fishery's been closed down for almost five years," Gray said softly. "The Bay raised our grandkids, our kids, most of us old-timers, and generations before us. We're as tied to it as we are to one another."

"Times've changed," Jim said. "When Jack built this'un, it had a centerboard and sail. See here." He leaned over the hull and ran his hand over a part of the keel board where the difference in the wood grain was visible, although the joinery had been done very precisely. "His son did this back in sixty-nine when he come home from the Nam. Then he reinforced the transom to hang an outboard."

I moved my fingertips along the visible seams in the wood planks and felt nothing. "Almost seventy years old," I said softly.

"And this'un ain't the oldest," Cowboy added, jerking a thumb toward a large door panel hanging on a track by what looked like wheels from some kid's little red wagon. "That'd be the Williams brothers' skiff out on the dock. They're young, but hard workers. Their second great grandpa built it at the turn of the *last* century."

"Over a *hundred* years old?" I asked. "Can I see it?"

"Jesse's dad and grandfather were boat builders," Gray explained. "His grandpa raised him after his dad was killed during the Tet." He turned to me. "They were *both* Marines, right?"

My chest swelled. "Pap fought in the South Pacific—Guadalcanal, Cape Gloucester, Peleliu, Iwo Jima, and Okinawa. He went to college after the war, started an architectural firm, and built boats as a hobby."

"Is he still livin'?" Cowboy asked. "There's a fella whose hand I'd like to shake."

I shook my head. "He passed away nearly fifty years after the war and rarely spoke of it. He died just shortly after my grandmother. Like my dad, he was posthumously promoted to gunnery sergeant."

Jim's eyes widened. "Is 'at right?" he asked, deep respect in his voice. "And you?"

"Retired gunny," I replied, then glanced toward the rolling door. "I'd really like to see a hundred-year-old oyster skiff."

"You like wood boats like your Pap?" Cowboy asked, leading the way.

The question made me realize that I liked a lot of things because of Pap. He'd been a surrogate dad when my dad deployed. A few times, we spent summers where Dad was stationed, but mostly it was just me and Mom in Fort Myers, a few blocks from Mam and Pap's place on the Caloosahatchee. He retired and sold his business shortly after I'd gone to live with them. I didn't realize until years later that he'd done that to spend time with me. I was probably influenced a lot more by my grandfather than my father.

"I've built a few," I replied. "Helping Pap, that is. And I designed *Taranis*."

Just then the front door opened, and a tall, broad-shouldered man stepped inside, pulling a ball cap off with one hand and holding a large green bottle with the other. He was at least a decade younger than any of us.

"Hey, guys," he said, tossing his cover on a wall hook with practiced ease, then placing what I could see was a bottle of Mountain Dew on a desk by the door.

Tank rose lazily and went to the newcomer, stopping a few feet away and wagging his tail.

"Whose pooch?" the man asked, pushing his hair back with his fingers to get the hat-bowl shape out.

"Hey there, Wyatt," Gray said. "Come and meet an old friend of mine, Jesse McDermitt. The dog's his. Jesse, this is my son-in-law, Wyatt Hamilton."

Hamilton?

He was as tall as me, or taller, and had the same oysterman's grip when I shook his hand. He probably weighed less than me, but not by a whole lot.

"Pleased to meet you, Mr. McDermitt," he said. "I thought I knew all of Gray's friends."

"Just call me Jesse," I replied. "Gray and I served together."

"Ah, that explains all three of them being here at one time," he commented, his eyes taking in Jim and Cowboy. He bent and rubbed Tank's side for a second. "It's hard to get them all to come to work at once."

"We're old men, Wyatt," Jim said, almost pleading. Then he winked at me. "Ya can't work us like we was half *your* age."

Wyatt chuckled and turned back to me. "Don't let Jim fool you, Jesse. He can run circles around his *great*-grandson out there on the water."

"But I don't *have* to," Jim said, eyes twinkling with mischief. "I'm retired, remember?"

These four men knew one another very well. This boathouse was where they socialized, this small Gulf Coast town where everyone knew one another was their home. They'd been here all their lives— of that, I was sure. Except maybe Wyatt. He didn't have the accent of the others, so maybe he wasn't *born* in Apalachicola. But I sensed that he had deep roots in the area.

"This is some undertaking," I told him. "How many of these skiffs have you repaired?"

"These three will make an even forty," Wyatt answered. "All I did was throw out an idea and help organize the paperwork. Seriously, these three old knuckleheads are the talent."

"He's done more'n that," Jim said. "We joke around a lot, but Wyatt fits right in with us. And as it turns out, he's got a good feel for the wood."

Pap had mentioned the natural ability that some had and some didn't in the same way. The physical part was easy—the hands and fingers transmitted texture and contour to the brain. But it's what the brain *did* with that information that Pap had been referring to. How the wood feels in your mind and soul, the enticing smell of sawdust, the fair curve from a noble plan.

"Gray says that men have an innate need to build things," Wyatt added. "And I guess that's true. It sure beats getting shot at."

Shot at? I thought. Was Wyatt a vet also?

"Wood therapy," I said. "That's what Pap called it—he was my grandfather. When I was just a kid, he and I would get lost in the work for hours."

Jim looked at me somberly. "He had demons to deal with, same as me, and I reckon same as you, son. Workin' the tongs was my therapy."

"We brought oyster skiffs up here from all up and down the Forgotten Coast," Cowboy added.

Wyatt nodded. "It was Gray's idea. He was working on rebuilding his father's skiff up on Scipio Creek when he was forced to retire."

"And then *you* retired and got bored," Gray added, turning toward me. "Wyatt used to be the sheriff here in Franklin County. He helped me and my grandson finish dad's old skiff about the time the fishery shut down."

Not a vet, I surmised. Law enforcement.

"I looked into some things," Wyatt said, "and found that we might qualify for federal aid. Mostly in the form of subsidies to do needed repairs while the fishery was closed."

"When it reopens," Gray said, "there'll only be a limited number of boats a day, and the forty we restored are at the top of the lottery list."

"I met a *Captain* Hamilton yesterday," I said. "Any relation?"

Gray chuckled softly. "You ran into Maggie already? That's not the first time you met her. You danced with her once."

My eyes widened. "That was your little girl who pulled me over on the causeway?"

Wyatt's eyes narrowed. "Whatever you were doing, it had to have been something serious. She's Franklin County's chief investigator. It's not her job to make traffic stops."

"I was driving the car of a friend, who your wife knows," I replied, going for a disarming grin. "She thought I'd stolen it."

"Been a lotta that goin' on," Cowboy said. "Damn dopeheads. When I was a kid, the worst we ever got into was to syphon off a little of Old Man Caleb's mash. These days, they're makin' weird shit outta cold medicine and Drain-O."

Wyatt turned to face me. "Maggie told me last night about stopping someone driving a car belonging to Charity Styles, but didn't say who it was. So, you're a friend of Charity's?"

Normally, I'd be quick to answer yes to that question. But Charity had a way of stepping on the toes of local law enforcement and, retired or not, Wyatt was still a cop. And he slept with one too.

"I hope that's not an *unwelcome* thing," I said.

"You kiddin'?" Jim said with a cackle. "I heard she and that one-legged pirate fella took down a whole drug operation over in Panama City. Folk like that are good to have around, ya ask me."

One-legged pirate? That could only have been DJ Martin, one of Jack Armstrong's investigators.

Wyatt's gaze came back to me. "Nothing was ever proven, and nothing ever will be. Local PD there wrote it off as two gangs warring it out, but... there *was* some talk. Charity came back a few months later, she and Maggie became friends, and Charity told me and her what really happened."

I met his gaze steadily. "And that was?"

"That she worked for a company called Armstrong," Wyatt answered, watching my eyes. "A company that does certain things local law enforcement and governments *can't* do."

I couldn't read in his expression if he considered that to be a good thing or a bad one. "I haven't seen her in some time," I said, noncommittally. "Has she been back here since then?"

"A couple of times," Gray said, looking from me to Wyatt, apparently bewildered by our conversation. "We had a cookout at your place, Wyatt. Remember?"

"I'm not a cop anymore," Wyatt said, then shrugged. "But Miss Styles is welcome here."

"*Welcome* here?" Jim said, then cackled once more. "She's a gorgeous woman who won an Olympic medal. Don't see many like that walkin' 'round these parts." He patted Cowboy on the shoulder. "So maybe she killed some dirtbag that needed killin'. We ain't gonna hold that against her. Right?"

Cowboy grinned. "Not a chance. And I second the drop-dead gorgeous part."

CHAPTER TWELVE

I'd heard bits and pieces about what Charity and DJ had done in Panama City but was surprised that she'd divulge anything about Armstrong. Unless she thought Wyatt, or more likely, Maggie, could be an asset.

"Your wife mentioned meth use here," I said to Wyatt. "After the misunderstanding over Charity's car was straightened out, that is. But later that day, someone actually *did* try to steal it. Dwight Schultz was first on the scene, and he mentioned the same thing. How bad is it?"

"Four ODs last year," Wyatt replied, stone-faced. "Five so far this year. All kids, fifteen to eighteen. Dozens of arrests. Dozens of bail jumpers. A few convictions. No charges of intent to sell."

"They skip town?" I asked.

"Not always," he answered. "We're a very rural county, and out there where the blacktop ends... well, they've lived out there for generations and have extended family and they set their own rules. Even professional skip tracers won't go back in there. Our guys go after them, and they fade into the wetlands like the fog."

"And it's a local lab producing the meth?"

"That's what Maggie thinks," he answered. "Way out in the sticks, where it can't be found. Those involved are very tight-lipped. No leads on who the supplier is."

Why was he telling this to me? There's no way Charity would disclose anyone else connected to the organization; not by name, nor description. Did Wyatt simply suspect I was a part of it, due to my connection to Charity?

I looked around at the others. You could take the uniform off the man, but you could never take the man out of the uniform. I guess that applied to life-long law enforcement types also. I sensed it was worse than Wyatt was saying, and in some subconscious way, maybe he was reaching out for help to anyone.

Tank gently nuzzled my hand, and I absently scratched him behind the ear. Then he returned to his spot in front of the TV.

"Deep in the woods, huh?" I asked.

Wyatt arched an eyebrow.

"How did you conduct the searches?" I pressed him. "A wide sweep with dozens of uniformed officers?"

Gray clapped his hands together. "That's right! You moved over to Recon just before I got out."

"What's that?" Wyatt asked.

"The Marines is like a big ol' spear," Cowboy said. "It gets flung way out ahead of America's military might. And Marine Recon is the pointy tip of that spear."

I couldn't help but chuckle. It was almost word-for-word what Russ Livingston had explained to Rusty and me, way back before we applied to Recon School.

"Marine Corps reconnaissance," I said. "Our job was to go deep into enemy territory ahead of the main body, identify enemy troop movement and deployment, assets, and other targets of opportunity. Among other things, I once taught cover and concealment to Recon Marines."

"No shit?" Cowboy asked, surprised. "What other things? How long were you with Recon?"

"Except for two years as a drill instructor," I replied, turning toward him, "my whole career—twenty years. And my last billet was sniper instructor."

"Sniper *instructor?"* Gray asked, seeming impressed.

Tank lifted his head and looked toward the door. A second later, I heard the crunch of tires on gravel outside.

"Wonder who that could be?" Gray said, then started for the door.

Tank got up and lumbered after him, his body swaying side-to-side with each step.

"What kind of dog is that anyway?" Wyatt asked. "At first I thought he was a Lab, but his head's too big."

"He's not really a dog yet," I replied. "Not quite nine months old."

"Nine months...?"

Gray opened the door and looked outside, then smiled and spread his arms wide. "Hey, how's my girl?"

Captain Hamilton stepped through the door and accepted a quick hug from her father. She looked nothing like Gray but a lot like Georgia.

Gray was over six feet tall, and the top of Maggie's head barely reached his shoulder. Georgia was probably average height, around five-six, but the two women had the same facial features and hair color.

For a moment, my mind flashed back to the birthday ball in 1979 when Maggie was a toddler, standing on my shoes while we "danced" beside the table where Gray and Georgia sat with Russ Livingston and his wife and son.

One of the Corps' traditions was the cutting and serving of the birthday cake by the youngest and oldest Marines in attendance. At the time, I was seventeen years and eight months old, four months younger than the next guy in the battalion, and the battalion sergeant major was the oldest at forty-nine.

Gray's daughter ended up being a police captain, pulling me over for suspected car theft, and Russ's son wound up being my business partner and close friend. If they met today, they probably wouldn't remember that evening, when they were just toddlers sitting at the same table.

It often amazed me how small the world really was if you just moved around in it.

"Mr. McDermitt?" Maggie said, walking toward us. "I wasn't expecting to see you here."

"Captain Hamilton," I replied with a nod. "Gray and I served together."

Her eyes cut to Jim, then Cowboy, then Gray. "Well, that explains things a little."

Wyatt glanced over at Jim with a half grin. "See? I'm not the only one who notices." Then he turned to Cowboy. "Why are y'all standing back here by the door anyway?"

"Jesse wanted to see the Williams's old skiff," Cowboy said. "We was just fixin' to go out back when you came in."

"Don't let me hold you back, Wayne," Maggie said.

Cowboy grinned at her, then leaned against the handle and shoved the door aside.

Outside was a back porch, or covered dock, depending on how you looked at it. Just a bare deck with no rails or steps, and an extension of the roof, supported by three posts.

Tied up to the dock was a slightly larger version of the three boats inside. The hull was painted teal green, inside and out, with white cap rails and exposed ribs.

And it was rigged to sail.

"It's quite a bit bigger," I said, stepping over to it. "And rigged for sailing?"

"Thirty-six feet," Jim said. "Biggest one we've done yet."

"John Williams, the oldest brother," Gray began, "already had his smaller outboard skiff refitted. He and his brother worked it before the ban. He convinced Thad to use their share of the grant money to restore the boat that three generations of their ancestors once used. It'd been upturned in a barn for the last thirty or forty years."

"I thought it'd be best to take it apart," Cowboy added. "It was pretty far gone. Those pallets out front are what's left of three that were in worse shape."

It was a simple workboat, rugged and strong, long, and wide. But the craftsmanship in the joinery, and the little details to the gunwales and working part of the deck, really set it apart.

It had a beam of at least thirteen feet, and the ribs of the nearly flat bottom were covered with a narrow lattice of what looked like teak, which would allow water and debris to drop into the bilge space below to be pumped overboard.

The sailing rig was a simple short mast, fore and back stays, and shrouds with no spreaders. It had a gaff-rigged, triangular sail, which, when hoisted, would be almost double the mast height. In the center, a daggerboard was raised five feet above the deck and locked in position.

There was no cabin, no helm station, no shelter of any kind, no chart plotter, nor even a compass. Just the mast, the daggerboard, and a long, curved tiller that seemed carved from a single piece of wood.

As I walked along beside the boat, admiring the detail and workmanship, I could easily imagine it loaded down with oysters as the captain stood at the tiller, bringing his catch to shore.

"Jesse was saying that you conducted your search wrong," Wyatt said to Maggie. "He's an expert in finding things in the woods."

I bent to inspect something on the gunwale. "I didn't say that."

An oarlock? There was another on the opposite side. I guess as a backup, some other means of propulsion would be needed in case the wind died while out pulling oysters. I'd be very laborious, and I couldn't imagine the strength required to row a thirty-six-foot boat loaded with a ton of cargo.

I straightened and turned to face them. "I asked if the search was conducted by a large group of uniformed officers, moving through the forest in a line."

"Do you know a better way to find a hidden meth lab?" Maggie asked.

"I do," I replied. "But it'd take months of intense training for one or two of your deputies to learn. The people you're after are apparently at home in the woods?"

She nodded.

"Then they won't be found except by someone experienced in the task," I said. "I have a friend down in Southwest Florida who can track an otter through the Glades without a sound, or he could suddenly appear right beside you, unseen, standing in an open field. He's a Recon Marine too. But more importantly, he's Native-American and was born and raised in the Glades by a father who learned the old ways from his elders, and was like an uncle to me, growing up. I don't think you have much chance of finding woodsmen without being one of them."

Maggie glanced up at Wyatt for a moment, bewildered. Then her eyes cut to me, and she seemed riled. "Are you like, looking for work or something? This is an interview?"

Looking for work? Where'd that come from?

I shook my head. "No, I'm not—"

"Did ya see that big, fancy, multihull at Battery Park Marina?" Cowboy asked her. "That's Jesse's boat."

Her expression changed. "I apologize," she offered. "We've hired a few so-called 'experts' in the past. So I'm a little leery of strangers offering help."

I shook my head. "I wasn't offering to teach them, and besides, we're only here a few days. What I meant was, if you sent one or two of your guys to *be* trained, and I *can* give you a few reputable facilities, it would take months. But then they could come back and teach others. Hunting people in their natural habitat is difficult enough without knowing that habitat very deeply yourself."

"Hunting people?" Maggie asked.

"A euphemism," I said. "Anything or anyone *can* be found. It's not just about the skill involved in tracking, but a lot of intuition. Some have it, some don't. Which is why I suggested sending two guys for training."

"But *you* could do it," Cowboy muttered softly. "I can see ya still got it in ya."

I gave him an amused look. "I'm only a few years younger than you and Gray, and also retired."

"Is that where you know Charity from?" Wyatt asked, right out of the blue. "Armstrong?"

"No," I replied slowly, shaking my head. It wasn't *really* a lie. "She and I were both attached to Homeland Security for a while, a few years after the terrorist attacks on 9/11." I turned to Gray. "You remember Russ Livingston?"

Gray nodded. "We went through NCO school and were squad leaders together."

"Do you remember his boy, Russell, Junior?"

"We called him Ace and the toddler Deuce," Gray said, his eyes drifting away for a moment, then coming back. "I heard Russ got murdered and the killer was never found."

I looked Gray in the eye. "Deuce brought Russ's ashes to the Keys, asking my help to scatter them on a reef. Then he and I found the man who killed Russ."

The realization hit Gray first, then Jim and Cowboy nodded.

"Deuce was a squid officer when we scattered Russ's ashes—a commander and SEAL Team Leader. He was hand-picked to run an elite team of counterterrorism operatives in the Caribbean." I turned to Wyatt and Maggie. "He was the one who recruited me and Charity into DHS."

"And the man who killed his father?" Maggie asked.

"Disappeared into the backcountry of the Keys," I replied. "It's a very inhospitable place for the unprepared. Without a fire, mosquitoes could drain the blood from a horse overnight, then crabs would pick the bones clean before noon. He's dead."

"And Russ, Jr is still with Homeland Security?" Wyatt asked.

"No," I replied, choosing my words carefully. "He went on to become an Associate Director at DHS, then retired from government service. He and I opened a small investigative service in Key Largo."

"That little runt?" Cowboy asked. "I remember him always gettin' underfoot when we went fishin'."

I couldn't suppress a laugh, remembering when I first met Deuce as a two-year-old boy, just learning to talk and curious about everything.

"He's married to my goddaughter, Julie, and they have two boys," I replied. "Trey and Jim are named after Deuce and Julie's fathers. Her dad is Jim Thurman."

"*Rusty* Thurman?" Gray asked. "I remember you two were close."

"He helped me get settled in when I retired to the Keys," I said, remembering it like yesterday. "And now, twenty-some years later, Deuce and I are business partners, and I'm kind of a surrogate grandpa to Trey and Jim."

Maggie was a cop, and even if he was retired, Wyatt would be curious, and either one of them could probably get all that information before the day was over. So, I figured it best to divulge what they could easily find out anyway.

Besides, I was intrigued by people who couldn't be found.

CHAPTER THIRTEEN

Gray, Jim, Cowboy, and I shared a steel-like bond that tied us and every other Marine together forever. It was forged aboard naval warships and hardened in long-forgotten land campaigns, going back many generations to before the birth of our country. The steel was tempered, honed, and sharpened by men like my father and grandfather into the mameluke sword every Marine NCO earned.

Our brotherhood was strong and unbreakable.

Yet, when Maggie asked, she got a lot of different reasons why we'd all served.

Jim was almost drafted into the Army, but when his number came up, he'd already enlisted in the Corps.

Cowboy had joined on a dare from Gray when the prospect of no work in the Bay loomed after high school graduation.

And I had enlisted by tradition. I'd known I was going to well before puberty and solidified my choice before high school.

Regardless of what motivated us to enlist, we were all Marines and would hold that almost familial bond, as well as the title, until the last breath was taken.

Maggie was bound to Gray by blood, and to the Corps by virtue of being born while Gray served. Wyatt was connected by marriage.

All family.

"Why did you join, Dad?" Maggie asked, then nodded toward Jim and Cowboy. "You hardly ever talk about it, unless you're hanging around these two and then you clam up if anyone comes in the room."

"Same reason I did," Cowboy answered. "The bottom fell out of oystering."

"A ban like this one?" I asked.

"Nothing like this one," Gray answered. "The beds began to grow very soon after this ban went into place and every month, they get stronger." He blew out his breath. "No, what he's talking about started several years *before* we enlisted, back in June of 1972."

"Well, you were only..." Maggie began.

"Fourteen, at the time," Gray answered. "I'd been working the boats after school and weekends since I was twelve. But that summer was when Hurricane Agnes hit the Bay. It wasn't a powerful storm, barely a Cat-1, with gusts to ninety-five."

"She was a slow-movin' *witch*," Jim added. "Brought a six-foot storm surge and waves on top of that, and completely covered the barrier islands and brought the salinity of the Bay way up."

"At least a third of the beds were destroyed by the surge," Gray continued. "Then Agnes moved north, dropping a ton of rain all the way up to Atlanta, flooding the watershed and bringing huge amounts of freshwater downriver. Apalach was under water for a couple of days and the water in the bay was mostly fresh, killing lots of fish and more of the beds. Then we learned the flood had brought toxic chemicals from the farms."

"We lost over ninety percent of the Bay's oyster beds in a week's time," Jim said. "Put a lot of people out of work for a long time. The recovery from the storm was quick, but the bay took years."

"When your mom and I decided to get married," Gray said to his daughter, "the beds had only come back a little bit and oystering was all I knew. So, I talked to a recruiter, figuring I could do pretty good in the Marines, and it'd leave one more job open to someone else, and the bay'd be recovered by the time I got out."

"I remember that season," Jim said. "Eight years after the storm, and things was finally gettin' back to normal around here." He nudged Cowboy. "Then you two come home."

Cowboy laughed. "Did we ever clean up that year! And Gray didn't get out until the season was almost over."

Jim joined him, cackling. "Yep, them ole boys couldn't keep up with us doin' reveille at three o'clock."

I could easily picture the two of them—Jim, the salty old Nam vet, and Cowboy, fresh out of the Corps, probably within days of the last time I'd seen him—rising before the town even thought about it and motoring out into the darkness, determined and disciplined for anything.

"I need to get back to work, Daddy," Maggie said. "I only stopped because I saw Wyatt's truck."

"Yeah, I need to get back to the boat, myself," I said. "My wife and son went shopping and they should be getting back soon."

"Can I give you a lift?" Maggie offered.

"No thanks," I replied. "We've been on the boat for a long time. I think Tank and I prefer walking."

"Okay, then," she said, then kissed Gray on the cheek. "See you."

"I'll walk you out," Wyatt said, then turned with her toward the door.

"Nice to meet you, Jim." I smiled, shaking his hand and then Cowboy's before turning to Gray. "Great to catch up with you. We're here for a few days. How about you and Georgia come to *Taranis* for dinner tomorrow night? All of you."

"Me and Jim'll have to pass," Cowboy said. "I'm drivin' him to the VA clinic in Tallahassee and we're spendin' a coupla nights."

"We can do that," Gray answered. "What time?"

"About eighteen-hundred and stay for sundowners?"

"You're on," Gray answered.

"Come on, Tank," I called, slapping my thigh with the leash, then turning to Gray. "I'll see you tomorrow."

When Tank and I stepped outside, Maggie had already left, but Wyatt was waiting, leaning against the fender of a Dodge pickup, one foot propped behind him on the tire.

As I clipped Tank's leash on, Wyatt pushed himself off the truck and strode toward us, adjusting the fit of his ballcap.

"Do you work for Armstrong Research?" he asked bluntly. "My guess is you do, and you're here because of Maggie's request but couldn't say anything in front of the others."

Later, as Tank and I strolled back toward the marina, passing little shops selling everything imaginable, small cafés with outdoor seating, and boutique clothing stores, I considered the discussion Wyatt and I had and what he'd told me.

As a rule, Armstrong tried to avoid operations on American soil, but more and more, it seemed like America was becoming a Third World country in many ways.

The fact that Maggie's request had gone unanswered didn't mean Armstong Research couldn't or wouldn't help. It took time to weigh the benefits versus the cost, and in a case like this, in a rural Florida town, they had to factor in the risk of exposure and collateral damage.

The fact that Charity had disclosed details and given Maggie and Wyatt the number to the Armstrong "hotline" meant that she trusted them.

That was good enough for me. But I still wanted to talk to her, and we had our own untraceable means of doing so.

It was this same kind of networking with local law enforcement that had created Jack Armstrong's vast army of informants, investigators, and operatives. Some could be trusted to make judgment calls in the field to expand the network. It didn't happen often, though.

Most of the time, if an investigator collected enough evidence to put a criminal behind bars for a long time, they turned it over to local law enforcement in a manner that would make the evidence legit in a court of law. Occasionally, other assets were sent in—operatives like Charity and Deuce. They didn't often interact with the cops, but usually left destruction behind for the authorities to try to figure out.

The part of Franklin County the sheriff's deputies had been searching was about twenty square miles of high, dense pine forest that ran along a natural limestone ridge. It was surrounded by wetlands near the boundary of the state and national forests.

The area contained some of the highest parts of the whole county, which wasn't saying much; it was only fifty feet above sea level and miles inland.

Their searches had been conducted in a grid pattern, as I'd figured, broken up into square parcels that could be searched before dusk. Yet, somehow, though they'd explored the whole area on foot, the lab hadn't been discovered.

Finding the people who *worked* the lab would be easier. My guess was, and Wyatt agreed, that the lab made meth at night, when there was less chance of discovery.

Wyatt had explained that 'no sane man would go out there at night,' yet that statement precluded adaptation. Marines, particularly Marine Recon, were well-trained and highly skilled at adapting to whatever environment they worked in, from frozen tundra to scorching desert sand and everything in between.

Sound traveled well at night. There were fewer noises to contend with and the air was cooler and denser. Darkness was an ally to the criminal.

Local law enforcement was constantly being forced to adapt to the criminal environment but was always reactionary—they responded to events on the ground as they came up.

What I'd suggested to Wyatt was a proactive stance.

Get ahead of the lawbreakers.

Finding the people by sound, as they moved or worked, would have to be done at night.

And whoever was doing the searching had to be silent.

I'd once spent thirty days alone in the desert in Kuwait, moving at night, sleeping when I could, eating MREs dropped fairly accurately from a high-flying surveillance plane with a low-opening drogue chute to slow it down a few hundred feet from the ground.

I remember having to watch the package from half a mile away, sometimes for hours, waiting to see if the drops had been noticed. On a few occasions, they were, and usually by non-combatants. So, I'd go hungry for a night, while some guy fed his family.

I once slipped into the kitchen tent of an Iraqi general and stole a bowl of stew while I recorded the GPS coordinates and placed a listening device and tracker high on a tent pole.

I'd had to adapt to a far more difficult environment then. Hiding in the woods was easy compared to desert sand and rocks.

Maybe the lab wasn't even a building at all, but just the equipment, concealed so only knowing precisely where it was located would enable a person to find it, set it up, and do whatever it was they did.

Bad guys adapted to technology too, and GPS trackers were a lot more accurate today than when I was in the desert. Tank had one on the back of his collar. It was buoyant and if he fell in, with or without his life vest and EPIRB, it'd ride up behind his head and we could find him using a tracking app on our phones.

The fact that deputies covered the whole area by grid pattern told me that the lab could possibly even be mobile. It wouldn't take much—a couple of ATVs with high-ground-clearance trailers. Even a small operation could produce a lot of meth.

Wyatt had explained to me that some meth users had their own little kits and made enough for themselves using a camp stove in the back of a car. Too often those were the people who were killed, either by overdose, inhaling toxic fumes, using the wrong chemicals, or in a fiery explosion.

"Sometimes, all of the above," he'd said. "But that's not these guys."

Wyatt had gone on to explain that he believed the lab turning out most of the meth in the county was run by smarter people than the backseat cooks—people who were at home in the dark forest.

The only chance the police had of finding the lab was finding the people. And that would have to be done under the cover of darkness.

Tank and I walked unhurriedly, as was Tank's natural pace. He kind of lumbered along like a bear on paws that were still oversized for his body, a forecast as to how big he would soon be. He was thick through the chest, with widely spaced front legs, so his walk shifted his body weight from side to side, as if he were sauntering. He kept his neck out straight, parallel with his spine, his big head up, eyes forward, and nose slightly down.

Several people asked if they could say hi to him. So, we stopped, and Tank made a few friends. I always got the same reaction when I told them he wasn't full-grown yet.

Most who saw him coming as we walked simply made room on the sidewalk.

Warren had said that Tank and all his siblings had learned to heel very quickly. He attributed that to the mountain dog lineage. Since they were known to be very noncompetitive due to their size, trying to establish dominance by pulling on the leash was a habit that didn't need to be broken.

In Tank's mind, "Heel" simply meant "Walk," and he enjoyed walking. Mostly, he walked beside me, the leash dangling, but if he noted a narrower passage ahead, he'd move slightly ahead of me, so I wouldn't trip over him.

It was hard to believe, as we strolled along the busy little streets of Apalachicola, hearing snippets of friendly conversation and inhaling the scent of fresh pastries in the air, that a town so quaint could have such a large drug problem.

Wyatt had explained that Apalachicola's full-time residents only numbered a little over two thousand, and another ten thousand lived in rural Franklin County, which was a thousand square miles.

One person for every sixty-some acres.

The vast wetland areas that were considered uninhabitable dwarfed the few small towns. No wonder they couldn't find the lab.

Law enforcement knew the general location, based on stories from hikers who reported smelling a strange chemical odor. They came from the same general area, deep in the state forest called Tate's Hell, where it bordered on the larger Apalachicola National Forest.

Though the reports of the odor came from a fairly small area, it was still thousands of acres of dense woodland.

When we reached the boat, the others were still not back, so I punched in the code for the alarm system and unlocked the sliding hatch to the salon. When I opened it, I felt a rush of cool air.

Though water and electric were available at the dock, we hadn't hooked up. While spending days in quiet anchorages, we'd learned that without the electric motors running, *Taranis's* solar panels and batteries could power everything on board, plus make water and power available to others, all day and all night for as long as we wanted.

Tied to a dock, where food was a short walk away, *Taranis* could stay unplugged indefinitely.

I rinsed and refilled Tank's water bowl, then went to Savannah's and my stateroom behind the wheelhouse, and then straight down into the head, which took up most of the starboard ama.

Turning aft, I opened my top drawer and reached under my T-shirts to retrieve a cell phone. It was an old flip phone, still active, and fully charged.

I'd bought two, years ago, and kept both activated for just me and one other person to communicate.

I turned it on and saw there were no new calls or messages. But I hadn't expected any. There was only one number stored in its call history.

I pressed the *Redial* button.

My call went straight to her voicemail with a beep, as I figured it would, since it was most likely powered off, like mine had been.

"Call me when you get this," I said into the phone, then closed it and dropped it into my right pocket.

From up in the salon, I heard Tank's low chuff, and the thump of his tail against the lounge cushion. I went back up to the stateroom and out into the wheelhouse just as Savannah was coming through the sliding hatch, Alberto and Maddy right behind her.

"I didn't know you'd be back so soon," she said, unloading a couple of large canvas bags onto the dinette table, then turning to reach up on her toes to kiss me. "How was the boatyard?"

"Very interesting," I mumbled, looking through the bags.

"There's nothing there for you," she said, as Maddy and Alberto added several more tote bags. "This is all stuff for the boat. How was it interesting?"

"Gray and his two Marine buddies, along with his son-in-law, who used to be the local sheriff, have been refurbishing oyster skiffs during the harvest ban. One was over a hundred years old. Where's Florence and David?"

"Still souvenir hunting," Maddy replied, pulling a dark brown shirt from a bag. "Here, Jesse. I saw this and had to get it for you."

I caught the shirt when she tossed it and held it up. On the left breast was a logo for Apalachicola Chocolate and Coffee Company.

"Thanks," I said. "I think Tank and I walked past this place coming from Gray's."

"Look on the back," Alberto insisted.

I flipped it over and held it up, then laughed. "Support your local caffeine dealer?"

CHAPTER FOURTEEN

We unloaded the canvas bags, one of which held half a dozen more bags, which Savannah said were the first things she'd bought from a local boutique shop, knowing she was going to do some serious shopping.

She moved things around the salon—a black-and-white photo of the Apalachicola waterfront, a wide-bottomed vase with cattails, and other things—plus several more decorative items in our stateroom, telling me how an item would look nice there, then changing her mind several times.

Then she decided she had to think about it some more.

I knew there was no sense in rushing her. She'd done the same thing aboard *Salty Dog*, and our little house in the Content Keys.

So, we went up to the flybridge lounge to relax with a beer and a glass of wine.

"I asked Gray and Georgia to come to dinner tomorrow." I said, looking out toward the open Gulf.

Savannah smiled and started to say something, then hesitated for a moment. "I like her," she finally said. "And it seems everyone in town knows and likes her, too. *And* Gray. We can grill the mahi up here."

"Mom?" Florence called out from behind us.

Savannah stood and looked down toward the dock. "Up here, sweetie."

"Where do you want me to put this?" David asked. "The fridge or the pantry?"

"I'll be right down," Savannah said, patting my shoulder and heading toward the stairs.

I followed her, curious about what they'd bought that might need refrigerating. We had plenty of food aboard, including filets from four nice-sized mahis we'd caught on the trip up through the Gulf.

When I stepped into the salon, David was placing four large grocery bags from Piggly Wiggly on the galley countertop, along with two more of the same canvas bags Savannah had bought.

"What'd you get?" I asked.

Savannah smiled. "Well... I needed some jasmine rice and sweet potatoes to go with the mahi Alberto and David caught. So, David and Flo volunteered to go to the grocery store."

"I'll be in my room," Alberto said, picking up his tablet and heading toward the port ladderwell.

I looked in the tote bags and found two bottles of rum in the first—Pusser's and Mount Gay—along with three bottles of different mixers.

The second bag held several large mangoes. I picked one up and sniffed it. It was very ripe and had a great aroma.

"I also invited the Redmonds," Savannah confessed. "And they're staying for sundowners, which the mangoes are for. They're grown locally."

I grinned at her. If I'd not noticed the contents of the bags, she would have continued letting me think *I'd* invited Gray and Georgia. She'd caught herself from saying it on the flybridge.

Mangoes were a tropical fruit that wouldn't normally grow more than twenty-five degrees north or south of the equator, which would be the Keys, and the southern tip of the Florida mainland around Cape Sable.

The Panhandle was a long way from the tropics.

"This far north?" I asked.

"A man in town has an orchard," she replied, unloading the other bags' contents onto the counter. "He donates most to the local farmers' market and the proceeds go to buy nonperishables for the food bank."

"Brings a whole different dimension to the term 'farm to plate,'" I said, curious. "I imagine it'd be a lot of work taking care of mango trees outside the tropics. Seems pretty industrious."

She looked up. "He's also the biggest employer in the area. His name's Bennett Boudreaux."

I carried the mangoes back to the dinette, where Savannah had strung two triangular nets in the corners of the overhead for storing fresh fruits and vegetables.

Maddy followed me. "Remember what we were talking about last night?" she asked, as I began transferring the yellow and red fruit to one of the nets. "Up on the flybridge?"

I glanced over at her. "We talked about a lot of things."

"Some kid about fifteen offered me a free taste of his 'cookie' earlier today. That's a street name for meth, right?"

I slowly turned toward her and nodded. "Yes, I think it is. You said a fifteen-year-old?"

"Probably," she replied. "Creepy kid."

"What'd you tell him?" Savannah asked.

"I shoved him away and called him a dickweed," she replied. "Then I told him to get lost."

"But... you were with us," Savannah said.

"It was outside that store where you bought the painting of the two dolphins," she said. "I was looking at something, and when I came out, you were going into the next shop. You probably walked right past him."

From past interactions I've had, I knew most drug dealers preferred peddling their junk at night, and Wyatt had said the meth problem was more rural than in town.

Kids selling drugs in broad daylight in town meant they felt no fear.

And at fifteen, a kid wouldn't get hard time for a first conviction, maybe not even a second.

"Remember the cop who stopped us?" I asked Savannah.

She nodded.

"She's a captain with the Franklin County Sheriff's office," I explained. "And their chief investigator. I ran into her again this evening at Gray's boatyard. The former sheriff I mentioned is her husband. They were both there."

"Why?"

"Oh, yeah," I caught myself, then backpedaled. "Captain Maggie Hamilton is Gray and Georgia's daughter. The last time I saw her before last night, she was three. Anyway, Wyatt—the former sheriff and Gray's son-in-law—explained to me the seriousness of the meth problem in the county."

"Can't they do anything about it?" Maddy asked. "That kid wasn't much older than Alberto."

"They know there's a local lab making it," I explained to her. "But they can't find it." I turned to Savannah. "They've even asked for *outside* help."

Her pupils dilated slightly; she understood. Captain Hamilton was a friend of Charity's and Charity worked for Armstrong.

We got the rest of the stuff put away, and while Savannah started moving pictures, small potted plants, and knickknacks around, trying to find the perfect place for them, I went back up to the flybridge.

My input on interior decorating was neither needed nor would it be considered if offered. And I was okay with that.

David soon joined me, and we cracked open a couple of beers and leaned on the aft rail, looking back at the marina and the town beyond it.

"Want me to see if Mr. Stockwell has anyone on it?" he asked, then took a drink. "I couldn't help overhearing and I know Charity has some connections here."

David had helped create the software that ran Armstong's massive, centrally located, Multi-Encrypted Technical Interface System, or METIS, named for the Greek goddess of wisdom and knowledge. He'd also worked some as a junior analyst and had access to the assignment roster.

"Correct assumption," I said. "I spoke with Wyatt outside the boatyard before I left. He told me that Maggie had called the hotline for Charity."

"Correct assumption, as in... you want me to check, or that I guessed they'd called Armstrong?"

"Both," I said. "That is, if you can do it without anyone knowing."

He looked over at me for a moment, then pulled his smartphone out and began thumbing through apps and filters, typing with his thumbs.

Finally, he put it away and looked up at me again. "A call was received nearly three weeks ago from Maggie Hamilton in Apalachicola, and a field investigator was assigned last Thursday. But no operations log has been created."

That meant that the nerds in the bowels of Armstrong's facility on North Bimini had investigated the caller and the reason for the call and had recommended sending an investigator in person. No operations file meant that no direct action was planned. Yet.

"Who's the investigator?"

He shrugged. "That's the 'multi' part of the encryption. From there, the communications are directly between the handler and the investigator. No other access. Even Chyrel couldn't hack that part."

I turned to face him. "Who's the handler?"

"Mr. Stockwell, himself," David replied.

"Travis?" I asked, getting a nod in return. "That could only mean one thing. DJ Martin and Jerry Snyder."

"Not necessarily," he replied, leaning on the rail. "I know he personally handles a couple other undercover investigators, as well as some very *deep* cover investigators and operatives, like Charity."

"It wouldn't be her," I conjectured. "She knows we're here and would have said something by now. Do you know who any of the other investigators are who he handles?"

David shook his head. "No. They're *that* deep."

"Do you think we should tell Travis we're here?"

He looked me in the eye. "Only you can make that call for yourself, Jesse. I feel like I'm sort of obligated to, now that I know an investigator is coming. But I will tell Mr. Stockwell that I'm with Flo and we're on vacation, getting ready to close out our apartment and move the boat."

I grinned at him and held up my stubby brown bottle. "You're getting devious as to how you tell the truth, Mr. Stone," I said, trying to mimic Stockwell's gravelly voice.

He clinked my bottle with his. "It probably rubbed off from someone close, Mr. McDermitt."

We both looked out toward the well-lit fish market, the pale orange lights from the park off to the left, and the glow of downtown Apalachicola beyond.

About two thousand residents were getting ready for bed and a couple of deputies were starting their shift.

And somewhere out beyond the lights and city limit signs, someone was manufacturing methamphetamine, and using kids to sell it to other kids.

I sighed. "Yeah, tell him we're all here, including Savvy, Maddy, and Alberto."

CHAPTER FIFTEEN

I woke early, slid quietly out of bed, and pulled my skivvies and shorts on. Savannah lay comfortably on her side, blond hair tossed all over the pillow and the sheet barely covering her hip.

Silence was something I was having a much greater appreciation for, and the latch made no sound when I turned the knob, nor did the hinges, when I pulled the hatch open and slipped out of our room directly into the wheelhouse.

The motion sensor turned on low-level red accent lights angled down at the deck, and higher ones pointed up at the overhead. The wheelhouse was pitched in an eerie red glow.

I closed the hatch softly and slowly released the handle, so as not to disturb Savannah.

The coffeemaker had finished brewing just a moment earlier. The soft beep when it finished was what had awakened me. After pouring a cup, I took a quick sip, then filled a small Thermos bottle full. At the sliding hatch, I disabled the alarm, then went out to the cockpit and up to the flybridge to wait for sunrise.

I took another sip, placed the Thermos on the dash, then sat down at the helm. With our stern toward the lights of town, the view of the Gulf of Mexico over the bow was incredible.

Due to her massive beam width, *Taranis* would almost always be tied up to a face dock any time we stopped to reprovision, which pretty much would mean an unobstructed view fore and aft.

Where I sat was a good seventeen or eighteen feet from the same dock the Chris-Craft ahead of us was tied to, and she was a big girl, easily fifteen feet wide, but she didn't impair my view. Her deck space was semi-cluttered, probably a dock queen. But I could see past her to the other boats, and all the way out to the end of the jetty.

The usual morning marina sounds reached my ears; the gentle splash of a wave against the hulls, docks, and jetties, the creak of a vessel's dock lines, or the soft, tinking sound of a halyard against an aluminum mast were universal in places where boats gathered.

Across the fairway and far out at the end of the lighted east jetty, a couple of old timers were setting up rods and reels, organizing their tackle by the light of a small lantern on a stand, and situating a pair of folding chairs, as if they were planning to be there a while.

The fish house at the other end of the far dock was open, with lights spilling out onto the water from an open unloading bay door. Apparently, it ran twenty-four hours.

A number of pelicans were gathered on pier posts and a few more in the water moved in and out of the pool of light from the open bay door, waiting for their breakfast of fish heads and guts. Not very filling, but they didn't have to work hard to get it.

There was a splash, and several pelicans dove toward the fish carcass someone tossed out the back door of the fish house. The victor came away, flapping its wings hard to reach the pier, then turning its beak toward the stars and swallowing.

The scene was as peaceful and serene as any Norman Rockwell picture, and reminded me of Pap's boathouse on the Caloosahatchee River, back home in Fort Myers.

Home.

It was such a relative term for me. I'd made my home in many places over the years. From Japan to the Horn of Africa, to the frozen Arctic, to the jungles of South America, and "every clime and place where we could take a gun," just as was written in the Marine's Hymn. The Keys have been my home for a long time, but I was constantly leaving there.

It was unusual for Colonel Travis Stockwell to dwell on things or be indecisive. Yet, he hadn't replied to David's communication.

That made me think that what was happening here, as well as the request Maggie Hamilton had made, weren't a high priority for Armstrong Research, and whoever was coming to investigate would likely be whoever Stockwell could scrape from the bottom of the roster.

The sky over the fish house was starting to turn purple with the coming of first light, and behind me and to starboard, the dawn chorus of songbirds was just starting in the park. I didn't have to look at a clock to know it was half an hour before sunrise. Nor did I need to consult a tide chart to know that since it was a new moon, dawn would bring a rising spring tide.

The setting was quiet, tranquil, peaceful, even nostalgic in a way, and it drew me in, creating an idyllic place in my mind—a place that wasn't ugly, like the rest of the world.

Yet I knew there was a layer of grime just below the surface, even here, far from the big cities and glam tourist destinations.

It was like a powder keg of addiction was slowly exploding across the American landscape, turning old Norman's drawings of simpler times into scenes from some hellish nightmare.

I could sense the tension in some of the people I'd met. The way Dwight Schultz's mask had slipped, melting away to expose his caring nature when he'd talked about the kids. I'd seen it in Wyatt and Maggie, as well. Cops always saw the worst side of humanity, and I could only imagine how hard it'd be to not become jaded, witnessing it day in and day out.

But I'd also felt the tenseness in Gray and Cowboy. And Jim didn't even attempt to suppress his distaste.

And there were others.

While Tank and I walked back from Gray's boatyard, people had been drawn to him first, even before saying hello to me. I'd tried to appear nonthreatening—just a guy out for a stroll with his pup—but once their attention shifted from Tank to me, I could *feel* the wariness emanating from some of them.

I knew part of that was just me. I was six-three, weighed well over two hundred pounds, and had almost no body fat. A big, scary guy, and I'm sure the many acts of depravity I'd witnessed over the years were visible in my eyes, too.

Something was about to happen here; I could feel things teetering on the brink, and it revolved around the production of methamphetamine.

I also knew there would probably be just one guy controlling most of it. One supplier, one kingpin, one major dealer. That guy either made the meth himself or bought it wholesale for local distribution. But the reports from hikers about a chemical smell deep in the forest seemed to point toward the former. The search not turning up anything didn't rule out its existence.

I could hide a five-ton truck in the forest and a person would have a hard time spotting it from just a few yards away.

Then again, the hikers may have smelled some naturally occurring odor and described it as chemical. Some springs had a heavy sulfur content and smelled like the depths of Hell were opening up. The corpse flower is native only to Western Sumatra and grows up to ten feet tall, with a single bloom the size of a man's head. When it opens, it releases an odor that's easily mistaken for decomposing flesh.

But there were other things that pointed toward the odor in the woods coming from a meth lab—the high use of meth in the county being the most prevalent.

That one person, whoever he was, would have a team of people under him. Not a lot, but more than a couple. I'd think at least two to do the actual manufacturing part. And probably one or two more to help move and sell the product.

That meant at least two people were moving around in the deepest parts of the forest at night, when no human should be there, according to Wyatt.

I wondered how many nights a week they did it. I wouldn't think it'd be very often unless they were transporting it out of the area. With only twelve thousand residents in the whole county, the customer base would undoubtedly be very small, probably no more than a couple hundred, which led me to consider how much of the stuff users consumed.

Wyatt had said that the average user was young, poor, and the demographic tended to lean more toward males. I knew meth was very addictive, which meant those poor young men, who'd given up on everything, could easily turn to crime to support their addiction.

I also knew it wasn't cheap, costing a hundred or more for just one gram of the stuff. Which was *why* those stereotypical lost youths turned to crime to fund their very expensive habit.

A couple of grams a week per user? For someone struggling at the bottom, probably out of work, two hundred bucks was a lot of money.

Wyatt had also briefly explained how easily a home lab could be built, requiring very little room to be able to manufacture a couple hundred grams of meth at a time, or "per cook," as it's called on the streets.

Moving it didn't require any great security measures. Two hundred grams wasn't even half a pound—easily hidden in someone's pants pocket. But it had a street value of $20,000.

Follow the money.

I looked back over my right shoulder at the little town, still mostly asleep, with a vast, sparsely-populated rural area beyond.

One of those twelve thousand people was suddenly making a lot of money. And likely spending it—new car, new clothes, new house.

Ahead in the distance, barely visible in a light mist, I saw the red and green glow of navigation lights with a steaming light high on a mast—a sailboat coming into the marina.

You'd think someone flashing twenty grand a week around in a small town would draw attention. Of course, any business, even an illegal one, had overhead. Wyatt had rattled off some simple items that were used to make the stuff and how purchases of those things had become a lot more scrutinized. One of the ingredients was a simple cold remedy, but if you were to buy more than a couple of boxes, they'd ask for your name and address.

That just meant the criminal had to adapt to avoid detection, and not buy some of the components in volume. A smart one would spread the purchases around, going to different stores and businesses over a wide area. And that likely meant a small organization of people getting the materials.

Again, if they could find the people, they'd find the lab. And the easiest way to find the people was to look for someone who was spending a lot more than usual.

It was getting lighter as I poured another cup of coffee from the Thermos and stood up to greet the day.

The approaching sailboat was at the last marker, just a couple hundred yards away, gliding silently ahead of a V-shaped ripple in the water, just visible in the gathering light.

It was an older production boat, and as it got closer, I decided it was a Catalina, less than thirty feet. The mainsail lay in a sail bag, but it wasn't closed up, meaning the sails had recently been doused or the crew was just lazy.

But lazy people didn't arrive at first light.

The sound of the little diesel, chugging at low RPM, didn't reach my ears until the boat was less than a hundred yards away.

A big, bearded man with long hair stood shirtless at the helm, only visible behind the cabin from the waist up. He was staring at *Taranis*, which we'd come to realize happened anytime anyone saw her.

The sound of the diesel dropped to an idle, then the transmission clunked out of gear as the boat drifted down the middle of the fairway, slowly coming alongside *Taranis*.

The name board on the side of the bow, below the toe rail told me her exact length—*Whole Nine Yards.* As the man in the cockpit came into full view, I could see a prosthetic lower leg and foot.

"I didn't figure on seein' *you* here," DJ Martin said in a low voice across the intervening fifty feet of water.

I grinned and lifted my mug. "Unfortunately, I *was* sort of expecting to see you. I take it you're still on the colonel's shit list?"

CHAPTER SIXTEEN

Leo Bishop drove slowly along the unnamed dirt road. It'd been cut through the woods a century earlier and abandoned long before anyone in the area was born. The road, as well as the overgrown canal next to it, were completely unknown to most of the people in Franklin County.

After a mile, he turned off of the dirt road onto asphalt that was only slightly better. The Mustang's headlights bore through the light mist, illuminating the broken line on the edge of the pavement, which was only partly visible in places. Like the dirt road he'd come off of, this one had no name and had also been left to the elements for decades.

He drove slowly. Deer season was still a couple of months away, and they were active all through the forest just before dawn. Also, the potholes would play hell on his tires and suspension.

After several agonizingly slow miles, he reached the state road that headed south. Low hanging limbs hid the entrance to the deserted sideroad from the average motorist speeding by, and they lightly brushed the roof as Leo pulled out onto the highway.

He was able to open the muscle car up a little on the highway. Not a lot, though. The last thing he needed was to get stopped for speeding at five o'clock in the morning with over 200 grams of ice hidden in the trunk.

He thought about his sister, Karin, as he drove toward home. If she were still alive, she'd be twenty-five. He wondered what she'd think of his current endeavor. She was wild at times, liked to party, and before she'd overdosed on Oxy, she'd have thought he was a genius for coming up with the idea.

A lot of people tried cooking their own meth, and it was a lot of trouble, not to mention dangerous. But if you could get all the right ingredients and did it the correct way, it was a lot cheaper than buying it.

All he wanted was to make enough money to get out of the trailer park, out of Eastpoint, and out of Franklin County. A fresh start anywhere.

Karin did it. She'd made it all the way to California.

And since Karin and their mom were both now dead, nothing still held him in Eastpoint. His father had left when Leo was just three and they'd never heard from him again. He had no other family that he knew of. So, why stay?

Leo was on his way home from his latest excursion deep into the backwater swamps of Tate's Hell. He was exhausted, both physically and mentally, and was looking forward to falling into bed for a few hours.

He'd used the fourth lab, which was the hardest to reach, being half a mile deeper in the forest. On the way in, he'd actually passed Lucas in the woods as he was on his way back from charging the battery. The encounter had startled both of them.

Aside from that one time when the police search had passed close to where Leo was hiding, he hadn't come across a single soul in the woods, nor had any of the others ever mentioned seeing anyone.

When Leo crossed Old 98 into the trailer park, he saw a blue Impala sitting in front of his trailer and recognized it instantly.

Rupert "Root" Valdi considered himself a gang leader. All he'd really done was give a group of local backwoods malcontents and thugs a name—the Roaches. Mostly, the Roaches just laid around blowing clouds all day, listening to music, and planning outlandish bank heists.

Hardly what would be considered a "gang."

"Man, it's too early for this shit," Leo muttered as he parked the Mustang.

He only had like four hours before he had to start the shift he'd promised himself he'd do.

Leo slowly climbed out of the car, leaving last night's product safely hidden in the trunk until he got rid of the guy.

"Mornin', Leo," Root said, rising from one of his lawn chairs. "Late night, huh?"

His kid brother got up quickly from another chair but didn't say anything.

"You know Lee, right?" the older Valdi said.

Leo glared at the kid. "I heard you got yourself busted."

"He did," Root agreed, nodding his head. "But when he went up in front of the judge yesterday afternoon, they were missin' some paperwork and hadda let him out on OR."

The same thing had happened to Leo once, and he'd heard stories of similar things happening to others, where the circuit court often lost paperwork and had to release people on their own recognizance.

"Lucky you," Leo said, then looked at the older brother. "What do you want?"

"Mr. Tobias sent us," Root replied, just a shade nervous. "I kinda owe him and he's gonna let me work it off for you."

Tobias was the giant bald guy who'd visited Leo and his friends a few days earlier, along with his boss, who'd threatened to shut down their whole operation.

Only after the boss man left did Tobias tell Leo that from then on, he would stop by to collect ten percent, and they had to increase production by fifty percent. He'd also demanded they take him to the labs way out in the woods.

"Work it off how?" Leo asked.

"Lee here's gonna be your new salesman," Root said. "He's already sold that two grams we got from ya yesterday."

The kid extended his hand, a wad of bills in it.

"Not here, shit-for-brains!" Root said, pushing his hand back down.

Against his better judgment, Leo nodded toward the door. "Let's go inside."

Tobias was a scary guy. Leo knew he'd done time and knew the gun he carried would land him right back in prison if he was caught with it.

But it was the ex-con's attitude that was scary. Anyone who didn't give a shit about going back to prison wouldn't think twice about snuffing trailer trash like Leo and his friends.

A cut of the profits every cook in exchange for "protection" was one thing. But the increase in risk by doing two cooks a week, not to mention double the work to get supplies, was all on him and the others. Their gear and their recipe weren't set up to do half a batch. Any increase over what they'd been doing was double the product, and that meant double the ingredients and double the work to get it.

And now, the guy wanted to use Leo's operation to let Root work off his debt.

Leo plopped down on one of the recliners, draping a leg over the arm. "Put it on the table."

The kid put the cash down, but neither of them moved to take a seat.

Leo was unworried about being alone with either of them or even both. The kid was no bigger than a girl, and Root wasn't much bigger.

The guy had a hugely inflated opinion of himself, though, and he always had. Around others.

But Leo'd kicked Root's ass in sixth grade and from that point on, the pecking order had been established. Even if Root became the president of the United States, he'd still be the guy who Leo'd whipped in a fair fight.

"How much is it?" he asked.

"Three hundred," Root replied. "The kid's got an angle."

"A buck-fifty a gram?" Leo asked, impressed. "How?"

"Tourist kids," Lee replied.

"You just...what? Walk up to kids when they're visitin' the lighthouse or some such shit?" Leo asked. "Good way to get popped again. Or just flat out beaten to a pulp by a mad dad."

"Yeah, well, it happens," the kid muttered, shrugging a bony shoulder under an oversized T-shirt. "Some little rich bitch got all loud and shit just yesterday."

"What happened?" Root asked him.

"Little bitch called me a *dickweed* in public and shoved me off a curb. But I stay away from the dads. She was with...like her mom or somethin', another old lady, and a little kid."

"You didn't tell me about that," Root said, turning to his brother.

He shrugged. "It was the last cookie, man. I offered to give her a free taste and if she didn't think it was worth one-fifty..." He grinned at Leo, exposing stained teeth. "I told her she could *try* to walk away."

"And she shoved you?" Root demanded. "Ain't no call for that shit, right, Leo? Know where she's stayin'? What's she look like?"

Lee grinned up at his big brother as he dug a cell phone from his pocket. "I got her picture, man," he said, showing them both.

"How'd you get her picture?" Root asked, looking at the screen.

Lee's face reddened. "Well... I was followin' her, ya see... waitin' for the right time."

CHAPTER SEVENTEEN

DJ Martin had been a part of the Armstrong organization as long as me, Deuce, and Charity, but where we'd moved straight into covert operations and then command positions, DJ had remained in the periphery, drifting in and out as it suited him, doing mostly investigative work with Jerry Snyder.

In my opinion, after losing part of his leg in combat, he had that right.

I knew Stockwell had ridden him hard at times, either because of their shared Army Ranger ethos, or because the colonel saw something others didn't. I could never really be sure.

The physical change was obvious as he motored on to his slip. He'd trimmed down and added muscle. When we'd first met, he'd been overweight, out of shape, easily agitated, and he tended to drink too much.

Again, in my own opinion, he had those rights, too, so long as his bad habits didn't become a liability to himself or others.

It looked like, at least physically, the man had turned his life around.

I got another mug from the galley and topped off the Thermos before setting up the coffeemaker for another run. Ten minutes after returning to the flybridge, I heard uneven footsteps approaching and went aft to the rail.

"C'mon up," I said quietly. "The others are still asleep."

Martin stepped over to the starboard ama's swim platform and came up the steps to the cockpit. A moment later, he ascended the steps to the flybridge.

He wore shorts, and his upper legs looked as strong as his upper body. The prosthetic's sleeve extended all the way up over his knee, but I knew the only part missing was from mid-shin down, below the cup that contained what was left of his lower leg. That part of the prosthetic was a gray rod about an inch thick and covered with stickers, which extended into a normal-looking running shoe.

"Who's still asleep?" he asked quietly, looking around, then accepting the mug I extended. "Thanks. And where the heck did ya get this cool trimaran?"

"I'm here with my family, on vacation," I replied. "And I had the boat built over the last couple of years. This is our final shakedown."

"Dang, I thought Dep's old catamaran was big with *two* hulls."

Jerry Snyder's boat, *Wayward*, had been destroyed while he and DJ were conducting an investigation in the Virgin Islands. I'd given him the use of *Floridablanca* for one dollar, until Jerry and Alicia got a new boat.

"This is a third more *marans*," I jokingly replied.

He chuckled, then looked at me, serious. "You asked if I was still on the colonel's shit list, and the answer's yes. It just don't seem like there's any pleasin' the man."

"Stop trying," I replied. "Stockwell's no different than anyone else. You don't *have* to please him."

"Yeah, well, that's easy for you to say," he replied, then looked at me questioningly. "You just *happened* to be here on vacation then, huh?"

"We *were*," I replied. "But I know why you're here and have already met some of the players. When I found out the local sheriff's investigator had reached out to the Armstrong hotline, I had David contact the colonel and let him know we're here if needed."

"You mean the daughter of the local crime boss?" he asked. "A police captain named Margaret Hamilton?"

"Crime—? Whoa! Wait a minute, Deej. I know her dad. I've known Gray Redmond since my first year in the Marines. No way he's involved in what's going on here. He's as straight as they come."

He cocked his head slightly. "Redmond isn't Captain Hamilton's father. A man named Bennett Boudreaux is."

The mango grower?

"I'm not following, DJ. Gimme the grunt version."

"Chip dug deep into Captain Hamilton's background," DJ began, referring to one of Armstrong's analysts. "Though it ain't exactly *public* knowledge, it's been determined that this Bennett Boudreaux is her real father."

I sat down on the aft lounge and waved a hand for DJ to sit also.

Maggie wasn't Gray's biological daughter?

That would explain the lack of resemblance. I remember him telling me once that he and Georgia had dated all the way through high school, so that one time I'd met her as a little girl, I'd just assumed she was his daughter. That's what he'd called her.

Georgia had become pregnant by someone else during that time.

"You're certain about this?" I asked him.

"Now, you *know* it wasn't me doin' the diggin'," DJ scoffed. "I just parrot what they tell me. But from little bits and pieces Chip dug up, it sounds like when he married his wife, your friend already knew the baby she was carryin' wasn't his."

The fact that Armstrong's analysts could find out something like that with any degree of certainty was a bit of a surprise, though it shouldn't have been.

And it dovetailed with what I knew of the man. It was exactly what the Sergeant Gray Redmond I'd once known would have done in that situation. The only right thing.

To protect his girlfriend and her reputation, he'd dropped out of school to marry her and joined the Corps because the bay was wiped out and his family would be taken care of until it recovered.

Head on a swivel, but always moving forward.

"And Maggie's biological father is involved in the meth production here?" I asked.

"That's what I'm here to find out, *compadre*," DJ replied. "Nobody's pointed a finger at him, and Chip couldn't find any connection between him and *any* kind of drug distribution..." He looked up at me. "But man, this Boudreaux character's fingerprints are on quite a few illicit enterprises all along the Gulf Coast."

"He's also the town's biggest employer," I said. "And he grows mangoes."

"Mangoes," DJ repeated flatly.

I shrugged. "Maggie's husband is the former sheriff here."

"Wyatt Hamilton," he said, nodding. "Originally from over on the East Coast, Cocoa Beach. Took the job as sheriff here after the death of his first wife."

"Even though he's retired," I told him, "I got the sense that Wyatt

Hamilton's mind is still on the job. He knows about Armstrong, too. Freely told me, thinking I'm still with y'all."

"And... you ain't," he replied with an exaggerated wink.

"No, DJ, not in any way," I replied. "Except I know a bunch of you, David's my son-in-law, and I'm still friends with Jack. Anyway, I talked to Wyatt about some possibilities the sheriff's office might've overlooked."

"Like what?"

"They did a thorough search of the area in question and turned up nothing," I replied. "A line sweep through the woods during daylight with enough deputies and local police to maintain sight of one another."

"Not too covert," he said, nodding. "And overlooks the notion it might be mobile. A lot of 'em cook the stuff inside their cars."

"Wyatt said the same thing," I replied. "But the location isn't accessible by road."

"Ya know the colonel ain't no fan of conducting ops on American soil..." He paused and met my gaze again. "But he's got a real hard-on for drug dealers."

"What did Travis tell you to find out?"

One by one, DJ ticked off some fingers on his left hand. "One—find out for sure if there really *is* a large meth lab in operation around here and then locate it. B—figure out who the mastermind is and if it turns out there's local law involved, turn the evidence over to the state police and walk away. If not.... Then there's Three—shut down the lab with extreme prejudice and absolute covertness with no collateral damage."

Covert?

DJ was an investigator. He had the makings and background to become a good covert operator, but so far as I knew, he and his partner, Jerry, hadn't made that transition.

"That's a little more than investigators usually handle," I said, curious. "Where's Snyder on this?"

"Dep? Oh, he's off on a sailin' trip with Alicia. Won't be back 'til the end of the month. I was actually on vacation too. Hanging out in Cedar Key." He looked up and grinned. "He ain't there, ya know."

I chuckled. "That's where John D. left him." Then I sighed. "Look, the family connection between Maggie and the local crime boss notwithstanding, I can guarantee that she, her husband, Wyatt, and Gray Redmond are not involved."

"How can you be that sure?" he asked.

"I don't know," I replied. "I've always been able to get a good read on people, especially men. But since Paladin, I'm not so sure..."

"One missed bad guy out of the millions of people you've met?" he asked rhetorically. "Okay, I'll trust your call and go in assuming they're legit. But Boudreaux ain't."

I heard the sliding hatch open and leaned over to look down the steps.

"Who are you talking to?" Savannah called up.

"An old friend," I replied, as DJ and I stood. "Come on up."

When she saw DJ, she charged up the last few steps and gave him a warm hug.

"DJ Martin! As I live and breathe! What are you doing—" The realization hit her, and she stepped back. "Travis sent you."

His eyes cut to mine for a second, and I nodded slightly.

"Yes, ma'am," he replied. "To conduct an undercover investigation."

"And possibly a covert operation," I added, getting a sharp look from

DJ. "Relax, DJ. Savvy knows more about what goes on at Armstrong than Chip does, without even asking any questions."

She looked at him, the smile gone from her face. "I don't know whether to congratulate you or pity you."

"A little of both, I guess," DJ replied with a shrug. "What's the story with you two? You in or out on this one?"

"In," Savannah replied before I could say anything. "Any way we can help you, just ask. One of those cretins tried to sell drugs to Maddy."

Again, DJ looked from her to me.

"You'll meet her," I said. "She's Rusty's cousin, and came with us on this trip, but she's flying back to Marathon later today."

"Who else?" he asked.

"Alberto," Savannah replied, "and Flo, who you know, and her husband—"

"David's here?"

"Yeah," I replied. "I told you. He emailed the colonel yesterday to tell him we were here."

"Ooh, okay. I thought you meant you *remotely* had him contact the colonel."

I heard the slider again, then the clicking of Tank's claws on the cockpit deck as he danced around excitedly.

"Is that you up there, Jesse?" David asked.

"Yeah," I replied. "With Savvy and an old friend. Come on up, after Tank's finished."

"Tank?" DJ asked, standing to look over the rail. "Whoa! That's a big Lab."

Savannah and I exchanged smiles as we got up and went to join him.

Tank lumbered over to the nearest pier post, hiked his leg, and relieved himself while holding his nose up in the air, testing the new scents of the day.

A moment later, Tank came up the steps ahead of David and stopped at the top when he saw DJ. Then he took a step closer, eyes fixed on the prosthetic.

"Tank, this is DJ," I said. "He's a friend."

"I 'preciate you pointin' that out to him," DJ said, a bit nervous. "I don't think I've ever seen a Lab that big. He's gotta be a hundred pounds."

"Mr. Martin?" David asked softly, passing Tank. "I'm David Stone. I recognized your voice, sir."

"What'd I tell you about that mister and sir crap?" DJ said. "It's DJ, like a guy who works at a radio station. Two easy syllables—Dee-Jay."

"Sorry," he said, as we all sat down. "I never really get a chance to meet you guys in person."

"DJ was just explaining how his assignment may turn covert," I told David, as Tank sat next to me for a belly rub. "And Tank here isn't all Labrador retriever, DJ. He won't even be nine months old for a couple more weeks."

Tank turned his head and looked at DJ, his dark brown eyes missing nothing, and his nose twitching, sending more information to his canine brain. Then he made a light chuff, flexing his saggy jowls.

"I think that means he accepts you," Savannah said. "He's a little aloof with strangers at first. Not afraid or nervous though."

"I can see it now in his face," DJ said. "Definitely not all Lab. How much does he—"

"Ninety pounds," Savannah replied, "as of last Thursday, so your guess is probably very close today. He's gaining almost five pounds a week still."

"What kinda dog has a nine-month-old puppy this big?"

"He has a lot of Lab traits from his mother," I replied. "Webbed toes, sleek coat and a thick underfur, and a rudder for a tail. So far, about the only thing he got from his Tibet mountain dog father is his size, his high forehead and jowls."

"And the chillest attitude of any dog *I've* ever known," David added.

DJ leaned closer, put a tentative hand under one of Tank's front legs and lifted it, exposing the white marking on his chest.

"You named him after your friend, right?" DJ asked, looking up reverently. "The Nam vet with the Medal of Honor."

"We picked the name before we picked the puppy," Savannah said.

"What's this about covert?" David asked. "Who's your analyst?"

DJ leaned back in his seat and gave David a quizzical look. "You being here just saved me from writin' an email. I'm here."

"Um... what do you mean?" David asked.

DJ leaned forward and rested his elbows on his knees. "As of two hours ago, you're my analyst."

CHAPTER EIGHTEEN

DJ explained that when he'd been given the investigation, Chip had been assigned as his analyst. They'd worked together many times before, along with Jerry and Alicia Snyder, and a couple of times on solo investigations. But when he was ten miles from Apalachicola, his cell phone picked up a signal and he'd received a communication telling him of the change.

David dug his phone out of his pocket. "It's been on silent," he said, tapping the screen and swiping. He looked up at me. "I have an email from Mr. Stockwell, assigning me as analyst for Mr. Mart—er, DJ."

"That's it?" I asked. "No apology for interrupting your vacation?"

DJ tilted his head slightly, arching an eyebrow. "An apology? From the colonel?"

"You better figure out some way to explain it to Florence," I said, hearing the slider opening down in the cockpit. "And most rikki tik."

A moment later, she came up the steps, followed by Alberto and Maddy, whose eyes cut immediately to DJ's missing right appendage.

"DJ, you remember Alberto and Flo?" Savannah said, as DJ jumped to his feet. "And this is Madison Thurman from Wyoming—Maddy to her friends. Maddy, this is DJ Martin, an... old sailing friend. He's docked here, too."

DJ took her hand in his big paw. "That's a shame, right there," he said with a crooked grin. "The nickname, I mean. Madison's such a pretty little name. But Maddy it is. That is, if you'll be my friend."

She blushed slightly.

Was DJ hitting on her? He had to be at least—

It suddenly dawned on me that DJ was just a few years older than I was when I first met Savannah, and she'd been only a couple of years older than Maddy was now.

As the sun began to peek over the horizon, we paused and went to the rail, even Tank. For those who go around on boats or live in the places where the map turns blue, sunrise and sunset are special times.

"If you're not busy later," DJ said to Maddy, "maybe we can—"

"Maddy's going to be leaving shortly," I said. "She has to be back to work down in Marathon tomorrow."

"Yeah, about that," she said, turning toward me. "I know you were planning to give me a ride to the airport in your friend's car, but it's way on the other side of town, and you and Savannah are going to be busy all day. I checked and, believe it or not, there's a rideshare service here, with *three* whole drivers. I've already arranged for my ride to the airport."

"You don't have to do that," Savannah said, as we returned to the lounge seats. "Jesse's just going to be in my way, as it is."

She smiled at Savannah as she sat down next to Alberto. "It's no big deal. I use the same service in Marathon and have even used it back home in Greybull. Besides, I have to leave just before your guests will arrive."

"It's a shame you have to rush home," DJ said, also taking a seat. "I've been here before, and it's a really nice little town."

"Well, my plane's arriving this afternoon," she said, her usual confidence restored. "And I haven't packed anything yet. Maybe when you come down to the Keys, I can show *you* around."

I knew she didn't have much to pack and could accomplish that task in a matter of minutes. But I couldn't read anything into that.

"That's a done deal," DJ said, rising as Maddy stood up. "I look forward to it one day."

"It was nice to meet you," she replied.

"The pleasure was all mine," DJ said.

After she started down the steps, he turned to me. "I gotta get to work on a project, myself," he said, then dropped his voice to a low whisper. "Thanks for the intel. I'll stop by this afternoon and let ya know what I find out, or at the very least, I'll update David. Right now, I just want to listen to what folks in town talk about."

"Actually," Savannah said, "we're having the Redmonds over for dinner this evening. You should join us."

He looked at me questioningly.

"I do not institute the social calendar, my good man," I said with an aristocratic flair, as I leaned back in my seat. Then I grinned as an idea came to me. "In fact, I'll call Gray and ask him to invite Wyatt and Maggie too."

DJ nodded. "Okay, I'll just concentrate on listening for things about Mr. Boudreaux then."

"Start at the farmer's market," I advised. "And have a mango."

"I'll walk you down," Savannah said. "I need to get another fillet out of the freezer."

"Just one fillet?" he asked. "For three extra people? And me bein' one of 'em?"

"Well, you look like you've slimmed down a good bit," she said, as he turned and started down. "I just assumed you were on a diet." Then she winked at me. "You're all skin and bones."

"Don't worry, Deej," I called after him. "The smallest of the four mahis we caught on the way up here was eighteen pounds."

They talked for a moment in the cockpit, but I couldn't hear what they were saying. Then I heard the sliding hatch open and close and saw DJ go down the steps to the swim platform and step over to the dock.

He turned around and tipped a finger to his brow. "Really nice boat."

I nodded. "Thanks. See you about 1730. Wear long pants."

"Long pants? Why?"

"I don't know if anyone around here knows exactly *who* it was who helped Charity in Panama City, but it's rumored he's an ugly, one-legged pirate."

He arched one eyebrow in surprise, then nodded. "Yargh..."

As he walked away, his footfalls sounded symmetrical. I guess being made aware of it made him self-conscious as well.

I stood and looked out over the marina, wondering what the hell Stockwell was thinking by changing DJ's analyst. Had Stockwell simply ignored the part of David's message about being on vacation? The colonel was target-focused pretty much all the time, and often overlooked the fact that most others weren't.

I was very tempted to call him, but figured that might just as easily be the reason he'd made the switch. To get me to call.

He knows I'm here, I thought. He can call me.

Just then, I was startled by the phone in my right pocket vibrating against my thigh.

I didn't need to check the caller ID, since only one person had the number, and I was expecting her to call back.

I flipped the phone open and held it to my ear. "Hey, Charity."

"I just powered my phone on and got your message," she said, sounding out of breath. "What are you doing in Apalach?"

"It's a trip we've had planned for a year," I replied. "Last shakedown before we disappear to paradise."

"You're really going to do it this time?" she asked.

I stood up and turned, looking out over the bow at the open Gulf of Mexico. "Who knows? Look, sorry about the incident with getting pulled over in your car. I promise, I wasn't hot-rodding."

"You should," she replied. "That's what a car like that is for. So, uh... why did you call?"

I gave her the short version of meeting up with Gray, then his daughter and son-in-law, who thought I was there to help.

"Given our relationship, a logical assumption," she replied, then waited.

"So, naturally, I had David check to see where Captain Hamilton's request was," I went on. "He and Florence came on the trip with us, and he found that an investigator had been assigned and was on the way, and then this morning, he learned Stockwell had switched the roster and made David the analyst on the investigation."

"Who's the investigator?" she asked.

"DJ Martin."

She giggled, then sighed. "Good luck keeping him corralled. Is Snyder with him?"

"No, he's flying solo."

"He'll break things, Jesse," she warned. "His heart's in the right place, but the man has a short fuse and a long boom."

"Still the loose cannon Stockwell said he was," I said.

"Yes, but he has an ally there," she replied. "His spiritual advisor."

"Spiritual... advisor..." I stated flatly.

"DJ's gone holistic," Charity said. "I introduced him to a sound healer I'd met there, and well... One thing I've learned about DJ Martin is this: he doesn't take up interests lightly. Last time I was there, Jojo told me that he'd turned fully to a meditative lifestyle."

"Jojo Lag...harry?"

"A little more from the throat," she said with a snicker. "Jojo *Laghari*. You've met him, then? It is a small town. DJ will probably see him as soon as he gets there."

"He arrived about an hour ago," I replied. "We all compared notes and he's going...'listening.'"

"A new talent he's picked up," she said. "Well, not really a talent, but a miniature hearing aid. By turning his head, he listens to conversations at a distance. He says he sometimes spends days just listening to what people in town say about someone he and Snyder are investigating."

I turned and looked back toward DJ's boat. "A hearing aid? Not very covert."

"For him it is," she replied. "Think about it. A long-haired, bearded guy with a prosthetic leg and a hearing aid, doing nothing but sitting around all day—a homeless vagrant. He's invisible in plain sight."

"Well, he'd have to wear an oversized hoodie or something now," I replied. "Have you seen him lately? Without a shirt, nobody's going to mistake him for a homeless guy."

"I saw him a few weeks ago," she replied. "I think his new spirituality kick is a good thing. He's lost weight, and single handing his boat without his prosthetic has made him stronger and more self-reliant. He quit drinking too."

"What do you know about a man named Bennet Boudreaux?" I asked. "Supposed to be the big man around here."

There was a pause before she answered. "I've met him," she said, a bit vague. "He comes across as a refined, well-mannered Southern gentleman, but I picked up a hard vibe that he was hiding a dark side. Be careful around that one. And um... there are some extenuating circumstances revolving around him."

"You and Captain Hamilton became close," I said, watching people moving around the dock area. "Did she tell you that Boudreaux was her biological father?"

Charity sighed again. "And because she *did* confide in me, *you* know about it. Hold that information close, Jesse."

CHAPTER NINETEEN

Maddy had been right; there was a ton to do before dinner and not all the work that needed to be done was in the galley. After DJ left, she told me that she wanted to make another round of the souvenir shops, and that's why she'd declined his offer to show her around.

I didn't press the issue about the invitation to the Keys.

Not my circus; not my monkeys.

It was our first full day in port and there were a thousand and one maintenance items I had to address. Plus, all the pictures, plants, and stuff that Savannah had bought needed to be hung, arranged, or situated in just the right place, and that sometimes meant me holding two things in outstretched arms against a bulkhead while she looked at them and swapped different things in and out of my hands.

Once that task was complete, Alberto was finished with his lessons, and looking for something to do.

Savannah glanced at me, nodded toward him, and then cut her eyes to the forward steps to the lower deck, where more boat maintenance waited to be done.

"I need to go down to the mechanical room and take an oil sample," I told her. "We didn't run the Cat long, just an hour, but it was pretty high revs the whole time, and it's not even broken in yet."

Alberto grabbed his tablet from the table. "I'll look at the engine data for that whole hour."

"Good idea," I said, winking at Savannah, then following him forward. "What is it you say all the time? Information is king?"

"Data," he corrected me, leading the way forward. "Information is open to... interpretation."

I couldn't help laughing as I followed him down the steps.

For the next hour, Alberto and I took oil and coolant samples, checked all the belts and hoses, and inspected the hydraulic lines, pumps, and connections. Not just on the main engine, but both generators as well. At some point, I'd find a UPS Store and send the sample to Caterpillar for analysis.

Alberto connected his tablet to a USB port at the control console and pulled up the data from the engine's running time since we'd left the Keys almost a week ago.

All of it was from the mad dash to get into Apalachicola Bay ahead of the fog.

"We used almost forty-eight gallons," Alberto advised.

I looked up from my position lying on the deck, where I was inspecting the output shaft. "Whoa, that's a lot. Are you sure?"

"It was nearly an hour, running wide open," he replied, then pulled up something else on his tablet. "The design specs say fifty-three gallons per hour at top speed."

I nodded. "At least it's better than design specs. But we'll need to be more judicious with the Thunder Button when we head to Dominica next month."

He looked down and grinned. "Yeah, right," he replied, with Savannah's trademark *snarcasm*.

My head and right shoulder were under the engine and my chuckle caused me to bump my head.

"Seriously, though," I said, rubbing it as I looked up at him. "What did we gain for that $250 in fuel?"

"Oysters!" he exclaimed. "But yeah, I see what you mean. We did it just to get in ahead of the fog. But as calm as it was, we could've just anchored near the barrier islands."

"Everything looks good down here," I said, then sat up.

"I'm looking at the, um... *performance* data," he said, flipping from one chart to another on his tablet. "I don't see anything.... Wait. Here, look. Twenty-three minutes and fourteen seconds after startup, the coolant temperature went up three degrees."

"That's not much," I said. "Did it come back down?"

He started flipping through more charts, each one a performance readout spanning two minutes of running time. "Here, it came back down twelve minutes later."

"Can you pull up our route?" I asked. "Find out where we were during those twelve minutes? I bet we passed over a shallow spot. Well, shallow-*er*."

After a few seconds, he looked up at me, puzzled. "How'd you know?"

"What was it?" I asked.

"An underwater hill or something. The bottom went from over two thousand feet to just five hundred, then it got deep again."

"Shallow water is warmer," I said with a shrug. "The closed loop cooling system in the keel is dependent on seawater temperature around it. I bet the water in that shallow area was several degrees warmer."

He sat down on a small stool. "Will there be other kids where we're going to go?"

I turned and sat cross-legged between the engine and one of the inverters. "There are kids everywhere, son. You getting bored with us old folks?"

"No, it's not that," he said, then looked at me with a grin. "Well, kinda."

"I wouldn't worry too much about *where* we go, so far as meeting others," I told him. "We're going to log a lot of sea miles on *Taranis,* and it'll mostly just be us and occasional crew."

"Like who?"

"Well, like Maddy," I replied. "Or Rusty and Sid. I'm sure Florence and David will join us again somewhere, and Kim and Marty'll take a couple of vacations a year. We could even get Eve and Nick to bring Fred to stay aboard for a passage. Or Deuce and Julie can bring Trey and Jim."

He looked over at me, his dark eyes twinkling. "I hadn't thought of it like that."

"Like what?"

"You could say *Taranis* is a... um... vacation destination," he replied. "And everyone will want to come. And it's free."

I grinned. "Think we should charge them?"

He crossed one arm, the other propping his chin in thought for a moment. "Naw, they're family."

"Jesse," Savannah called down from the wheelhouse.

"We're just about finished," I yelled back.

"Jojo and Rudy are here," she said. "They brought Charity's car."

I got up from the deck and went to the watertight hatch. "We'll be right up. Just gotta unhook the diagnostics computer."

"Got it," Alberto said, rolling his USB cord around his hand and stuffing it into his pocket.

When we reached the wheelhouse, we found Jojo and Rudy waiting, but no Savannah.

Tank sat on the settee, watching the two men.

"She said she had a few last-minute things to get," Rudy said. "Your dog was keeping us company."

I laughed. "She just wanted to drive the car again. Alberto, take Rudy down and show him the mechanical room. I need to talk to Jojo."

The two went forward and disappeared down the steps, as Jojo, then Tank, followed me out into the cockpit.

"Have you seen DJ Martin recently?" I asked, point blank.

He smiled. "No, but I have seen his boat, *Whole Nine Yards*. I was not aware you and he were—"

"Sure, you were," I said bluntly, cutting him off. "You were with Savvy in the Yucatan. DJ was there too. And you know our connection with Charity."

"I assumed but did not know."

"What's he like now?" I asked. "I haven't seen him in some time."

"He is coming closer to being a perfect being," Jojo replied. "What was he like before?"

"He tended to drink too much," I replied. "He was overweight and out of shape and lacked direction."

"You have a very critical eye," Jojo said. "I do not know about the first. I have never seen him drink. However, DJ most certainly has direction in his life now, and it manifests itself in his physical being as well as his spiritual."

"Being critical went along with my old job," I replied. "I was a career Marine. What *kind* of direction?"

"Toward spiritual enlightenment," he replied. "A higher plane of awareness and physical well-being."

I didn't lean toward all that spiritual stuff. But being more aware and physically stronger were both good things.

"Is there a specific reason DJ is here?" Jojo asked.

"That'd be up to him to tell you," I replied, as Rudy emerged from the forward steps.

"I don't think I've ever seen a neater, more well-designed use of space than your engine room," Rudy said, joining us in the cockpit. "And there are electric motors as well?"

"Come have a look," I replied, pulling the key fob from my pocket.

I pressed one of the buttons and the steps and rear deck of the port sugar scoop started to rise up.

Tank cocked his head a little, ears up as high as they'd go, his brow knitted in curiosity. He was okay when the boat moved, and he'd been fine riding in my old truck, but when the boat started moving its parts all by itself, it was puzzling to him.

"Both amas have a ton of storage aft," I said, stepping over onto the vertical ladder and descending. "We keep our kayaks and paddle boards in this one."

I stepped off the beam-width platform that covered the motor compartment, which could be converted to a crew berth with no more work than putting a mattress on top of it. Then I raised the cover for the electric motor.

"How powerful are they?" Rudy asked, looking down at the motor.

"Fifty kilowatts," I replied. "One in each ama. About sixty-eight horsepower each. Not a lot, but we can cruise at four knots all day and night without burning fuel, and the top speed is about eight knots for four or five hours."

"Why is it mounted vertically?" Jojo asked.

"It's not a typical horizontal shaft drive turning the prop," I replied. "Below, the shaft housing and prop are hinged and can fold up into a recess in the hull when using the main engine."

"And no transmission?" Jojo asked.

I shook my head. "Doesn't need one. A three-phase electric motor runs equally well in either direction. Moving the controller to reverse is really just changing the phase rotation of the motor. Plus, everything you see here, the motor, its mount, the output shaft and gear-driven prop assembly are a single, hermetically sealed unit, which can be removed or replaced from in here, or from underneath."

"Very innovative," Rudy said. He knelt and leaned in to see the rest of the large lazarette. "That is a *lot* of space. Is it the same on the other side as well?"

"We have a dive shop over there," Alberto said.

I nodded. "We can outfit and fill tanks for eight divers, and there's a hookah rig with four hoses."

"The hookah will mostly be used for cleaning the underside of the boat and fixing things," Alberto added.

"Do you dive?" Rudy asked him.

"Dad's teaching me," he replied. "I'm old enough to take the course, and can do all the math stuff, but Dad says I have to be a little bigger."

"He's right," Rudy said. "A diver should be able to carry all their own gear before becoming certified. But I'd say you're just about there now."

"He'll be taking an open-water course in November," I said, closing the motor hatch and stepping up on it. "With a couple of friends of mine on Grand Turk." I climbed back up the ladder and joined them in the cockpit, then pressed the button to close the sugar scoop. "Do you dive?" I asked Rudy.

"I'm NAUI advanced scuba-diver certified," he replied, referring to the National Association of Underwater Instructors. "But it's a good distance out to any dive sites from here. Heather and I do most of our diving in the Caribbean or Western Pacific."

"We must be going, Rudy," Jojo said, moving toward the steps. "You asked me to remind you."

"Oh, yes," Rudy agreed. "I told Heather we'd be back in an hour."

I walked them down the steps and joined them on the dock.

Rudy glanced back at the boat. "Do you have the same storage in the main hull?"

"That's the garage," I replied. "There's a jet-drive tender in there."

"Amazing," he said softly.

"Thanks for bringing Charity's car," I said, shaking both men's hands. "We may actually need it when Savannah gets back from her joyride."

CHAPTER TWENTY

After Jojo and Rudy left, Alberto and I sat at the dinette table, and I helped him with his math lesson—one of the few things I could still help him with. At twelve, in the state of Florida, he'd be in sixth grade. But he was taking a couple of courses meant for kids who were several years older: computer science, English literature, and algebra.

Savannah actually did have a reason for leaving, besides driving Charity's little sports car again. David and Florence had missed one important item on her shopping list the previous evening. Or so she said.

It took her an awfully long time to get back.

Florence and David had gone with Maddy on her last-minute souvenir hunt, something I insisted on after what'd happened the last time. Until DJ reported in, David had little else to do.

So, when Alberto went to his cabin to study, and nobody else was around, I managed to finish up a few more boat chores before Savannah returned.

When the kids got back, I was in the galley helping Savannah.

"Did you find everything you needed?" I asked Maddy.

"I did," she said, holding up a wooden cane or walking stick. "I got this for Dink."

"He might be insulted," I said, examining the intricate carving that ran the length of the stick. "And it looks expensive."

"Only forty-five dollars," she replied. "I honestly think it's because on a boat, a person has handholds everywhere. Even if he doesn't need them, Dink knows they're there. And he doesn't have a grab rail on land. You'll see when you get back."

Dink Wilcox was a local fishing guide who was in high demand because he could always find the fish. He was a big man but moved around on the deck of a boat like a dancer. However, as soon as he stepped ashore, his legs got wobbly, and he was prone to tripping over his own feet. "Perpetual sea legs," he called it.

Florence placed a bag on the table. "Where's Mom?"

"She went down to get the electric mixer," I replied.

"Okay, I'll be downstairs with Maddy helping her pack."

David lingered in the galley until they'd disappeared.

"DJ emailed me a little while ago," he said in a low tone. "Actually, he updated the investigation report, which sent an automated email to me and Mr. Stockwell."

"What'd he say?" I asked, seeing Savannah coming up the steps.

"What did who say?" she asked, placing the mixer on the counter.

"DJ has something," I replied.

"Well, not much," David said. "He only reported that he'd arrived and had found a good location to not only pick up information but also see the target's office."

"He has an office in town?" I asked.

"Boudreaux owns the fish house," David replied, opening the fridge and reaching for a bottle of water. He held it up. "Want one?"

I nodded and he tossed it to me, then got another, removed the cap and guzzled half. "It's hot out there. Anyway, DJ also mentioned a person was selling drugs right out in the open at the park."

I shook my head. Only two thousand people lived in Apalachicola, so there shouldn't have been *any* visible drug activity. It was just too small a town.

"How sure was he?" Savannah asked, carefully carving the fillets into individual servings that probably weighed half a pound each.

"Very," David replied. "He made a buy."

The water bottle stopped halfway to my mouth. "Really?"

"I've worked with him a few times," David replied. "He's probably the most street-smart investigator we have. He can pass for a bum pretty easily when he wants to."

Maddy came up from the port ama with two backpacks, which she placed out in the cockpit before disappearing below again.

"That's something I couldn't pull off," I said. "Drug dealers don't trust people my age."

"Me neither," David agreed. "Not that I've tried or anything. But I have friends who I know smoke weed, and they stash it as soon as I walk in. So don't think it's on account of you just being older."

"You're both squares," Savannah said. "Or 'un-cool,' or whatever the new term is." She paused and looked up. "If fire is the new cool, then wouldn't cool be the new un-cool?"

I grinned at her as Maddy re-emerged from the port ama again, Florence and Alberto right behind her.

"That's everything," she said, picking up the walking stick. "Except Dink's third leg."

She looked up at me, horror in her eyes. “I’m so sorry. That was awful of me. How did your friend lose his leg?”

“DJ was in Afghanistan,” I replied. “An IED took his foot and lower shin and killed his radioman.”

“Oh, my God,” she breathed. “I’ve never met anyone who lost a friend in combat before.”

“Yes, you have,” I replied. “Me, Rusty, Gray… We just don’t talk about it.”

Maddy regarded me solemnly as she digested this information.

“We’ll go upstairs and get the deck ready,” Florence announced, taking David’s hand. “It was great to see you again, Maddy.”

“What time’s your taxi?” I asked her.

“It’s a uh… rideshare, not a taxi,” she replied nervously, still a bit flummoxed. “I requested two-thirty.”

Savannah looked at the clock in the wheelhouse. “It’s almost that now. Jesse can still—”

Maddy’s phone began emitting a sound like a sonar echo and she picked it up. “No need. My driver’s ten minutes away.” She tapped the screen and scrolled. “Oh, it’s a Mustang. I wonder if he’d let me drive it.”

“Want me to carry your backpacks?” Alberto asked her. “And he’d probably say no. Insurance.”

“Wouldn’t hurt to ask,” she said. “Sure, you can carry the blue one.”

“Where’s it meeting you?” I asked.

“Across the street,” she replied, giving Savannah a hug. “At Battery Park.”

I glanced through the hatch, noting that most of the dock was visible all the way to the office, as well as the parking lot beyond it and the boat launch. One of the advantages of a thirty-two-foot beam.

"See the boat ramp?" I said, pointing directly astern as I stepped out into the cockpit with them. "Wait there for the rideshare, or whatever it is, and Alberto, stay with her until it does, then you come straight back."

He shouldered the smaller pack and grinned. "Most rikki tik."

I laughed and gave Maddy a hug. "Tell Rusty I'll see him in about three weeks, but if he and Billy are still planning to work on that sub next week, we'll be in that area."

My old friend, Billy Rainwater, had found a German U-boat stranded deep in the Everglades, and for the past year he and Rusty had been working with the state and National Park Service, as well as with the Seminole Nation, to not only recover the sub, but tow it through existing canals *and* ones that hadn't even been built yet, to get it to open water. It was an uphill battle, and in the meantime, they'd built a more permanent caisson around the conning tower and were actually attempting to restore the sub's electric propulsion system.

"I'll tell him," Maddy said, as she shouldered the other pack and followed Alberto down the steps of the starboard sugar scoop.

I went back inside and began mixing the ingredients for the marinade, looking toward the dock every few seconds to check the kids' progress.

The marinade's base was a simple mixture of an eighth of a cup of pineapple juice to a quarter cup of liquid amino for each serving of mahi. It was the tablespoon of Rufus's "Swimmers" spices mixed in that was the secret, and he wasn't telling anyone what was in it, except to say, "Dey are rare herbs and spices from all over de Caribbean, mon."

So, there was some math involved in preparing enough for ten people and I was a bit distracted.

"He'll be fine," Savannah said, when I glanced aft for about the seventh time. "I think he's going to miss Maddy's company, though."

I looked back again. They were on the ramp where I'd told them to wait, packs grounded, laughing and talking.

"Florence and David are good with him, too," I commented, though I knew she was right.

Maddy was eight months older than Florence, and quite wealthy, though it didn't show. She liked things simple and disliked flashy, so to meet her, a person would never guess that she'd once owned and sold a huge piece of land in the Bighorn Mountains, where rare gems and rare metals were mined, and several oil wells were pumping. And she'd had no debts to pay off after the sale.

In the short time since she'd arrived in Marathon, she'd become not just a well-liked and integral part of the community but family. Alberto loved spending time with her, as did many younger people. She even volunteered every week at the fishing and sailing school for at-risk kids.

She'd grown up in a small mining town in Wyoming and in many ways, she struck me as more of an adolescent, seeming years younger than Florence. But she was very smart, and not the least bit afraid of hard work. She'd proven that many times over during our trip.

A late-model black Mustang turned slowly toward the ramp and even at that distance, I could see the sticker affixed to the corner of the windshield. I'd looked up the whole rideshare thing after Maddy had told me, and found that Florida had enacted some serious rules for rideshare companies in recent years to make sure all their drivers were vetted, trustworthy, and identifiable.

"There's her ride now," I said, stirring in Rufus's spices.

We watched as Maddy spoke to the driver through the passenger window, then accepted something from him. She looked at it for a moment and then looked at something on her phone before handing whatever it was back to the driver.

Savannah nudged me. "See? She checked his ID against her phone, so there's nothing to worry about."

The driver popped the trunk open, then got out and helped Maddy with her two packs. He even paused to shake hands with Alberto. He was on the smallish side, just a few inches taller than Maddy, clean-shaven, and, at least from a distance, he looked neat and squared away. He closed the trunk, then went to the passenger side to open the door for her.

A moment later, the car was pulling out of the lot, and Alberto was trotting back along the dock.

"Is that ready for the fish?" Savannah asked, sliding a large casserole dish toward me.

"Oh...yeah," I replied, still stirring.

I set the spoon aside and began pouring the marinade over the neatly trimmed mahi steaks resting in the dish.

"Do you think they'll be on time?" Savannah asked. "The Redmonds, I mean."

"If he's as punctual as a civilian as he was in the Corps," I replied, "they'll board at precisely eighteen hundred."

"Then we should plan on everything being finished at that time," she suggested. "I'll bring the jasmine rice and mashed sweet potatoes upstairs when they're done and put them in the warmer."

"Or we can do all the cooking up there, like I suggested," I said, as Alberto came in.

"I know you like to conserve electricity," she countered. "But for this, I prefer the induction cooktop."

"She's on her way home," Alberto said, hovering at the dinette.

I looked at the clock. It was 1430. "Yeah, Buck will be landing in about half an hour."

CHAPTER TWENTY-ONE

When he logged on to the app for his day job, Leo was still tired from the long night in the woods and hiking out before dawn. He'd forgotten his bug spray and was also covered in red welts.

He never knew what the day would bring and often, he could be signed in all day and not get a single request. Other times, he could be busy all day if he wanted to. That was one of the perks of his job; he set his own hours.

Once, several months earlier, Leo had gotten a request from a salesman who'd missed his flight to Jacksonville, where he was supposed to connect with another flight home to Atlanta. The guy was a talker and kept Leo entertained, and he'd managed to get the guy to his destination before his plane would have landed. He'd left Leo a hundred-dollar tip on top of the three hundred for the ride.

Earlier in the day, when Leo first got home, he'd told Root and his brother to come back in the evening and he'd give them four grams, but they had to leave the three hundred in cash, up front. After they left, he moved the ice from the trunk to his stash location in the trailer and was able to get a few hours of sleep.

Leo didn't like being forced to do business with anyone he didn't want to deal with, and although he wasn't *afraid* of Root, he didn't trust the guy as far as he could throw him.

Having his kid brother sell ice to pay off a debt to Tobias would take too long. Even at twenty-five bucks off the going rate, he was only making seventy-five a gram, and planned to do it four or five grams at a time.

Tobias would only get ten percent of that, or thirty bucks every time the kid sold four grams.

They didn't need to discount the price to sell in quantity. He, Lucas, Kenny, and Marc had always sold out in a matter of hours.

And Leo didn't even know how much Root was into Tobias for, but at that rate, it'd take months if it was as much as Leo thought.

"Penny ante shit," he muttered to himself, just as his phone dinged.

He picked it up and looked at the screen. There was a ride request to the airport. He opened the app and saw that the pickup was at Battery Park, so it was a short ride, maybe ten minutes.

"Not worth my time," he said with a sigh, and started to put the phone down. Then he remembered he needed to make an occasional appearance on the dispatch board, and he hadn't signed on in days. Not just to maintain his appearance as gainfully employed, but just to keep the rideshare license that he'd worked so hard to acquire.

The pickup was in fifteen minutes. If they were ready, he could be at the airport half an hour later, and home before an hour was up.

So, he clicked on the button to accept it before one of the other two drivers, Wendy and Sharon, snagged it. The two old ladies drove almost full time, but only during the day. When he'd first started, Leo had worked only at night, and still did for the most part. But he hadn't signed on to the app since last week.

Battery Park was just across the causeway, no more than five or six minutes. So, he quickly put on a clean white shirt, pulled his shoes on, then grabbed his wallet and keys.

Leo was halfway across the causeway from Eastpoint when his dash-mounted phone dinged again. He glanced at it and saw that the pickup point had changed to the office at Battery Park Marina.

He touched the OK button, sending an automated reply to the company and the passenger. It was only a couple hundred feet from the park and actually easier to get to.

Three minutes later, as he turned into the parking lot, he saw a young woman with a dark-haired boy, both of them with backpacks. He angled toward them and pushed the button to put the window down.

I've seen you before, he thought, as he focused on the girl.

Leo stopped and looked at her, smiling. "Are you Madison?"

It's the snack in the picture Root's kid brother had shown us, he thought, and his smile widened

She asked for his ID, and he handed it to her as an idea began to formulate in his mind.

"Are both of you riding?" he asked, taking his phone from the mount and starting a quick text message.

"No, just me," the girl replied, looking at her own phone, then extending his license back. "Here you go, Leo. Thanks."

Leo pushed the button to open the trunk, then got out of the car after quickly finishing the message and sending it.

"Thanks for being cautious," he said, with a smile that was neither genuine, nor happy, but he knew looked sincere.

"I don't suppose you'd let me drive?" the girl asked, returning his smile.

"Sorry," he replied, feigning the innocent look that had worked so well before. "I could get in a lot of trouble for that. Where are you flying to today? Back home?"

"Yeah," she replied, as she and the boy met him at the trunk. "I'm flying back to the Keys."

He looked up at her as he placed the first backpack in the trunk. "Oh, man, I'd love to go there one day."

"Maddy," she said, extending her hand. "And this is Alberto."

He shook hands with both of them, then put the second pack in the trunk and went to the passenger side to open her door.

She gave the kid a hug, then got in. Leo hurried around the back of the Mustang and just as he got in the driver's seat, his phone pinged an incoming message. He looked down at the screen.

deal cun 10

Root had accepted Leo's offer and would see him in ten minutes at the closed down hangar Leo had mentioned in his text. Now, if the guy could just follow through and be there on time. It was risky, but the private hangars were little used and mostly out of sight.

While he had his phone in his hands, Leo entered the pickup and destination information, then put the phone back in its cradle so his oh-so-cautious passenger could see the route.

"Busy day?" she asked, as he started driving.

"It might be," Leo replied, glancing over at her. "I just got a really good offer, and it's right there at the airport."

"Well, that's good," she replied politely.

As he stopped the Mustang at a crosswalk, he looked over and smiled at her again. "Looks like it'll be a pretty profitable day after all."

CHAPTER TWENTY-TWO

The large gas grill on the flybridge was *probably* overkill. But I figured it was better to have a thousand square inches of grilling surface, heated by six burners, and not need them, than need the extra cooking space and not have it.

I could put one of the cast iron griddles over one burner at medium heat for just the three of us. The griddle had room for four large fillets or steaks and plenty of space between them. Then, once the meat was cooked to the desired temperature, I could flip it onto a custom-made grill grate, also cast iron, and have *that* one over a different burner set on high, for a final sear.

Or fire up the whole shebang and broil fifty lobster tails at one time.

The topside kitchen was on the starboard side, forward of the steps down to the cockpit, and facing the rail, with plenty of room for the "chef" to work behind it and still be engaged with everyone.

And it was only four steps from the helm.

That was one of the most important design functions of the boat. No matter what the activity I might be involved in, whether it was in bed, asleep, on the flybridge, cooking, or down in the cockpit, fishing, I had to be close to the boat's controls. If not, another set of controls had to be added.

With *Taranis* on autopilot, I could cook a steak dinner and have only to turn my head slightly to check the water ahead. Four knots was a fast walk or slow jog, and it took her more than a minute to cover the length of a football field.

Florence and David had converted the large sun pad into a table that could seat fourteen. They'd also brought out the plates, glasses, and silverware, set the table, and even extended the sun canopy to shade the aft seating area.

A couple of weeks earlier, knowing where and how we lived, Warren had suggested adding a little fish to Tank's diet and if he liked it, we could start weening him off the puppy food. He seemed to like it fine, but we'd learned quickly he wasn't picky about what he put in his mouth, so whenever I grilled, he was always there, knowing he'd get some of the day's catch.

When he chuffed his impatience, I looked down at him. "I just lit the grill, Tank. It'll be a while."

"Hey, Jesse," DJ called up from the dock. "Permission to come aboard?"

"Come on up," I called out. "You're early."

His footfalls on the starboard steps sounded normal. He disappeared into the covered cockpit for a moment before reappearing at the top of the flybridge steps clad in neatly pressed jeans and a button-down fruit-juicy shirt.

With his hair pulled back in a ponytail and all but the long goatee gone, he looked like a hipster college professor on vacation. Which was maybe what he was going for.

"Yeah," he replied. "I figured ya might need some help." He looked around the deck and nodded at Florence and David. "But it don't look like ya need any."

"Grab a coupla beers from the fridge there at the end," I offered, just to see his reaction. "I just fired up the grill."

To my surprise, he took a pair of Red Stripes out, used the opener on the door to remove the caps, and handed me a bottle.

"I thought you quit drinking," I said.

"Me? Naw. Well, yeah, I don't drink the hard stuff anymore, but a beer or two in the evenin' ain't gonna hurt a man. Who said a dumb thing like that?"

I glanced over at him as I opened the grill's hood. "Charity."

His face flushed slightly. "Well... I mighta told a little white lie last time I saw her."

"When was that?" I asked. "Never mind. None of my business."

I pulled the casserole dish closer and removed the lid as DJ slid past me to see what was on the menu.

"Holy smoke," he said. "Those gotta be a pound each."

"Not quite," I replied. "But one's going to be enough for anyone."

His finger moved over the dish, counting. Then he looked up at me, puzzled. "I thought you said ten people were comin'. But ya got a dozen big-ass mahi steaks there."

Tank chuffed again, and I laughed. "You get three guesses who gets the leftovers, and the first two don't count."

DJ hadn't spotted Tank lying at the end of the counter and was startled at first.

"Just kneel down to eye level and scratch him behind the ear," I instructed. "He'll be your buddy for life."

DJ knelt cautiously as I began to move the fish from the dish to the three cast iron griddles on the right side. Living on a boat, sacrifices had to be made as to how much weight you brought aboard. And we'd all made sacrifices. But the cast iron was an absolute must.

"Hey, I think he likes me," DJ said. "Hey there, Tank."

I moved another mahi steak to the griddle. "He's never met anyone he hasn't liked."

DJ rose, caught David's attention, and motioned him over. Florence followed. He nodded toward her as he faced David. "Okay to talk openly?"

David grinned. "I don't think Tank's been read in, but Flo knows everything I do."

DJ glanced at me, and I barely nodded my head.

"Okay then," he began. "I *did* find out a whole lot of interestin' stuff today. Man, I wish all my assignments were in small towns. Everybody knows everyone and they gossip like it's nobody's business."

"What did you find out?" I asked.

"Your buddy, Gray, and his family are completely off my radar. Not just on account of what you told me, but everything I put together in town today. No chance any of them are involved." He took a pull from his beer and continued. "And I can't even say I learned anything damning about Boudreaux, either. Heard some talk of his past, which ain't the cleanest, but far as I can tell, he's a pillar of the community now."

"And you found out all this just by listening to gossip?" I asked.

"Listenin' and *organizin'*, man," he replied, tapping a finger to the side of his head. "Puttin' all the little pieces together up here. Somethin' Dep's been helpin' me with. Hell, it was so easy here. Like I said, everyone's all up in everybody else's business." He paused and winked at Florence. "I even know who's cheatin' on who, and there's a good bit of that goin' on, I'm here to tell ya."

I poured the remaining marinade carefully from the dish onto the fish, some streaming off onto the griddle, causing a sizzle of steam as I gave each piece of fish a good coating. Then I closed the hood and faced DJ.

"Somebody's making methamphetamine here," I said. "I don't suppose you heard any talk about *that*?"

He grinned. "Yeah, I sure did. No names or addresses or anything actionable, but I know it's a group of locals working out in the deep woods like moonshiners used to."

"That's something the sheriff's office pretty much already suspects," I said. "They just can't find it."

"*Them*," DJ corrected, his grin turning into a smile. "*Four* meth kitchens. And they're *underground*."

CHAPTER TWENTY-THREE

The Mustang turned right off of the highway, through an open gate in a high fence, and onto a side road. It immediately curved left to run parallel to the main road, and ahead, Maddy could see large metal buildings on the right. It didn't look like much of an airport, but the one back home was probably smaller.

Her driver slowed, then turned between two of the buildings and stopped. "The public gate is closed at three," he said. "This alley goes out to the flight line, where the pilots park their cars. But I'm not allowed to drive out there."

He pressed a button on his armrest, and Maddy heard the pop of the trunk lid as he opened the door and got out.

"So I have to walk the rest of the way?" she asked, getting out on her side. "How far?"

"Oh, sorry," he said, pulling one of the packs out and looking at her sheepishly. "We're already here. The entrance is just around the front of this building. But like I said, I can't drive out on the flight line." He grinned at her as he pulled the other pack out. "Pilots are a weird bunch, and well... I don't back up so good. Hope you don't mind."

She picked up her two packs, slinging the heavier one on her shoulder and stuffing her phone into a side pocket of the blue one. Then she looked toward the other end of the alley. "Just around that corner then?"

"Turn left and it's the first door on the left," he replied. "That's where your pilot'll be directed to meet up with you. You *did* say it was a private plane, right?"

She nodded.

"It's sort of a lounge area where the pilots hang out while their planes are gassed up. There isn't a terminal or anything like that here, just the Fixed Base Operator that runs things out of this hangar."

"Okay," she said, turning, but still a bit hesitant. "Thanks for the ride."

"No, thank *you*," he shouted after her.

Maddy started toward the other end of the alley and was halfway there when her phone dinged in the blue backpack.

She paused, unzipped the side pocket, and pulled it out to see a notification—a partial receipt for the ride, waiting for her to confirm the amount or provide a tip.

After opening the app, Maddy added a five-dollar tip and stuck her phone back in the pack's pocket.

Looking back, she watched the Mustang slowly back away to the access road, turn, and then speed away.

She felt a little apprehensive, but let it go. South Bighorn County Airport, twenty miles from her old home in the Bighorn Basin, was only a cluster of hangars like these and a small building housing the FBO, where one old man worked.

She shrugged off the edgy feeling, muttering, "At least there aren't any mountain lions jumping off the roof on top of me."

As she reached the corner and turned, she heard a quick crunch of feet on gravel as someone came running up behind her.

Suddenly, she was grabbed from the rear and nearly went down as her attacker pinned her arms to her sides, causing her to drop the blue backpack. She tried kicking and stomping, but the man behind her squeezed harder, lifting her off the ground.

She struggled and started to scream, but another man quickly appeared in front of her and stuffed something in her mouth before roughly pulling some sort of bag over her head.

The new guy took hold of her, hugging her from the front, and even through the bag she smelled a chemical odor on him.

When the man behind her pulled her backpack off, freeing her hands for a moment, Maddy went into full attack mode, fighting hard against the man hugging her.

She stumbled as rough hands grabbed at her wrists, pulling her arms behind her as the guy who'd put the bag over her held her tightly to his chest, grunting in her ear as she struggled.

In seconds, her hands were bound and the two men each took an arm, turning her around, then hurrying her away.

Maddy stumbled again, tripping and going down. She felt the sharp pain of the gravel grinding into her knee and winced as the two men pulled her up again.

Her muffled screams were barely audible, even to her, and after several more stumbling steps, the men stopped and turned her again. Then she felt hands on her legs, and she was suddenly lifted off the ground, one man holding her from behind and the other lifting her legs at the knees.

The man holding her legs laughed sadistically as he got his arms fully under her knees and lifted, spreading her legs around his torso.

She struggled against them, thrashing wildly with all her strength while trying to spit the rag out of her mouth and scream.

Then they dropped her, but not on the ground. Her feet were up on something.

The guy who'd been holding her legs forced them into her chest as both men rolled her onto her side.

She smelled gas, and something else—something foul.

Then there was a bang and a metallic click, and it was suddenly pitch dark under the bag.

She heard two car doors open and close and realized instantly they'd put her in the trunk of a car.

Why me? she asked herself. *What do they want?*

She froze and shivered.

Are they going to rape me? Did they come here from Wyoming?

"Let's get outta here," she heard someone say, the voice, with a Southern accent, muffled by the back seat of the car.

What's going on? Maddy wondered. *Have they found me?*

Maddy had been stalked back home in Greybull, Wyoming. Not by an ex-boyfriend, or anything like that, but by her whole family going back many generations.

She'd learned in recent months that she was the product of a pure bloodline, each marriage and subsequent child arranged by a secretive organization that dated back to colonial days. She still didn't know the purpose, or even the name of the organization.

One of their bunch, a ranch hand named Marshall Grey, the one sent to bring her back to the old ranch to be bred, was now in prison.

If Jesse hadn't pulverized him in a tackle exactly when he did, Savannah would have blown his head off with a shotgun.

For dozens of generations, her ancestors had been born within days of the mother's and father's twenty-fifth birthdays in November.

Maddy herself had been born right in the middle of both her parents' birthdays in mid-November, just as they had been.

And each firstborn on her paternal bloodline, for over the last hundred years, had been a boy.

Similarly, women of other pure bloodlines were married into the organization, each willingly submitting to whoever the organization chose for them to marry and have a child with.

Maddy was the first girl in her father's line. And her twenty-fifth birthday was just a couple of months away, so whatever the reason for it, she was past any chance of being impregnated by one of them in time to give birth this November.

"Now we got the rich bitch," another muffled voice said, "what the fuck we do wit' her?"

They know about my money, she thought.

"For now," a man answered,"let's go see Tobias. We can ransom her little city ass for what we owe him."

The car started and the loud rumble of the exhaust silenced the voices on the other side of the backseat.

Ransom? The people who'd been after her didn't want her for money. They wanted her to breed like livestock.

Maddy concentrated on remembering everything she could. That quickly became impossible as the car made a succession of lefts and rights before finally making a left and accelerating to a high speed.

They had to be back on the highway to town, but as soon as she thought it, the car braked hard and turned sharply to the left, sliding Maddy across the trunk and scraping her other knee.

There was another succession of turns, both left and right, seemingly at random, until the car started going fast again, once more on a highway, the engine droning on for a long time.

Maddy lost track of the turns and curves.

What seemed like an hour later, the car slowed and turned to the right. The road curved a few times, then the car braked again, turning to the left.

The tires dropped off the pavement and the car continued onto a bumpy road where all she could concentrate on was keeping her body rigid, so she didn't get hurt being bounced around.

The exhaust sound stayed low as the car moved cautiously down what she was sure was a little-used dirt road.

Time again became immaterial as the suspension bounced the back of the car, constantly throwing her around.

She forced the tears from her eyes, and finally got both feet planted firmly against the underside of the trunk to at least hold her lower body in place. She was twisted around, her hands bound behind her back, but with supreme effort, she got her body into a crunch position with her hands splayed out behind her butt on the floor of the trunk.

When Maddy clenched her muscles, pushing with all she had, the bouncing of the car only affected her head and neck.

Finally, when she was about to give up and let the metal around her just beat her to death, the car came to a stop.

Then the engine was shut off.

She had no idea where she was or how far they'd come from the airport, and she was clueless as to how long it'd taken. All she knew was that she was badly beaten up and bruised.

And she was angry.

If those assholes want it, she thought, wincing as she repositioned herself, *then they're sure gonna pay for it.*

She turned her body so both feet were against the trunk lid on either side of the latch.

Her shoulders burned with her arms and hands cramped up beneath her torso. But she waited, hurt, afraid for her life, and extremely pissed.

Was the rideshare driver in on this? she wondered.

He'd seemed very nice, so she didn't think so. But he *had* dropped her off and left her in a secluded place.

"Where the hell you been?" she heard an angry voice shout from outside the car.

It startled her. Nobody had gotten out. So now there were at least three of them.

"Go ahead and do it," a voice from inside the car whispered. "It takes 'em a minute to trace a call. Just keep it short, like I told ya, and I'll take care of Tobias."

One of the doors opened, but didn't close, and Maddy could hear two men talking some distance from the car. But she couldn't tell what they were saying.

"Don't bother tryin' to trace me," a voice on the other side of the backseat said, sounding drunk, high, or just plain dumb. "I ain't gonna be on that long. We done snatched, uh... Madison Thurman. And we want fifty grand. But we don't know who to get it from."

There was silence for a moment.

"That's right," the dim-witted voice continued. "It's up to y'all to find out who we need to get hold of. One of us'll be callin' ya back at six-thirty and you better have an answer."

Maddy heard footsteps approaching; more than one person.

She set herself, waiting.

The lock clicked, and Maddy pushed hard.

The trunk lid flew open with great force, and she heard a satisfying crunch as the lid caught one of them in the face.

He went down screaming as another man cursed.

CHAPTER TWENTY-FOUR

After divulging all he'd learned about the people involved, which wasn't much, DJ went below to say hi to Savannah. Apparently, at least one person in what he thought was a group of four or five meth makers was bragging about their accomplishments and word had spread among a certain segment of the population.

Nobody ever mentioned names, but DJ had heard several people talking about *four* underground labs.

I considered all he'd said as the mahi slowly cooked under the hood.

Building just one underground lab would be a big undertaking, especially way out in the state and national forest area, where it was suspected of being.

But building four?

The logistics of getting material and equipment out there on foot was staggering. And both Wyatt and Maggie had insisted that there were no roads and few trails in that area. It was as wild as Florida got.

During our drives, I'd seen how dense the forested area around town was and where it wasn't dense, it was low wetland. In such a remote location, a lot of things had to be moved on foot.

I had no idea how big they'd have to be to make as much as the county police thought was being manufactured locally. But if you could make it in the backseat of a car, I wouldn't think they'd have to be *too* big, especially with four of them going.

But why four different labs, instead of one large one?

The countdown timer on the front of the grill beeped, and Tank rose to a sitting position, ready.

"Not yet," I told him as I opened the hood, then began turning the mahi slices over one-by-one on the cast iron griddle. "It'll be a while."

Dogs had little concept of time. We'd all started using the same phrase in an attempt to help Tank learn patience. "It'll be a while," to him meant he would soon get to go swimming, or play fetch, or in this case, taste what he'd been smelling for five long minutes.

But it wasn't going to be right now. He had to wait.

Florence went down to the galley to see if Savannah needed anything, and David joined me at the grill.

"Not a lot to go on," he commented. "But probably more than the police have. And speaking of which, how do you want me to treat Captain Hamilton?"

"Why are you asking me?" I replied, then sighed. "I'd just play it by ear. Don't offer anything that isn't asked for. Your and DJ's job here is to investigate deeper than local law enforcement is allowed, then arrange for them to *discover* the evidence on their own."

"Don't offer anything. Got it." He glanced back toward the marina in thought. "But I still remember the look in that cop's eyes when he talked about that boy's mother.... We can't even offer hope?"

"Unless you need local law enforcement's help with the investigation," I began, "then there's no need to even let them know of your presence. DJ proved that today. Just by hanging out, blending in, and listening, he learned more in a few hours than the cops have in months. None of it's admissible in court but is almost certain to be true and can lead you to more. How can the police help speed things along?"

"They can't," he replied. "Not with the constraints they're under."

"And the best part is," I suggested, "DJ did it without asking any questions or drawing attention to himself. Law enforcement has to have a reason to ask questions and a warrant to look for things. These people are so brazen, they speak openly when they should be keeping their yaps closed. But they don't talk so openly when a cop's around. Or even 'squares' like you and me."

He chuckled nervously.

"My point is," I said, "when you and DJ leave here, nobody will remember you or him asking questions. They'll just remember how the cops found the bad guys red-handed."

David nodded aft. "They're here."

I glanced up the dock and saw Gray and Georgia approaching with Wyatt and Maggie walking behind them.

"*My* question is," I said, turning back to David, "why four labs?"

He shrugged. "Maybe they started with one small one, and then needed to make more, so they added a new one as demand grew."

"Makes sense," I said. "And two are harder to find than one. Then their operation grew to require three. Then four. But at some point, wouldn't they have just enlarged one? Multiple locations increase the odds of detection."

Just then, Florence came back up, along with Alberto, both of them carrying large, covered bowls.

"Mom said to just put these in the warmer," Alberto said. "She's going down to meet your friends."

I already had the infrared heater turned on and had set it at the temperature Savannah told me, so I opened it, and they put the warming bowls inside, just as the timer on the grill beeped again.

Once more, Tank rose, but this time all the way up onto his feet.

I opened the hood and inserted a thermometer in the thickest part of the biggest piece—one-forty-five.

Perfect.

I could hear cordial conversation from below, but I was too busy moving the fillets to the grate to get that final sear and the all-important grill marks.

Cooking on a gas grill was no different than a wood-fired one, except that it was a whole lot easier. Jimmy and I had cooked so many meals in our stone fireplace that we had damper and flue openings memorized for whatever we were cooking.

With the grill, I just turned it on, set the temperature for whatever burners were needed, and waited for it to beep, letting me know it was ready.

Since the fish was already fully cooked, I only left them on the superheated grates as long as it took to move all of them onto it, then started taking them off in the same order.

I turned each piece as I moved it to a diagonal position on the large platter, so the grill marks were up, and the word "*Taranis*" was visibly seared into the flesh.

They looked perfect, and I knew from experience that Rufus's "Swimmers" seasoning would make them taste just as good as they looked. Opening the warmer again, I slid the platter in on the top shelf and closed it, ready to greet our guests wearing my best Yachty McYachtface garb.

Entertaining had become an important endeavor for Savannah, and I didn't want to screw it up. Everything was done and would stay warm without drying out for as long as we needed it to.

Savannah came up first, followed by our guests, then DJ.

"Welcome aboard *Taranis*," I said in greeting, sweeping my arm toward the expansive deck. "Wyatt, Maggie, I'm glad you could join us on short notice."

Maggie's expression betrayed some discomfort. She was probably remembering how she'd kind of accused me of trying to milk money from the department.

Gray and Georgia looked around beaming, but Wyatt seemed singularly unimpressed. I guess in his job, he'd probably seen it all. And Apalachicola was a far cry from bustling Cocoa Beach.

"Is everything ready?" Savannah asked me, placing two large bread baskets on the table.

"I just pulled the mahi," I replied. "Everything's in the warmer. How do you want to do this?"

Georgia stepped away from Gray. "Can we help you with anything, Savannah?"

"Everything's ready," she replied, moving past me, then opening the warmer. "I guess the easiest way will be for everyone to just grab a plate, like we used to do for large gatherings back home."

Alberto joined Savannah and me behind the counter as she brought the bowls out and uncovered them, then followed with the platter full of fish.

"Oh, man, that looks good," DJ said, leaning over and inhaling. "And ya got the name of your boat right there on the fish! Cool! But are ya really gonna feed it to Tank? Looks spicy."

I chuckled as I removed the two fillets I'd set aside for Tank onto a small, stainless-steel platter to cool for a minute. "His aren't blackened."

The sun was still well above the horizon as we served our guests, and everyone took a seat. Conversation was light and friendly, mostly centered on the food.

Tank ate on the deck, but not far away, and unlike most big dogs, he didn't tend to wolf down his food. He knew there was plenty.

Some might scoff at feeding a dog by the dinner table or consider it rude with guests. But those weren't my people.

Tank was family.

Our surroundings were just beginning to take on that golden hue of evening as shadows began to grow longer.

The Golden Hour.

When dinner was finished, everyone pitched in to clear the table and put everything in the commercial-grade dishwasher mounted under the cabinet next to the drink fridge.

Savannah began mixing ice and rum in the blender with slices of fresh mango and different mixers.

"I see you've met Miss Evangeline," Wyatt said, picking up an uncut mango and sniffing it.

"The little elderly lady selling the mangoes?" Savannah asked. "She was very sweet and told me all about the orchard where Mr. Bou—" Her eyes suddenly came up, a shocked look on her face as she met Wyatt's, then Maggie's eyes.

One corner of Wyatt's mouth twitched, but Maggie's expression was neutral.

"So, what do *you* do, DJ," Wyatt casually asked, placing the fruit back and turning to face him.

And with that little bait and slip, I knew. Wyatt already suspected we were with Armstrong. And if we were, we'd know about Maggie and Gray not being biologically related. And now he was testing DJ.

"I try to do as *little* as possible," DJ replied jovially, passing on Savannah's sundowner, and opting for bottled water instead. "I live on my boat and just arrived here this mornin'. Some might say I'm a spoiled trust fund kid, but the truth is, I don't think I've found my real callin' in life just yet."

It was a near truth. Enough so, that if they checked his background, they'd find that he had, in fact, inherited a good deal of money and then dropped off the face of the earth.

Being financially independent was one of the requirements for being an active investigator or operator for Amstrong. It made it very easy for them to move around as if they didn't have a care, so could be anywhere for no reason.

A phone rang, and Maggie reached for her back pocket. She pulled it out and checked the screen, then glanced up at Wyatt before looking across the bar at Savannah. "Excuse me, I've got to take this."

"Go right down the steps," Savannah said, sensing the woman's urgency, "and through the glass slider. It's quiet in the salon. Everyone's up here."

"What about you?" DJ asked Wyatt, as Maggie started down the steps. "What do you do?"

"I'm retired law enforcement," Wyatt answered, watching DJ's reaction.

"Well, thanks for your service," DJ said without pause. "I got a good buddy who retired from bein' a cop out on the left coast; great guy."

"He's being modest," Georgia added. "Wyatt used to be the sheriff here in Franklin County."

Wyatt shrugged. "I gave it up when I married Maggie."

"Too dangerous, huh?" DJ asked, though I knew he was probably fully aware of every detail.

"There were... a lot of reasons," Wyatt answered. "Mostly wear and tear on the body, but it just didn't seem appropriate, being involved with one of my detectives."

Again, he watched DJ to get a reaction that was once more not what he wanted.

DJ gasped and looked toward the steps. "You mean that little wife of yours is a cop? Well, I'll be." He turned to Gray. "And good on ya, for raisin' such a woman."

Maggie came back up, a troubled look on her face, and walked straight over to where we were standing by the bar. She glanced forward, and my gaze followed hers to Alberto, who was sitting at the helm, showing something to Florence on the display.

"There's been a kidnapping," Maggie whispered to Wyatt, but loud enough for those at the bar to hear. "I have to go."

"What?" DJ asked, his eyes cutting to David's, then mine. "Here in this little town?"

She glanced over at Alberto again, then said, "Someone called Apalach PD with a ransom demand."

"They called the *police*?" Savannah asked, surprised. "Don't they tend to avoid that?"

"I know, right?" Maggie said. "Weird."

My phone vibrated and chirped in my pocket, and when I pulled it out, I saw that it was Buck Reilly calling. The time on the screen said it was 1845, so I figured he was calling to say they'd made it to Marathon.

I stuffed it back in my pocket, letting his call go to voicemail.

"Why would they call Apalach PD?" Wyatt asked. "Did the caller say anything else?"

"Only that they didn't know who to make the ransom demand to," she answered, shaking her head, somewhat bewildered. "And for us to find out."

"That's just weird," Wyatt said. "Was it a hard line or cell phone?"

"Cell," Maggie replied. "And it's registered. Apalach PD already contacted Judge Nevis to get a court order to release records."

My phone began chirping once more. It was Buck again. I felt a sudden drop deep in the pit of my stomach as I stabbed the *Accept* button.

"McDermitt," I said, holding the phone to my ear as Maggie and Wyatt started to head for the steps.

"Hey, buddy!" Buck said. "Sorry I'm late, but you know how it is with women and airplanes. Where's my passenger?"

"Maggie! Wait!"

I hurried past Savannah, and I could tell by the look on her face that she'd just thought what I now knew.

Maggie and Wyatt stopped at the steps and turned around.

DJ and David joined me, Savannah right behind them. I glanced back, and saw Florence holding Alberto's elbow, worried expressions on both their faces.

A thousand things ran through my mind at once as Buck repeated the word hello over the phone.

But my major concern was telling Alberto what I was about to do. Suddenly, I remembered the way he'd pitched in the last few months, doing grown-up tasks and taking on adult roles.

I nodded at Florence, and she rose and came to join us with Alberto as I turned to face Maggie.

"We're here to help," I said. "All of us. But you don't know us, never met us, and you know nothing about Armstrong Research. The only reason I'm telling you is because I need *your* help."

CHAPTER TWENTY-FIVE

Maddy had been gone for over four hours. She could be anywhere in a two-hundred-mile radius.

Buck confirmed that she'd never checked in at the airport FBO. He already had her picture—they'd exchanged photos to make it easier and less awkward—and he'd shown it to everyone there, a total of four people, but they'd all been there all afternoon and hadn't seen her.

Maggie was on her cell phone, getting a deputy out to the airport and Wyatt was using his to talk to the rideshare company.

David and Florence were using separate devices, digging up anything they could find, and informing Stockwell of the new development.

DJ was pacing the deck.

"You shoulda drove her," he mumbled.

"You think I don't know that?" I hissed at him. "I'm going to need your help when we find out who's behind this. Looking *forward*, not back."

He stood straight, head back, and exhaled slowly as he pushed down from his chest, with his palms toward the deck, as if he were pushing himself up out of a hole.

"Sorry, man," he whispered. "It's hard to keep it in check sometimes. I got it. I'm cool."

I remembered Charity's warning, *He'll break things.*

Wyatt turned around and came a step closer. "I just got off with the rideshare company supervisor. She was very cooperative and provided time of pickup, route, drop-off location at the airport, even the five-dollar tip Madison gave the driver."

"Okay, we have the information on the original 911 caller," Maggie said, moving closer as she lowered the phone from her ear. "I still can't believe anyone would be so dumb as to call us for help with a crime."

"Who was it?" Wyatt asked.

"Name's Jerome Cook," she replied. "New to the area, originally from Tallahassee. Small-time record, burglary, vandalism, weed. Hangs around with Root Valdi and that bunch."

My head came up. "Valdi? The kid who tried to steal—"

"His older brother, Rupert," Wyatt said. "Root's his street name."

"Other known associates are Lucas Rivera—a local kid, and..." She looked up from her phone. "Tobias Wilson."

Wyatt crossed his arms and exhaled, the first visible tell I'd seen him exhibit.

"Who," I asked him very deliberately, "is Tobias Wilson?"

Maggie's shoulders fell. "He works for my bio—"

"Tobias Frank Wilson," David cut in. "Age thirty-six, male Caucasian, five-eleven, two-twenty-five, brown hair, usually shaved, and brown eyes. A long list of prior arrests and convictions going back to 2003. He served a pair of five-year sentences, one in New Jersey, another in Texas, both for armed robbery."

Maggie was obviously about to reveal her paternal connection to the local crime boss, or former crime boss, if local *gossip* was to be believed.

But this guy worked for Boudreaux. It didn't necessarily make him dirty.

"Circle back to him later," I said. "Cook, Rivera, and the Valdi brothers." I looked over at DJ.

"That's four," he said, nodding. "All locals." He turned to Wyatt and Maggie. "Are these guys any good out in the woods?"

"The Valdis live on the edge of Tate's Hell," Maggie said. "It's a state preserve in the middle of the county. Cook is a cousin of the older brother —the Valdis have different fathers and were given their mother's last name. Yes, I'd say they know it well. Rivera lives in Eastpoint, just across the river."

"Three outta four," DJ said thoughtfully, as he looked deep into Maggie's eyes. Suddenly, he clapped his hands and pointed a finger, startling her. "Name one thing they all have in common."

"Meth arrests," she said instantly. "Rivera, as a juvenile, and the others more recent and more often."

Maggie's phone trilled and she looked at it, then held up a finger before tapping the screen and putting it to her ear. "What do you have, Dwight?"

She listened for a second, then said, "It's okay. Go through them and see if you can find anything that'll help. I'll wait."

She moved the phone away from her mouth as she looked up at Wyatt. "He found two backpacks between a couple of hangars."

"One small blue one?" Savannah asked, haltingly. "And a larger green one?"

She moved the phone back to her mouth. "Put on a pair of gloves and turn it on."

Maggie listened for another moment, then Savannah's phone started to ring. She took it out and looked at it, tears welling in her eyes.

"It's Maddy's phone."

"You can hang up now, Dwight," Maggie said. "Call me back if you find anything else. You're in charge of the crime scene. I'm on my way."

She looked up at Savannah. "I'm so sorry. It looks like she's been abducted. But we have some solid leads."

"Tell me everything you know about each of these four men," I said deliberately. "Beginning with Rivera."

"I don't see the connection," Wyatt said. "If they are the ones making the meth, why would they kidnap your friend?"

Savannah's hand went to her mouth. "Oh, no." She looked at Maggie. "Can you show me pictures of those men?"

Maggie went to work on her phone and in a few seconds turned the screen toward Savannah. "That's Lucas Rivera. Swipe up for the next one."

"That's not him," she said, then swiped the screen. "No... There! That's the boy who tried to sell Maddy the drugs."

"That's the younger Valdi," Maggie said. "He's in jail. For trying to steal Charity's car. Remember?"

"I didn't get much of a look at him then," Savannah said. "But that boy was outside the store where I bought the dolphin painting. And Maddy told us later he tried to sell her methamphetamine."

"On it," Wyatt said, waggling his phone at Maggie and moving to the aft rail.

"What else can you tell me about Rivera and Valdi?" I pressed.

David stepped forward, looking down at his tablet. Then he looked up at me, his face drained of color. "Valdi has a blue 1964 Chevrolet Impala registered in his name. License number—"

"HLB-174," I finished, looking at Maggie. "And it's an Impala SS."

"How do you...? Never mind." She turned back to Savannah. "You're certain it was him?"

"Not a hundred percent," she replied. "But I remember that he looked vaguely familiar at the time, then I ducked into another shop, just as Maddy came out of the one we'd been in before. It had to be him. He was the only one on the sidewalk."

"Released on his own recognizance," Wyatt said, rejoining us. "The court didn't have his rap sheet."

"Again?" Maggie asked in an exasperated tone. She looked up at Savannah. "What happened when he tried to sell her meth?"

"She shoved him away and insulted him," I replied. "The same as any moral person would do."

"Do you think that's why?" Savannah asked. "Retaliation for an insult? Then how would they have found her at the airport?"

"Wyatt, pull up the information from the rideshare again," I said, moving beside him to see his phone. "The route. Zoom in on the drop- off spot."

He pinched and spread his finger and thumb clumsily on the screen, zooming in on the end point.

"He dropped her off between two hangars," he said, then turned to Maggie. "Almost half a mile from the main gate and the FBO."

I pulled my phone back out and called Buck.

"Did you find out anything?" he asked without greeting.

"She's been abducted, Buck. Are you still at the airport?"

"Of course I am," he replied. "What do you need me to do?"

"Ask those four guys there if they've seen a light-blue 1964 Chevy around the airstrip today."

"Hang on."

I heard muted conversation and switched my phone to speaker.

"The Valdi boys?" Buck asked.

"I'll send a couple of uniformed deputies to pick them up," Maggie told Wyatt. "There's more than enough reason to bring them in for questioning."

"Thanks," I told Buck. "That's just what we needed."

"Hey, wait!" Buck said.

"Yeah?"

"Would a black Mustang be involved?" he asked.

Maggie's eyes opened wide.

"Why?" I asked.

"The guys said it stopped just past the gate on the side of the road and when the Chevy went by, the Mustang took off after it."

"Thanks, Buck," I said. "Yeah, that helps a lot."

"Anything else I can do?" he asked.

It'd be nice to have some wings if needed, and I wasn't sure if the county even had a helicopter.

"Are you planning to fly out?" I asked him.

"I'd have pushed on tonight if she..." Buck paused. "Well, let's just say... I'm here."

I ended the call and Maggie nodded. "I'll have deputies pick up Bishop, as well."

CHAPTER TWENTY-SIX

Ten minutes later, Maggie was informed via radio that Bishop was in custody at his home in Eastpoint.

"DJ and I are going with you," I told her.

"No," she answered flatly. "I did reach out to Charity for help, and we appreciate any assistance we can get on the meth case, but we don't know that this is *directly* related, and as far as the law and the courts are concerned, you're both civilians."

DJ gave her a mocking expression. "Civilians?" He pulled his small backpack off the lounge seat and opened a zippered pocket to pull out a black wallet. He flipped it open and extended it to her. "This look like a civilian ID to you, Captain?"

"DEA?" she asked, looking from the ID to DJ's face. "I thought you were with—"

"Side gig," he said, cutting her off. "And if you check, you'll find that Jesse here is still on the *active* roll over at DHS. We're *not* civilians."

His ID was a phony. I had a fake one too. But they were made by the best forger money could buy, and not even the head security people in those agencies could tell the IDs were bogus. If someone were to scroll through a list of all the names of the people in those agencies, they wouldn't find either one of us, but if they *searched* for our names on those databases, we *would* show up, thanks to Chyrel Koshinski, Deuce's computer guru.

Ten minutes later, all four of us were headed across the causeway, me riding with Wyatt and DJ riding in Maggie's Jeep, just ahead of us.

"If they grabbed her for spite," Wyatt began, "why in the world would they call Apalach PD with a ransom demand?"

"You're the one who used to be sheriff here," I said, looking over at him. "These are your people. You tell me."

He glanced over at me quickly, then back to the road. "The Valdis live under a rock. They *are* rocks. Very *dense* rocks. Stupid is as stupid does, I guess."

Maggie slowed as we reached the end of the long bridge, and then she turned right.

"Bishop lives at the end of this road," Wyatt said, turning after the Jeep. "A small trailer park overlooking the bay."

"How long ago did you step down as sheriff?" I asked.

It was a small town, sure. And he'd lived here a long time, so probably knew at least half the population by name.

But a twenty-something kid in the next town over?

"I retired about six years ago," he answered, braking for a stop sign, then accelerating across the road as soon as he was sure nothing was coming.

"So, this kid would've been in his first year of high school then?" I asked. "Maggie said he was clean, except for who he hangs around with."

"Clean *court* record," Wyatt said. "He has a few *juvie* convictions that've been expunged. But they don't seal arrest reports."

I could see a pair of squad cars ahead, one with city markings and the other, county.

"Your department and Apalach PD work together a lot?" I asked.

"Not my department anymore," he answered. "But yes, we all live here, and every deputy knows every officer in town."

"Not a lot of either, I assume."

He went past Maggie as she pulled in behind one of the squad cars, then turned into the yard.

"Small in numbers, yes," he replied. "Twenty-six sworn officers between them, last I asked."

Nationwide, the average was two cops per one thousand citizens, and using that ratio for both city and county populations, one or the other was one or two armed officers short-handed.

But most of the 12,000 residents here lived in a few small towns, and the sheriff's office covered the entire county, which seemed to me to be spread even thinner by geography.

We got out and joined Maggie and DJ, who were talking in front of her car.

"I know this is your investigation," DJ said. "And I know it's a kidnappin', which has nothin' to do with me. But I'll bet you a dollar to a donut that this guy's part of the meth ring you're after."

Both DJ and I were wearing the same black windbreakers that Maggie and Wyatt wore, with FCSO printed on the back in big white letters. She'd insisted on it, "just in case," since we weren't known to other law enforcement officers.

And both of us were openly armed.

I carried my SIG Sauer nine-millimeter in a holster clipped to my right hip, and DJ had a shoulder holster over his shirt, with a cannon tucked under his arm—a .50 caliber Desert Eagle, loaded with snake shot.

"Pistols put holes *in* people," he'd explained earlier, using his own form of logic. "Rifles put holes *through* people. But a shotgun's gonna remove a chunk of shit from the enemy and throw it on the floor."

I didn't argue. With a half-inch bore diameter, *anything* coming out of it would be lethal.

"Give me two minutes," I said, glaring at the Mustang parked in front of the trailer with the sticker in the windshield.

It was the same car I'd watched Maddy get into.

The guy driving it had shaken her and Alberto's *hands*.

"Yeah," DJ agreed. "We'll get him to confess to killing his own sister."

"Um, actually," Maggie said, "his sister overdosed on Oxy about a year ago—Karin Bishop."

DJ's eyes widened. "The Antoine Nucci—"

"I knew it!" Maggie exclaimed, kicking DJ's left shin with her booted foot. "You're the one-legged guy who was here with Charity!"

He fell against the Jeep. "Wrong leg!" he exclaimed, bending to rub the spot where she'd kicked him.

"It's your case," I told Maggie, ignoring him. "Your town. DJ and I are just observers. But we know things you don't, so if this guy *accidentally* gives up something either of us catches, and you don't pick up on..." I paused and looked at DJ. "We're both very skilled interrogators." Then I turned back to her and added, "So if you ask for our help in questioning, we can do so from the standpoint of Drug Enforcement or Homeland Security."

She looked up at me for a moment. She had a question in her mind. I gave her the time she needed to put her thoughts into words.

"You work for DHS, and he's with DEA, but you both work for Armstrong?"

"It's complicated," I said.

DJ's voice dropped an octave as he became serious. "By that, he means we don't work *for* anyone. Our federal salaries barely cover dockage and fuel. You've *seen* his boat."

As if a light went off behind his eyes, Wyatt's face lit up. "You're *not* motivated by income."

"Through our work with Armstrong Research," DJ began, "we can make a much bigger difference in the world without adhering so much to parent agencies' rules of engagement. Now, we *could* just leave these jackets in the car. And ya don't have to identify us at all while you leave the room. The girl's been gone almost five hours, Captain. The clock's tickin'."

Maggie glanced up at Wyatt, then at me. "Leave the jackets."

We quickly removed the windbreakers and tossed them through the open door of Maggie's Jeep.

"Oh, yeah," Wyatt said with a half grin. "*Now* you look like cops."

I glanced over at DJ in his pressed jeans and tropical shirt. I could see by his expression that he didn't think much of my khakis, blue-and-white striped sailor shirt and blazer, either.

He shrugged. "If it comes up, just say we're from Miami. Crockett and Tubbs."

Wyatt chuckled as Maggie led the way to the trailer's little patio and steps. There was a small fire ring in the front yard with brand-new lawn chairs around it. I looked out back, expecting to find a broken-down, seventies muscle-car with the hood up, but there was nothing but a hammock in a metal frame and a grapefruit tree.

Like the one at Gray's boatyard, this one was also half covered in very ripe fruit, with a dozen or more rotting on the ground beneath it.

Two uniformed cops stood in the living room as we entered. A young man, who I assumed was Leo Bishop, sat handcuffed on a couch that was flanked by a pair of matching leather recliners, all facing a massive, wall-mounted TV with a gaming console on a table below it. The wires from the console ended with four controllers on a coffee table in front of the couch. The table was hardwood, not laminated pressboard, and it had a magazine storage space inside.

Nothing in the room was cheap.

The trailer itself was old and rundown, as was the carpet, which held a visible and well-worn path that didn't fit the furniture arrangement.

Everything was brand new.

"Is this our man?" Maggie asked the deputy.

"Yes, ma'am," he replied. "He's been frisked. He's clean. Found his wallet and ID in his back pocket." He extended a hand with an evidence bag, which Maggie took. "When we rolled up, he was smoking something in that pipe that we both suspected was methamphetamine."

DJ looked over at Maggie and grinned.

She opened the seal on the bag and put her nose to it. Then she extended it to DJ before turning to face the deputy again. "Did you Mirandize him?"

DJ sniffed the contents as well and handed it back to her with a nod.

"Yes, ma'am," the young deputy replied. "And placed him under arrest for suspected drug possession."

She turned to the kid on the sofa and let out a soft sigh. "Mr. Bishop, my name is Captain Margaret Hamilton, chief investigator for the Hamilton County Sheriff's Office. You're under arrest for the use and possession of methamphetamine and possession of drug paraphernalia."

"Ain't no possession," he said nervously. "I found that thing out front and picked it up just as those guys pulled inna my yard."

Maggie stepped closer, looking down at the table. I followed her gaze and saw about half an inch of a pack of cigarette rolling papers sticking out of the closed lid.

"It seems there's more paraphernalia right under here," she said, opening the lid.

Bishop slumped into the couch as the rolling papers toppled into the table.

In the magazine storage space was a small electronic scale, a box full of tiny plastic bags, and another box that held a good dozen of those same little bags, all marked with a number and containing a tiny rock or crystal.

She turned to DJ and me. "May we speak outside?"

Wyatt followed us out and over to Maggie's Cherokee, where she turned to face DJ.

It suddenly *dawned* on me how incongruous our little group was.

Maggie was a foot shorter than the three of us and the only woman, but there was no doubt she was in charge.

Wyatt might have been at one time, and probably was at home, but I could tell by their posturing that his stepping down as sheriff hadn't been easy and had probably caused more than one squabble between them.

"We want a quick end to this," she said to DJ. "He's never been in any serious trouble before, but he has been arrested twice. The judicial outcome of those arrests was sealed by the juvenile court, but the arrest records are still there. I'll let you question him, alone, under one condition."

Wyatt looked down at her, surprised. "You're going to let a couple of feds—"

She wheeled on him. "The girl's been missing since the afternoon, Wyatt. Look closely at the data the rideshare company sent. He was already gone when she ended the transaction with the tip. It's dubious evidence at best and there's no way the DA will act on just that. You taught me to follow the evidence and you showed me when what I had wasn't enough to take to the DA. So maybe the fear of federal drug charges will loosen his tongue."

I hated it when Savannah used my own logic against me, and I could see in Wyatt's eyes she'd bested him with his.

"What's the condition?" DJ asked her.

"You can't actually hurt him," Maggie answered. "I'm guessing your parent agencies, like Charity's, don't even know you're here. You'll have to question him within the constraints of your badges. If he asks for an attorney, the interview is over."

"All zen-like, man," DJ said, glancing over at me.

"You be zen," I said. "I'll just be me."

"That's exactly what I'm countin' on," DJ replied, heading toward the steps ahead of Maggie and Wyatt.

CHAPTER TWENTY-SEVEN

I followed behind them, a slow rage building in the pit of my stomach as we reentered the trailer. The air inside was cooler, but there were so many foul scents it was hard to figure out where that came from.

"Remove his cuffs and leave," DJ ordered, when we went back inside.

"Wait...what?" the city cop protested.

"Uncuff him, Jim," Maggie said. "We're going to wait outside."

Reluctantly, the officer removed the handcuffs and followed Maggie and Wyatt out the door.

DJ's hand went quickly to his shirt pocket, right next to the grip of the big pistol. Bishop jumped and DJ grinned, having gotten the reaction he wanted. He pulled his wallet from the shirt pocket, flipped it open, and tossed it onto the side of the table closest to Bishop.

"I'm Special Agent Martin," DJ said. "And this big ugly guy is my partner, McDermitt. And if you even *think* about those talkin' M&M commercials, he's gonna clobber you."

Bishop looked down at the ID, then up to DJ. "DEA?"

"We're out of the Miami office," DJ said, moving to a recliner and plopping down in it, one leg over the wide armrest. "Hey, this is comfortable, man."

I remained standing.

DJ sat up and leaned forward. He picked up one of several games on the lower shelf and looked at it, then tossed it onto the table and looked at another. "*Counter Strike*? *Left for Dead*? Ya know these are just games, right? In real life there ain't no do-overs. Dead is dead." He leaned forward, big arms resting on his knees. "I understand ya lost a sister. I'm sorry for that. I can't imagine the pain of losin' someone so close and so young."

Bishop swallowed hard.

"Now, take my friend here," DJ continued, leaning back again, and nodding toward me. "Twenty years as a Marine sniper... fourteen confirmed kills in Desert Storm and the Mog, right?"

I stood with my arms crossed, eyes fixed on Bishop's, and simply nodded.

"Did any of those guys whose lives you ended get another life after you blew their brains out?" DJ asked.

I shook my head very slowly, my eyes boring holes through the back of Bishop's skull.

"See?" DJ asked. "No second chance in real life. You know the difference between real and fantasy, son?"

Almost as if he feared I'd reach over and strangle him if he looked away, Bishop carefully moved his gaze to DJ.

"You can't hurt me," he croaked. "I've been placed under arrest."

DJ looked up at me, presumably puzzled. "Did you arrest this guy, Jesse? I know I didn't."

"The cops," he blurted. "They—"

"Aren't here anymore," I finished, enunciating each word unhurriedly, keeping my voice low and menacing.

It was the standard good cop-bad cop routine. One pretended to buddy up to the suspect to gain trust, and the other pretended to want to pull the suspect's heart out of their chest and let them watch the final beats.

DJ was pretending, but I wasn't.

"Leonard," DJ said, "or can I call you Leo?"

The kid nodded.

"It's like this, Leo," DJ said, reaching into the table and pulling out a handful of those little baggies with the rocks in them. He looked at them, dropping them one by one back into the box. "Let's see what we got here. Here's .97 grams, and my nose tells me it's ice. This un's 1.02... here's .99...." He paused and then lifted the scale out. "Yeah... This ain't just about possession of a controlled substance anymore, son. Ya see, we know about the four labs up in the National Forest."

What little color remained in Bishop's face faded.

"We know about your three partners in crime too," DJ added, then glanced at the gaming station. "I bet their fingerprints are all over those controllers, eh, Leo?" He tossed the scale on the table, and it almost fell into the magazine storage area, coming to rest hanging over the edge. "And we know about Tobias Wilson, kid."

The look of both hatred and fear on Bishop's face when DJ mentioned the name was all he needed.

He grinned at the kid. "And we got you stone-fuckin'-cold for manufacturing and possession of more than an ounce of meth, I'm guessin, *with* intent to distribute. Those are felonies, son. That's why it's me and my partner talking to ya and not those local yokels outside."

"I think I need to talk to a—"

"Ain't no mouthpiece gonna get you outta this," DJ said, calmly, nodding down to what looked to be fifteen or sixteen grams of meth, individually packaged in roughly one-gram bags.

"The local cops seen you smokin' it," DJ went on. "That's probable cause, right there. They could tear this place apart if they wanted. No warrant needed. Even if seein' ya smokin' it wasn't enough, seein' them rollin' papers sure was reason enough to look inside that table. You're goin' up to Raiford, and that's just about the end of this story." He glared coldly at the kid. "How long some fat-ass bubba gets to use you as his little bitch depends on you."

"Wh-what do you mean?"

I bent forward, putting my fists on the end of the table, and leaned in close to him, the tat on my forearm—with the inscription around the spearhead that read *Swift, Silent, Deadly*—clearly visible.

"We also know you're responsible for the kidnapping of a young woman," I growled. "Big mistake for a dope dealer. Manufacturing, possession with intent, and kidnapping—three strikes."

DJ sat forward again. "The locals tell us you're twenty-two. Once we convict you on the drug charges, and there ain't no doubt you will be, you'll be forty-five before you're even eligible for parole." He paused, waiting for Bishop to look up at him. "I'm forty-five, kid. This's what you're gonna look like next time you're free. Deputies are pourin' plaster molds of your Mustang's tire tracks right now, not thirty feet from where they found the girl's backpacks and cell phone, *and* where your buddies, the Valdi brothers, abducted her less than two minutes after you dropped her off. Once your call records are accessed, here in about an hour, I'm bettin' they'll show that you made a call or sent a text to one of them boys just a little before she was kidnapped."

Bishop's face sank further.

DJ's face bobbed up and he grinned at me. "Man, I love it when they text each other. Sure makes our job easier, huh?"

"That woman is family to me," I hissed.

"If ya don't start talkin' now," DJ warned, "I'll just have to take all them cops out for coffee and donuts somewhere, and leave ya here... all alone... with just *him* to keep ya company... until you do talk."

The lid of the table was made of a single hardwood plank, about twenty-four inches square. Hardwood used to make furniture is kiln-dried and usually cut from near the center of the tree trunk, so it shows the growth rings in the wood as wavy lines, evenly spaced.

It also makes kiln-dried, hardwood planks easy to break for a karate demonstration.

I flipped the lid closed, and it fell on top of the scale, which propped it open just a little at one corner. Then I brought my right fist straight down hard on the center of the lid. The plank fractured along one of the growth lines, as I knew it would, and the hinged side flipped back open with enough force that one of the hinges broke. The loose end flew up and struck Bishop in the shoulder.

I looked over at DJ. "I think he misses his sister, Karin. Why don't you make that coffee run while I arrange a little family reunion."

CHAPTER TWENTY-EIGHT

"He's all yours," DJ said, after I motioned Maggie, Wyatt, and the two uniformed cops back in. "He copped to settin' up the kidnap to get Valdi out of his hair. Somethin' about a debt the older brother owed to Wilson."

"Take him in and book him," Maggie told the uniformed cops.

"The Valdi brothers took her first to Wilson's house," DJ went on, as Bishop was cuffed once more and led outside. "Then Wilson called Bishop here and told him to stay away from lab four."

"You think that's where they took her?" Maggie asked. "We know the general area, but never found anything."

DJ waved the packet of cigarette papers. "We got the GPS numbers."

"Where is it?" Wyatt asked. "What're the coordinates?"

DJ read them off the inside of the pack and Wyatt thought for a few seconds.

"That's close to the area that was searched," he said. "Maybe over into the national forest, if I'm not mistaken. But GPS numbers will only get us close. We'd still have to find it."

"We can organize a search party," Maggie suggested, "and head up there within the hour. It'll be hard going at night, though. Half the searchers will probably be eaten by mosquitoes."

"One man could get in faster and easier," DJ said. "If it's the right man."

I glanced over at him. Then my eyes cut to the grapefruit on the ground, and then the rope hammock in its rigid metal frame. The ground beneath it was littered with leaves, and grass was growing up through them.

An idea began to form in my mind as I pulled my phone out and called Buck again. He answered instantly.

"How much fuel do you have?" I asked him.

"They just finished topping me off," he replied. "About six hours of flight time. I'd planned to fly on to the Caymans after the stop in Marathon."

"Hang on a second," I told him, lowering my phone to speak to Maggie. "Does your deputy on the scene at the airport have any kind of night optics?"

"Nothing real high tech," Wyatt replied for her. "Dwight's a hunter, and I know he always carries a spotting scope to check open fields for deer during the off-season, and it *does* have night optics."

"Is he afraid of flying?" I asked.

Wyatt grinned knowingly. "No, I don't believe he is. You want a spotter in the air to guide help in. Is that it?"

"Exactly," I replied. "I can use my phone's screen to show him my location, and he can help guide me straight to the lab. They're bound to have a light on. That far out in the forest at night, there won't be any other lights, and night optics will pick me and the target up easily."

"You mean us and we," Maggie said.

"I can get there faster on my own," I replied, heading toward the back yard.

"And do what?" she asked suspiciously, following after me.

I snatched up one end of the hammock, pulled my knife from my pocket, and severed the line cleanly.

"Disable the suspects and get Maddy out safely," I replied, tossing a few grapefruit onto the hammock. "If you want to follow behind me, you can arrest them or wipe everything out—either's fine by me. But I'm getting Maddy out right now."

"What in the heck are you even doing?" she asked, as I parted the other line and rolled the fruit up, along with some twigs, in the hammock's rope webbing.

DJ and Wyatt joined us as I picked one of the grapefruit still hanging on the tree and cut it in half.

As I squeezed one half on one shoulder of the navy blazer, and the other on the opposite shoulder, DJ grinned. "A makeshift ghillie suit!" he declared.

I grinned back at him as I rubbed the two halves up and down my pant legs. "And a natural mosquito repellant."

"I'm still going to rally some deputies," Maggie said, as I carried the hammock to Wyatt's truck.

"You do that," I said. "I can be in place before you enter the woods, and if I need help, I'll wait." I paused and looked down at her. "But if Maddy's been hurt..."

"And just how do you plan to get there?" Wyatt asked.

I paused by the bed of his truck. "You're driving us."

"Us?" DJ asked. "Like in me and you, us?"

"When we get close," I told him, "I'll go ahead of you. Tonight's a new moon, and I might need someone to guide me in covertly *and* cover my six. They might have a sentry posted."

I put the rolled-up hammock and rotting grapefruit in the bed of Wyatt's truck near the cab as he got in and started the engine.

"We'll put in at the same place we did for the searches," Wyatt said to Maggie. "It's pretty close to those coordinates. I'll wait there for you."

"You better," she said, as DJ and I climbed in.

Maggie headed for her Jeep, while Wyatt backed out of Bishop's yard, then took off back toward the main road.

"Personally, I think you're nuts going in there alone," Wyatt said, as he turned right on the highway. "They call it Tate's Hell for a reason."

"I heard that name mentioned around town," DJ said. "Gotta be a story behind it. Where's it come from?"

"A man named Cebe Tate lived out there about a hundred and fifty years ago," Wyatt answered. "Local legend has it that he'd lived there a good long time, and when a panther got after his livestock, he took his dogs into the forest to kill it. They say he got separated from his dogs and was lost for seven days until he stumbled into a clearing near Carrabelle, where someone found him." He made a left, then looked over at DJ, his face lit by the dash lights. "They say his last words were, 'My name is Cebe Tate, and I just came from hell.' And that's why nobody goes back in there."

"Except folks who ain't bothered by that sorta thing," DJ replied. "Like these backwoods meth heads."

Wyatt looked over at me and I met his gaze for a second, until he looked back to the road.

"Is this what you did in the military?" he asked. "*And* Gray?"

"It was what I did," I replied. "Gray was a regular infantry squad leader, but he probably would've moved into Recon if he'd shipped over for another tour. He had the skills and could motivate his troops. I think he'd've made an excellent Recon Marine."

"He never talks about it," Wyatt said softly, accelerating along a lonely stretch of backroad. "Except when he's around Jim and Wayne, but mostly Jim."

"Ever hear of the *USS Spiegel Grove*?" I asked.

"The artificial reef down off Key Largo?"

"That's where she is *now*," I replied. "But in 1976, she was a dock landing ship in the Med, evacuating innocent civilians caught between warring factions in Lebanon's civil war. Infantry Marines normally do sea duty at some point in their first tour. Gray was aboard the *Spiegel Grove* and helped with the evacuees." I paused and waited for him to look over at me. "A Lebanese girl, just a few years old, died in his arms during the last flight back to the ship."

He stared at me for a moment, and then the right tires bounced on the rumble strip at the edge of the road, making him swerve back into the lane.

"I had no idea," he whispered, looking straight ahead. "Maggie was born that year—July first."

"Witnessing the death of an innocent child will haunt a man forever," I said, remembering all too well the broken body of a young boy I'd tried to save. "If he never told you about it... then you take that knowledge to the grave."

CHAPTER TWENTY-NINE

If I needed to find my way back on my own, I was screwed. Wyatt had taken more lefts and rights than an aged boxer, and after nearly forty minutes we were on yet another abandoned dirt road.

"Hardly anyone even knows about these roads," Wyatt informed us when we reached a dead end. "Over eight hundred miles of roads, with canals on either side, none of which are on any map. They were built by a private owner in the early 1900s, and when the land became the property of the state thirty years ago, some were filled in to allow water to move naturally, and the roads were left abandoned and blocked off."

"Like that little hill you hadda drive over?" DJ asked.

"This whole area is being constantly and slowly eroded," Wyatt explained. "A five-foot hill a hundred years ago is barely a speed bump today."

When we got out and closed the doors of the truck, we were enveloped in near total darkness. I looked up through the limbs of an overhanging live oak and inwardly grinned when I saw stars.

The sky was clear.

"No flashlights," I said. "In a few minutes, our eyes will adjust."

People rely too much on artificial light, but on a night like this, the stars would provide all the light I'd need.

"It's darker than Colonel Stockwell's heart out here," DJ said. "How far away is the GPS point?"

I'd already entered the numbers on my phone's land-nav app, so I opened it in dark mode, turning until I faced the blinking dot at the top of the screen.

"Not far," I replied. "Just over a mile."

"A mile of mosquitoes big enough to carry off a small child," Wyatt answered. "Not to mention snakes, alligators, panthers, and bears. I really wish you'd wait for backup."

"Gators and panthers and bears, oh my," DJ chanted. "We're not in Kansas anymore."

"The reason this road ends here," Wyatt began, "is because we're at the northern boundary of the land once owned by Cebe Tate. Beyond here, you'll be in Apalachicola National Forest."

I checked my watch. "Your deputies are still a good twenty or thirty minutes behind us, Wyatt. DJ and I will be within sight of the location before backup even gets here where you'll be waiting. But I promise, if I don't think I can get her out safely by myself, we'll wait for you."

He went back to the truck and opened the driver's door, then flipped the seat forward, revealing a rifle rack mounted to the back of it.

"You may need this," he said, pulling out a scoped hunting rifle.

I recognized it immediately. Billy Rainwater's favorite gun manufacturer had returned to the old-fashioned lever action, and he'd gotten one of the first ones they made. After firing it, I had to admit, if I had to choose between it and a bolt-action, at least for rate of fire, the lever-action was far superior. Less movement was required—just a quick down and up flip of the wrist, as opposed to moving the bolt handle up, back, forward, and down. There was also no need for the shooter to break cheek weld with the stock, allowing them to keep their sights on the target more effectively.

"Smith and Wesson Model 1854," I said, accepting the lever-gun from him. "A friend let me shoot his just before Christmas last year."

Wyatt nodded appreciatively, then looked puzzled. "It was only introduced this year. In January."

"Yeah, I know," I replied. "His was pre-production."

"It's zeroed at a hundred yards," Wyatt said. "Not that you can see that far in broad daylight out there. You've shot one, so you know the round drops a good eight inches in a hundred yards, so inside that range, aim low. The windage is also at zero, but it's doubtful there's any wind out there. It's chambered for the .44 Magnum."

"A .44 Mag?" DJ asked. "What the hell you hunt around here? Cape buffalo?"

Wyatt shrugged his shoulders. "I've seen gators in backyards that were bigger."

"Thanks," I said, racking the lever and finding the chamber empty. "I hope I won't need it."

Wyatt reached back inside and handed me a box of ammo. "Nine in the pipe, one in the chamber."

I closed the lever, doubting I'd need a full ten-round load, and didn't want to move through the forest with a round in the chamber, safety or not. At most, I expected to find no more than four tangos. So I began feeding nine of the big cartridges in the side loading port, one by one.

"Is that foot of yours going to be a liability in water and mud?" I asked DJ.

I didn't mean it as a slight and hoped he wouldn't take it that way. I just needed to know of any limitations he might have, and the uneven gait when he wasn't thinking about it meant it might slow him down.

He paused while slathering on a very noxious-smelling mosquito repellant. "This is Patty 2.1," he replied with a smile. "Titanium shaft and blade, with a latex-over-composite flexible foot. I can sprint for short distances. Mud might suck a shoe off, but I don't have to worry about stepping on a cottonmouth with a bare foot."

"Patty 2.1?" Wyatt asked.

"The first few models didn't quite do what I needed," DJ replied, then grinned at him. "And 2.0 got eaten by a shark."

I could see the shock in Wyatt's expression. "Well, if a *gator* bites you, I hope it's the leg Maggie didn't kick."

I reached into the bed of the truck and got the hammock out, squeezing more grapefruit juice over my body. At least it gave me a good excuse to burn the Yachty McYachtface attire.

"Why not just use this?" DJ asked, holding up the bug juice.

"They'll smell that from fifty yards away," I replied. "Which is as close as you're going to get."

"And how close do *you* intend to get?" Wyatt asked.

"I once snuck into an enemy encampment and stole food from the kitchen," I replied. "After planting a few listening and tracking devices. I can get close enough to hear and maybe touch them."

I unrolled the hammock on the ground and got to work removing the wooden spreaders at both ends and separating the lines, knotting them close to the ends of the weave.

Using some of the lines I'd cut loose, I knotted loops on either side, about eighteen inches from the end, large enough to fit my arms through, and tied four more pieces to where my ankles would be, to secure the net to my body.

I tried it on and found that the hammock would easily cover my entire body, with a flap I could pull over my head.

Then I cut a few small branches from a nearby scrub oak and weaved them into the hammock's ropes in strategic places, along with small clumps of Spanish moss and pine needles, which easily clung to the gnarly oak twigs. I'd add more forest detritus once I got closer, to better match the immediate surroundings. The last thirty or forty yards, I'd be on my belly with only the makeshift ghillie suit to hide me.

"You ready?" I asked DJ, as I pulled the improvised camouflage suit over my arms and shrugged it into place.

He nodded, and I slung the rifle over my left shoulder, then turned to Wyatt.

"When the cavalry arrives," I said, "tell them to move straight in to the coordinates of the lab. I won't get there for another fifteen or twenty minutes after they get here, so tell them to be quiet. We'll communicate through Buck, and Dwight can relay to you."

"Will do," he replied. "Good luck."

"I'll just follow you, man," DJ said, as I moved to the end of the road and a narrow footpath. "Gators as big as Cape buffalo? That shark, grabbin' Patty like it did, done left me psychologically scarred."

"As quiet as you can," I replied. "And don't lose sight of me."

The path we took looked like it was less abandoned than the road and showed signs of recent movement, probably a game trail. Or it might be how Bishop and his bunch accessed the denser part of the forest.

This close, I didn't want to use a light to check for signs, though.

We moved quickly along the trail, and I checked my land-nav app sporadically in dark mode. The trail seemed to be heading in the general direction we wanted to go, but I figured eventually we'd have to hoof it overland. It was unlikely they'd set up a meth lab right next to a trail, even an unmarked one off an abandoned, unmapped road.

But then again, they had called the police with the ransom demand.

The path, as well as the dead-end road, seemed to follow a naturally elevated ridge, with coarse sand under our feet, scrub and saw palmetto falling away on either side.

After thirty minutes, we reached a spot where the trail turned west, following the limestone ridge. I stopped and turned to find DJ five yards behind me, walking quietly.

"No telling if this trail curves back to the north," I whispered, crouching to look at my phone's subdued screen. High above, I could hear the drone of an airplane flying slowly. "Time to call our eyes in the sky."

DJ took a knee beside me, pulling his own phone out, unlocking it, and making sure to turn the screen away from our eyes.

Buck answered immediately, the sound of his plane's engines in the background. "What took you so long?"

"Says the guy flying a hundred knots through clear air while we walk through the jungle," I replied.

"This nice young deputy here says he can see the bad guys' lights clearly," Buck said, as I put my phone on speaker and turned the volume way down. "Or at least light where there shouldn't be any. He says he just spotted your light, and you're only about two hundred yards from them, due north."

I looked at the navigation app and it showed the distance to target was slightly farther and more north-northwest. Hopefully, the Sergeant Schultz in Buck's plane was a better navigator than the one on *Hogan's Heroes*.

"Roger that," I whispered, knowing that two hundred yards in a dense forest could take half an hour. "I'll have my phone in my pocket, so I can hear you, but its light won't be visible to you. DJ's going to leave his on until we split up about fifty yards out."

"How come I can't go all the way with you?" DJ asked.

I glanced over at him. "You're quiet, but not silent. Buck, I'll just be able to hear you but when I get close, I won't be able to respond. So I'm going to add DJ to this call."

A few seconds later, DJ's phone vibrated. He tapped the screen and whispered, "Okay, I'm on."

"Let's do this," I said, then started through the dense undergrowth, ducking under and around brush and trees and avoiding the saw palmetto altogether.

At first it was rough going. Not so much dangerous as it was time- consuming. Moving through heavy brush quietly is a hard test of proprioception, or the body's ability to know where other parts are without the mind interfering. Babies learn it with a spoon, but not before covering their face with apple sauce for weeks.

Stepping over a low branch, then balancing on one foot to lift the other one over while at the same time, not kicking the twig you spotted with the first step, then ducking under another branch and pushing a third one away before lowering the second foot—and doing it silently, in ever-so-slow-motion—requires a lot more skill than hitting your mouth with a spoon.

And behind me, DJ was doing it with one foot, though perhaps not as silently.

We moved slowly, our eyes now fully accustomed to the low light from the stars. Fortunately, the canopy was low and sparse. Within minutes, we started down an incline and were soon up to mid-shin in swamp water. But there was less vegetation to contend with and a clear view all around.

We continued northward, keeping small and moving slow, trying not to disturb the water. With no other lights to diminish our night vision, we could see the other side of the open swamp. The downside was, we could also *be* seen.

On a moonless night, with no other lights around, pupils dilate fully to allow as much light to reach the optic nerve as possible. Trying to look directly at an object is difficult, because in low-light situations we see more with our peripheral vision than directly what we try to focus on.

With practice, the thousand-yard-stare can be adapted at night to see more and see better, allowing each eye the maximum peripheral vision possible by leaving them unfocused on infinity.

DJ was staying a good ten yards behind me now, using his phone's land-nav app to quietly guide me with voice directions over the phone as we came out of the shallow swamp and onto another low ridge.

I would have preferred better comm devices, but I knew Savannah had employed low-volume cell phone communication a couple of times as an alternative.

When I stopped, he stopped. And I stopped a lot to listen and watch, and DJ didn't have to ask why.

Being in the open meant trusting my camouflage. All DJ had was some mud smeared over his forehead and cheeks. Of course, his beard helped break up the outline of his face, and the fruit-juicy shirt looked dark and mottled in the starlight.

The hammock wasn't ideal camouflage, but crouched low and standing still, I knew that under these conditions, anyone seeing me would see a dead tree trunk sticking up out of the water, its broken limbs draped in Spanish moss and ferns.

I was hyper-aware, my eyes catching a night bird flitting from branch to branch fifty feet away, and my ears picking up the sound of its wings.

I was also aware that even though I could hear the minute sounds DJ made behind me, nobody else would, unless their adrenaline was also elevated, and they knew how to channel it.

Reaching the other side of the swamp, I paused and knelt on one knee, pushing the tied ends of the hammock back off my forehead. I raised a hand and signaled DJ forward.

The hammock, draping down from my shoulders, covered my entire body leaving my face visible, but with the loose end pulled up over my forehead, I knew it was enough to break up the outline of my head from a distance.

When I got closer, I'd pull the whole thing up over my head. The hammock's woven netting was far easier to see through from the inside than the outside.

DJ knelt silently beside me as I holstered my SIG. He did the same with the big Desert Eagle, then took his phone out once more, unlocked the screen, and held it over his head.

"Dwight said you're sixty yards away," announced Buck's muffled voice from my pocket. "Due north."

"Let's get a little closer," I whispered. "Top of this ridge."

I rose and started moving up the slight rise.

From the top of the ridge, the ground sloped down again, but this time, it looked like it ended at a creek instead of swamp. I could hear moving water.

We continued downhill as noiselessly as possible, the limestone ridge giving way to a pine forest, until we reached, then forded the creek. As we made our way deliberately through open woodland carpeted with soft needles, I heard something ahead, movement maybe.

I stopped and dropped to a crouch.

There was a laugh, and quiet voices.

DJ knelt beside me.

"I go alone from here," I whispered.

DJ turned his head slowly, looking all around. Finally, he pointed at a tangle of pine needles over a long-dead tree trunk. "I'll cover you from there."

I waited until he got into position a little ahead and to the left of the direction I'd heard the voices. When he was in position, he signaled me to advance.

There was another laugh.

I unslung the rifle, dropped into a rifle crawl and proceeded slowly forward, up the slight embankment from the creek.

I hadn't gone far when a light came into view. A couple of minutes later, I could see some sort of encampment, a dim light illuminating the undersides of the lower tree branches.

Moving my chin toward my chest but not taking my eyes away from what looked like a small, open campsite just over the next rise, I whispered, "DJ, move up. I have eyes on target."

CHAPTER THIRTY

I couldn't see exactly where the light was coming *from*—it was just there, bathing a large area with a soft luminescence. Like seeing the glow of a campfire but not the fire. It was steady though, not like a flickering flame, which told me it was probably a lantern or light of some kind, close to the ground.

The scope didn't help. The camp seemed to be just over another slight rise no more than forty yards away, so anything at ground level was invisible to me.

DJ appeared beside me, almost like a ghost in the night. "Dwight just got a message from his boss," he whispered, his shoulder pressing into mine and his head no more than four inches away.

"They're just over the next rise," I whispered as softly as I could. "A lantern or flashlight sitting on the ground."

He held his phone to his ear and listened for a moment. My own was turned all the way down.

"The posse is entering the woods at the trailhead," he whispered. "Wyatt, Maggie, and four uniforms."

"Roger that," I whispered. "Let them know the GPS numbers are off by a good bit."

DJ moved his phone to his mouth and whispered quietly. “Buck, tell them to ignore the GPS numbers and stick to the trail until it turns sharply west, then proceed due north. They’ll cross a small, swampy area, then a ridge, then a creek. That’s where we are.”

“I’m moving in closer,” I whispered, going back down to my belly and starting up the low hill.

I paused several times to listen, as well as to toss a few pine needles onto my back, where they easily became tangled in the oak twigs and netting of the hammock.

I noticed a slight chemical odor when I did so, and I lowered my face to the needles in front of me.

The scent was stronger; the forest floor was covered in it.

I hoped burning my clothes would be enough.

Was Maddy here? If so, how long had she been exposed to the noxious chemicals?

Another five endless minutes of crawling put me within twenty yards of the camp.

With the scope at its lowest magnification, I moved it around the brightest part of the camp and found what looked like a trapdoor propped open on the forest floor.

They really *had* built the labs underground.

The light I was seeing was being reflected off leaves and branches from an underground light source.

Moving the scope, I saw a pipe sticking up out of the ground and followed it up to a low-hanging oak branch, where it was tied off.

A chimney of some kind? I wondered. *Were they making meth right now?*

Sweeping the scope farther to the right, I saw nothing more. Then a voice said, "Gimme another."

I moved the scope back to the left, and could just make out two figures, sitting on the ground about ten feet from the trapdoor.

They were so close, I couldn't get both of them in the field of the scope. In hindsight, it would have been better without the scope, but it was too late to remove it now. The slightest click from the rail would alert them.

In the dim light, I couldn't tell if they were facing toward me or away from me. One was bigger than the other. A lot bigger.

Suddenly, the big guy lit one of those torch-type lighters and hunched forward.

They were facing away from me.

I watched as he lit a pipe or something, the other guy giving him encouragement.

"Shine ya light, man," the guy with the pipe croaked.

A bright light came on as the other guy rose and pointed his phone down at the ground.

I quickly scanned the whole camp again, looking for anyone else. The light from the guy's phone illuminated a pair of hunting rifles I hadn't seen, leaning on the trapdoor.

The big man leaned over, and I could see Maddy, lying on her back on the ground, as the man bent over her face and kissed her.

My gut wrenched and my thumb moved to the safety.

But it wasn't a kiss, I realized, as the man sat back, blowing a cloud of smoke from his mouth, laughing. The other guy was also laughing, as Maddy's body spasmed in fits of convulsive coughing, expelling smoke.

Without hesitation, I rose to a standing position, racked the lever loudly, and began advancing quickly, no longer concerned with noise, but inviting attention.

I wanted them to hear and see me coming.

There was a loud crack from a large tree branch under my heel, and both men scrambled quickly toward the trapdoor and the rifles.

I heard DJ flanking me to the left, and knew he was advancing also, that big cannon of his leading the way.

Continuing steadily forward, time seemed to stop as my mind ramped up, taking everything in and processing it at lightning speed.

The bigger guy was quick on his feet and reached the trapdoor first, grabbing up one of the guns.

He turned, but I held my fire, still advancing methodically in a straight line, finger alongside the trigger guard.

His night vision was ruined by the bright light of his buddy's phone, and I was seeing clearly.

His first shot was far to my right as the second guy came up with the other rifle. As *he* raised the weapon and aimed, my finger moved to the trigger and pressed it.

The big .44 Magnum cartridge ripped a hole in the quiet forest before tearing through the bigger man's chest, just as he fired a second shot wildly into the air.

I racked the lever as I moved the scope to the second man. His aim was closer than the first guy's and when he fired, I heard the bullet thud into an oak just ten feet away.

But before I could press the trigger, two booms rang out from my left, and the smaller man spun around, falling to the forest floor.

The cracking sound of a small caliber weapon to my right was followed instantly by a metallic ting, then the whine of a ricocheting bullet to my left.

I spun to see another man, halfway out of the hole, as I heard the thud of DJ's body hitting the ground.

When my scope found the third shooter, I recognized the face of the kid who'd tried to steal Charity's car, lit grotesquely from below.

But my brain had already sent the electrical impulse to my finger, which pressed the trigger.

Lee Valdi's face disappeared in a pink mist.

CHAPTER THIRTY-ONE

Standing in the open, covered with the hammock, I looked quickly all around, taking everything in. Then I did another deliberate turn as I moved toward where DJ had fallen.

Nobody within the pool of light was standing, and only he was moving.

"I'm okay," DJ muttered, slinging his bad leg around in front of him in a sitting position. "He shot Patty. Go check on Madison."

I went to the trapdoor first. Valdi's body lay at the bottom of the hole, filling most of the empty space next to a camp stove on a couple of milk crates.

There was nobody else in the hole. So I hurried over to Maddy, who was lying on her back, still coughing, but appearing unconscious.

I knelt beside her and quickly untied her hands and feet.

She stopped coughing, and I lowered my head to her chest. Her heartbeat was very rapid, thundering like a crash of rhinos. Her breathing was also fast and raspy.

"Is she okay?" DJ asked, dropping down beside me, scanning the area for threats.

I could hear excited voices from DJ's phone, but it was turned too low to understand.

"They were blowing the smoke from a meth pipe into her lungs," I replied, untying the hammock netting, pulling it off my shoulders, and casting it aside. "Pulse is fast and her breathing's hard and labored."

DJ got his phone out and turned it up, switching to speaker as Maggie finished talking. "...him we're on the way."

"I hear you," I said to her, as I lightly patted Maddy's face. "Three tangoes are down. We need medevac now!"

Maddy started coughing again, then she gulped for air as her eyes fluttered open, unfocused.

"Maddy, it's me, Jesse. Wake up. You're safe."

Her eyes found mine and she reached up feebly, grasping my shoulders. "Jesse?"

She began sobbing uncontrollably as I pulled her to my chest and held her tightly. "You're safe now, Maddy. We're going to get you home."

Off in the distance, I could hear the sound of several people running headlong through the swamp to the south.

DJ stood precariously, waving his phone's light. "Over here!"

I could see the bullet hole in his pant leg, halfway between his foot and knee. And there was blood just above it.

Wyatt was first to leap across the creek and come charging up the low hill, handgun drawn. Two uniformed city cops were right behind him, also with sidearms drawn. Maggie ran up the hill behind them, carrying a .410 shotgun with two deputies accompanying her.

"Everything's secure," I said, lifting Maddy to a sitting position. "We have to get her to a hospital and DJ's bleeding."

"No, I ain't," he protested. "He hit the shaft."

"I think it ricocheted up," I said, turning to Wyatt. "You guys have a helicopter?"

"Son-of-a..." DJ muttered, hiking his pant leg and looking down.

"Somebody say they need an emergency evac?" Buck's voice came over DJ's phone.

I pulled my own out and turned up the volume. "Is it possible, Buck?"

"It'd be nice of you to check it out before I put her down," he replied. "But yeah, there's a lake very near you and time is of the essence."

"If it's the swamp we traversed getting here," I warned, "it's really skinny, just a foot."

"Farther north from you," he replied. "Maybe a quarter mile. Dwight says it's a deepwater lake, nearly a mile across, with a horse pasture just to the east for a shallow descent. I won't use half the lake. He says it's a state-run horse ranch for tourists. So, one of your cop friends there might want to give them a heads-up before I stampede their herd."

A horse ranch, I thought, my mind flashing back to the carcass we'd encountered forty miles offshore.

"The lake at the dude ranch," the city cop Maggie had called Jim said. "We used to fish there as kids. I'll call it in to let them know."

I stopped him. "Ask if they've had a horse go missing in the last week or so."

"Huh?"

"Humor me," I replied.

Wyatt and Maggie spent several minutes examining the bodies. She knelt down closer, pointing out several things on both the bodies *and* the guns. Then Wyatt rose and came back to join us.

"I'm going back with you," Wyatt said. "How many seats does that plane have?"

"With Dwight aboard," I replied. "Six more, but he can't get everyone out."

"Maggie's staying behind until the ME arrives," he said. "Along with her two deputies."

Jim returned, looking puzzled. "How'd you know about the missing horse?" he asked me. "It disappeared last Thursday, a quarter horse named Scout busted out of his stall in a storm."

"I'll tell you on the plane," I said, bending to pick up Maddy. "Can you make it on your own, Deej?"

"I think it's just a flesh wound," he said, standing and moving his leg around. "Yeah, let's go."

I lifted Maddy off the ground and she clung tightly to my neck, sobbing and still afraid, as we started out down the slope. I didn't know enough about meth use to know what she was experiencing, but paranoia seemed close.

It was fairly easy going, just tall pines and a dense and sometimes slippery carpet of pine needles. Wyatt and both deputies had powerful flashlights and Wyatt walked beside me, his light illuminating my path.

"Tell me what happened," he said softly, holding his phone out in front of him. "Maggie's listening."

"When I saw them," I grunted, "they were blowing smoke... from a meth pipe... into Maddy's lungs."

I knew Maggie and Wyatt were faced with a dilemma. They had multiple shooting victims who were believed to be kidnappers, and who were killed by someone not with their department.

"She was bound," I said. "Hands and feet.... They laughed while she coughed."

"Then what happened?" Maggie asked over the phone.

"They spotted me," DJ said. "And grabbed up their guns."

I looked over at him and he gave me the slightest of nods.

I'd intentionally sought their attention, knowing they'd go for the guns. And I'd waited until they'd both raised their weapons and fired before I returned fire.

I knew the forensic evidence would show that.

"The bigger of the three... fired as I rose," I lied. "I shot him in the chest."

"The second guy shot at me," DJ added. "I returned fire, and he went down."

"Lee Valdi was in the hole," I grunted. "He came up shooting."

"And you shot him between the eyes," Wyatt finished.

"With your rifle," I added.

"And what did you return fire with, Agent Martin?" Maggie asked.

"My two shots were .50-caliber snake shot," DJ replied.

Wyatt moved his phone to his ear. "Get all that?"

He listened for a moment, then ended the call, just as we came out of the pine forest onto a narrow beach on the shore of a wide lake.

As we walked out onto the sand, I could hear the engines of Buck's plane to the east.

I started to kneel in the sand when suddenly, behind us, came the report of two gunshots.

Maddy clung tightly to my neck.

"It's okay," Wyatt said, grinning at DJ. "That was Maggie's shotgun; she doesn't like snakes either."

Could the two of them be doing damage control already? I wondered. I'd shot two men with Wyatt's rifle and DJ dropped the third with what was basically shotgun pellets from a .50 caliber handgun, meaning no ballistics.

Maggie carried a .410 shotgun. Very close to the same caliber.

I could see Buck making a slow flyover of the lake, landing lights on and a bright spotlight creating an elongated pool of light moving across the water's surface. He added power about halfway across the lake and banked sharply to the right as he climbed.

"He's checking for obstacles," I said.

"I think I can stand," Maddy said. "If you help hold me up."

I looked down at her and smiled, then gently lowered her to the ground. She wobbled a little, then her knees started to buckle, but with my arm around her waist, she gathered herself quickly.

Buck came in low over the field, flared at the shoreline, and brought his Goose down softly onto the water.

A few minutes later, he killed the engines as the plane drifted toward us, then at the last instant, he kicked the rudder right and the plane began to turn as it grounded on the bottom.

Dwight Schultz opened the rear hatch and sat down, then slid off into the water, which only reached his waist.

"Water's shallow!" he shouted. "Come on."

We quickly waded out into the dark lake, and I picked Maddy up again. Waist deep on a man as tall as Schultz was too deep for her in her condition.

Dwight climbed back aboard, then knelt at the hatch with Buck to help her get aboard. I came right up behind her, guided her into one of the backseats, then sat next to her, putting an arm around her shoulders.

"Um, Buck said you're a pilot," Dwight said, as DJ climbed in.

"Yeah," I replied.

"Scares the bejesus outta me," he said. "Maybe you oughta—"

"I'm staying here with Maddy."

"I'll sit up front," DJ said, squeezing past Dwight as Wyatt and the others boarded.

The former sheriff pointed to two seats for the two Apalachicola cops, then sat down with Dwight across the aisle from them as Buck pulled up the lower part of the door, then closed and latched the upper part.

"We'll be out of here in three shakes," he said, following DJ to the cockpit. "Back to the airport, right?"

"Yes," Wyatt answered. "We'll have an ambulance meet us there to take the young lady to the hospital to be checked out."

"And DJ," I added.

Wyatt scowled and went back to talking to Dwight and the two cops, which quickly became impossible once the engines started.

Unlike with the original equipment on my Mallard, the Goose came with reversible pitch propellors, so getting off the shoreline was a breeze.

The first time Buck had demonstrated the ability, I'd had his mechanic, Ray Floyd, order the parts needed to allow my Mallard, *Ocean Hopper*, to do the same thing.

The engines roared, and Maddy clung to me tighter.

"It's okay," I said into her ear, helping her put a pair of headphones on and adjusting the mic in front of her mouth.

I switched our controls to seat-to-seat and put on the other pair. "Can you hear me?" I asked her, putting my cheek to the top of her head.

She nodded as the port engine slowed, then the starboard.

"You're going to be okay, Maddy," I told her. "Nobody's going to hurt you."

She sobbed again as the engines roared once more, and the flying boat accelerated up onto the step. Then she looked up at me with tears in her eyes. “I thought they were from back home,” she said, holding back the sobs, then leaning on my chest again.

“The Keys are your home now,” I said quietly. “You’re safe there.”

The plane broke free of the water and began to climb into the night sky as she looked up at me. “You can’t tell Rusty about what happened.”

CHAPTER THIRTY-TWO

When we touched down at the airport, there was an ambulance waiting on the flight line, red lights flashing. Wyatt was out of his seat before the plane stopped. Dwight and the other two cops followed him quickly to the rear door.

Through the windows, I could see two paramedics, a man and a woman, approaching with a wheeled stretcher.

"Do I really have to go to the hospital?" Maddy asked me nervously.

"It'd be wise," I replied. "No telling what the drugs might have done."

Wyatt opened the hatch as the engines were shut down, and the two cops hurried down the steps, making room for the medics, who came aboard and straight to Maddy.

I rose and moved forward to make room as DJ came out of the cockpit.

"How is she?" he asked.

"I think she'll be okay," I replied, as the EMTs helped Maddy to the rear, where Wyatt waited.

We started to follow after them, but Wyatt and Dwight stopped us as the two cops outside helped Maddy down.

"I need a minute," Wyatt said.

I started to push past him, but he didn't give.

"You were never here," he said softly. "That's what you told us just a few hours ago, remember?"

"And?"

He nodded his head back toward the paramedics helping Maddy onto the stretcher. "I'll ride with her to the hospital, but you two aren't going."

Buck came out of the cockpit. "Is she okay?"

Wyatt nodded. "She's going to be fine. I'm going with her to the hospital, where she'll be treated and released. Then I'll bring her to the dock and all of you will leave Apalach. Maggie says there's no way to explain your presence without divulging names." He looked me in the eye. "If uninvolved civilians arrive at the hospital with us, there will be a paper trail."

"What are you talking about?" I asked gruffly.

"Acting as a reserve deputy," Wyatt answered, "I accompanied other officers on a search party into Tate's Hell tonight, and we found the kidnap victim." He paused, looking deadpan at me. "The kidnappers opened fire. I returned fire with my personal hunting rifle, hitting one suspect in the chest and one in the face. Maggie dropped the third with two shots from her four-ten shotgun. The forensics evidence will confirm our statements."

"I'm going with Maddy," I said, starting past him again.

He put a hand on my shoulder to stop me. "No. You're not."

I looked down at his hand and he removed it. "Look, you guys have been a huge help, and I'm sorry Maddy got caught up in it. But Maggie has decided, and I agree." He paused, searching my eyes. "We don't know you, and you were never here."

He was right, and I knew it. What's more, I knew our IDs were fake, and that if it came down to proving anything, DJ and I could end up facing charges. Maybe even Buck.

"Okay," I replied, "but let me tell her."

"Gray's on his way," Wyatt said. "He'll give you and DJ a ride back to the marina. I'm sure we won't be long, but she needs to be checked out." He turned to DJ. "How's your leg?"

I could tell by his expression that DJ didn't like the situation any more than I did, but it dissolved into one of resignation as he, too, realized the problem Maggie and Wyatt were facing, *and* that they were really sticking their necks out.

He nodded his head. "It'll keep."

I followed Wyatt down the steps and over to the ambulance, climbing in and moving alongside the stretcher.

Maddy gave me a feeble smile. "Thanks for coming for me."

"Look, we can't go with you to the hospital," I began. "But Wyatt and Dwight will be with you. They're good men. Once the docs check you out, Wyatt will bring you back to the boat."

"But I have to work tomorrow," she protested softly.

"Don't worry about that," I said. "Rusty did okay before you came along; he'll hold the fort down for a while longer, and we'll come up with something to tell him."

Wyatt squeezed past me and sat down in a jump seat by Maddy's head. "Hey," he said with a smile. "I'm Wyatt. The drug they gave you is starting to wear off a little. When we get to the hospital, a doctor can give you something that will counteract it, and I'll make sure you get back to your friends as soon as possible."

"Family," I corrected him. "You'll get her back to her *family*, as soon as possible."

CHAPTER THIRTY-THREE

The headlights of Gray's pickup swept through the dense pines as he turned out of the airport. He drove in silence for a while, with DJ sitting sideways in the cramped space behind the seat, his leg and prosthetic stretched out on the little bench seat as he worked on the straps.

"What happened out there in Tate's Hell tonight?" Gray asked me, without taking his eyes from the road.

"Three men died," I replied.

"And the fourth member of their little meth ring's in custody," DJ added. "Just like I said there'd be."

"Maggie stayed out there," Gray said, but meant it as a question.

Wyatt had told Gray what happened over the phone, as well as the basic story that he and Maggie had come up with while examining the bodies of the three men.

"She has two of her deputies with her," DJ said. "And there's likely gonna be a few more, plus the medical examiner."

Gray visibly shuddered. "She's almost died several times," he said quietly. "Wyatt, too. Maggie was lost at sea just a few years back. She has a terrible fear of sharks. We found her the next morning, clinging to a buoy." He sighed deeply. "Her mom and I would love nothing more than for her to quit that job. But each time something bad happens, we support her and nurse her back to health."

Whether Gray Redmond was Maggie's father or not didn't matter. At least, not to him. Any male could father a child, but being a dad was a whole different story. I'd seen for myself that it didn't matter to her. He was and always would be her daddy, and she would forever be his little girl. The bond was established at birth, and grew with each passing day into an unconditional love between a little girl and her dad.

I felt sorry for Bennett Boudreaux.

"You raised a strong-willed daughter, Gray," I told him. "You showed her how to do the right thing and be independent. I know; I've seen it. And she found a man just like her dad."

The brakes squeaked a little as he came to a stop sign and looked over at me. "It's been a long time since she was dancin' on your toes, Jesse. I'm not the same man I was then."

My mind flashed back to when I was a young Marine, newly married, with a baby girl in my arms. Gray left the Corps for the same reason my first wife left me. But, just like my father before me, I'd stayed, giving up so much time for what I believed was right and just.

Two months after my first daughter, Eve, was born, we moved to Parris Island; I'd been selected for Drill Instructor School. For two years, I was at work far more than I was at home, and when I was at home, I'd mostly just slept, physically and mentally drained.

During my two years as a drill instructor, I'd missed Eve's first words, her first steps, and her first fall. Instead of helping my little girl up, encouraging her to try again, I'd been shouting at a recruit who'd fallen on the obstacle course.

Gray finished his tour, performing admirably as a Marine, after holding a dying girl in his arms, knowing there was nothing he could do about it. Then he'd quietly slipped back into his former life in a small coastal town and become a full-time dad.

He definitely *was* the same man now as he was then.

"She's going to be just fine, brother," I told him. "She's as dedicated to her job as you've *always* been to yours—being her dad."

He made another turn, then steered the truck into a parking spot at the park across from the marina. The lights were on aboard *Taranis*, and I realized I hadn't called Savannah since we'd left.

I looked at my watch. It was 0130 and we'd been gone since shortly after sunset.

Gray turned in his seat, looking back at DJ. "Thanks for keeping us up to speed while all this was going on, son. Savvy told us a little about your background." He glanced at me and winked, then added, "Soldier or not, you're welcome at our dinner table any time."

I looked back at him. "You've been communi—"

"Per *your* handler's orders," he said, cutting me off. "I texted Savvy every fifteen minutes, until just now."

We got out, and I saw Savannah and Georgia coming across the lawn toward us.

"Is she okay?" Savannah asked, before falling into my arms. She immediately recoiled. "Eww, what's that smell?"

"Maddy's fine," I assured her. "Wyatt wanted to have her checked out at the hospital. Let's get inside so I can change." I turned to Gray and Georgia. "Please stay until Wyatt gets here. I'm sure he'll want to talk to you both."

We walked back to *Taranis,* where Tank and the kids met us in the cockpit. Tank was the first to retreat from the stench.

"You don't go inside with those clothes on," Savannah said, stopping me at the hatch. "Take them off in the port lazarette and put them in the trash; there are towels and a rinse hose down there."

Alberto grinned and grabbed the key fob from inside the salon. As the others filed inside, he opened the hydraulic hatch. I stepped down to the swim platform and stripped the yachty clothes off down to my skivvies and quickly rinsed my body in the cold freshwater shower. Then I dried off quickly and shit-canned the Yachty McYachtface garb, wrapped the towel around my waist, and climbed out.

"Did they...?" Alberto began, struggling with the words.

I knew what he was trying to ask, and sat down at eye level with him. "They forced her to do drugs, son," I explained. "Beyond that, I don't know yet."

"D-did you—"

"I did what I was forced to do," I said, feeling the sting of guilt.

I'd seen what they were doing to her and became enraged. It really was that simple. I intentionally drew their attention, knowing they would go for the weapons. I choreographed their movements like a dance teacher, then executed them for doing exactly what I wanted them to do.

"You did the right thing, Dad," Alberto said, moving toward the hatch.

I tried not to show the sting I felt at his words as I followed him inside, knowing that wasn't true.

"Give me seven minutes," I told the others, as I made my way through the salon to my and Savannah's stateroom.

DJ was sitting at the settee, his prosthetic lying on the table as Florence tended to the stump of his right leg.

"You were right," he said as I passed. "The bullet hit Patty at the top of the shaft and ricocheted up through the cup, just barely grazin' my calf."

He put his hand into the neoprene sleeve that went up over his knee, poking two fingers through a slit at the bottom and wiggling them.

"Gonna need a new sleeve though," he said. "Or at least some duct tape?"

I went down to the master head and grabbed clean clothes from my drawer—a pair of cargo shorts and a Rusty Anchor T-shirt. Then I quickly showered, dressed, and went up to the salon, just in time to see Wyatt's truck pull into a parking spot out on the street.

"They're here," Georgia said, rising anxiously.

Savannah was first out the hatch, and we all followed her down to the swim platform and over onto the dock, as Wyatt and Dwight escorted Maddy across the lawn.

Florence and Savannah quickly helped Maddy inside, with Georgia right behind them.

"She's been given a shot that counteracts the methamphetamine," Dwight said, taking my arm as I turned to follow Wyatt. "If I can have just a moment, sir."

I stopped and turned toward him.

"The doc said she'll be okay by morning," Dwight said. "The ER here is never busy, and Wyatt's in tight with a couple of the docs."

"In tight?" I asked.

"Maddy was treated and released," he answered. "No name asked for or given."

I arched an eyebrow.

"He's done it a few times," Dwight explained. "First time users; mostly kids. He helps them get off it without any record."

I glanced up the steps, to where the tall former sheriff stood in the salon, talking to Savannah.

"Does he make a difference?" I asked.

"Depends on which side ya look at it from," Dwight answered, as I turned to face him again. "It makes a world of difference to the one out of four or five he's able to get through to. It's the ones he knows he can't help that torture him."

Like the little girl Gray couldn't save, or the young boy I'd failed to rescue.

"At least we got all four of 'em," he concluded.

"No," I replied softly. "You only have one of the four. Those three guys out there in the woods tonight weren't part of the manufacturing ring."

"Wait, how d'you know this?" he asked.

"Bishop said that the Valdis kidnapped Maddy and drove her to this Tobias Wilson's house, where Wilson called Bishop and told him to stay away from lab number four. If those three were a part of it, why exclude the fourth? And if they weren't, wouldn't Wilson's order have also applied to Bishop's three partners?"

He thought for a moment, while looking out over the water, then said, "You're a hundred percent right, Mr. McDermitt."

"I know one of those dead men was Lee Valdi," I said, then waited for him to look at me. "You went to school with his mother; I'm sorry."

"You're certain it was him?"

I nodded solemnly. "And I know Wyatt explained to you and Jim and his partner why I can't testify to that fact. But I'll bet the other two men out in those woods were Valdi's brother and Wilson."

"Makes sense," he agreed. "They kidnapped her and took her out there, warning the guys who ran it not to interfere. But why? She wasn't beaten or molested."

"She insulted him," I explained. "The younger brother. In public. I can also tell you that a profiler advised DJ to look *closer* at Bishop. He didn't like those backwoods brothers, and he was afraid of Wilson. So look at his three closest friends and see if they also have brand-new furniture."

"That'll be Mags's job," he said, as Wyatt came back down the steps with Gray and Georgia. "But yeah, I noticed Bishop's new furniture and stuff."

"Savvy and Flo got her to bed," Georgia said. "The poor girl was almost dehydrated and after two bottles of water, I'm afraid she'll be awake again in a couple of hours."

"The shot they gave her will make her a little lethargic come morning," Wyatt said. "But her head should be clear."

"We'll be shoving off at first light," I said, then turned to Gray. "I'd offer to have you come to the Keys for a week of fishing in the Gulf Stream, Gray, but I don't charter anymore."

"We'd love to have you aboard *Taranis*, any time you like," Savannah said to Georgia. "We'll be cruising for the next couple of years, from the Caribbean to the Mediterranean."

"Great idea," I said, and took a card from my wallet. "We're going to try to do this without hiring a crew, so you'd have to *work* for your passage."

He took my card and looked at it. "That sounds like exactly my kind of vacation. The Med, huh?"

"The Greek Islands in the spring," I said.

"Right now, it's time to get you home," Georgia said, patting Gray on the chest. "It'll be a week for you to recover from all this excitement."

I shook his hand, and the women hugged.

"It was good to catch up," Gray said, then he and Georgia started across the lawn to where he'd parked, his arm around her shoulders and hers around his waist.

He was as much a part of Apalach as the river. It was doubtful I'd ever see him again.

Wyatt extended his hand, and I shook it. "Thanks for everything," he said, then glanced over his shoulder at his father-in-law. "Especially the insight."

CHAPTER THIRTY-FOUR

"The next five days, they're sayin' winds'll be dead out of the east at eighteen- to twenty-two-knots," DJ was explaining to David at the settee, as I walked out of our stateroom the next morning. "The sea'll be flat calm, and on a beam reach I'll make better than five knots all the way to Key West."

"That where you're going?" I asked him, heading toward the coffeemaker, where Maddy was filling a cup.

"For now," DJ replied.

"How are you feeling this morning?" I asked Maddy.

The display on the coffeemaker said it was 0930. Late start, but she probably needed the sleep. I know I did.

"I'm fine," she replied. "Inhaling that stuff was nasty, but those guys putting their ugly mouths on mine was worse. I'm sorry I put—"

"You have nothing to be sorry for," I said, taking her shoulders in both hands. "You didn't do anything wrong. You even checked out his ID. None of what happened was the slightest bit your fault."

"Thanks," she said, giving me a hug. "I called Rusty and told him I was taking a little longer."

"How long will it take you to get there?" David asked DJ.

"Sailing straight through, two nights and three days," he replied, rising and coming toward Maddy and me. "But I gotta get underway soon or it's gonna be three nights."

"Take me with you," Maddy blurted, turning to face him.

"Huh?" DJ exclaimed. "You need to rest and—"

"He's right," I said. "You're—"

"A grown-ass woman," she said, cutting me off. "I've fought off grizzly bears, mountain lions, outlaw trespassers, and land grabbers, Jesse. I need to get home. Your friend called Savannah a little while ago and offered a ride in his plane, but I think I need a couple of days to sort things out."

"I'd be obliged for the company," DJ said. "And I'm a pretty good listener." He grinned at her. "Ya won't have to do nothin' but enjoy the ride and make me a sandwich now and then. *Whole Nine Yards* is well rigged for solo passages."

She spotted her backpacks out in the cockpit. "I'm already packed."

"Packed for what?" Savannah asked, as she led Alberto, Florence, and David into the salon, with Tank bringing up the rear.

"She says she wants to sail back with DJ," I replied, knowing Savannah would quash that idea.

To my surprise, she smiled. "I think that's a wonderful idea. After what you've been through, a few days under sail would do you a world of good."

I gave her a surprised look. "She needs rest," I protested.

"And she'll get it," Savannah countered, then smiled at Maddy. "On a sail across the Gulf of Mexico with a man I'd trust my life to."

DJ's face flushed, then he stood and checked his balance on the prosthetic. "Well then, let's get goin'."

Maddy hugged me and Savannah, then turned to Alberto. "I'll see *you* in a few weeks. And maybe next spring, I'll fly to wherever you guys are, and we can resume our chess lessons."

He hugged her tightly, then smiled up at Savannah and me. "That'd be... cool!"

Beyond them, I saw a black Jeep Cherokee pull into the parking area by the street.

"I think our welcome in Apalachicola has worn out," I said, heading toward the sliding hatch.

"Just Apalach, Dad," Florence said, as they all followed me out to the cockpit. "You sound like a tourist when you say the whole name."

"We *are* tourists," I replied over my shoulder, as I descended the steps.

"Mr. McDermitt," Maggie said with a nod as she got closer.

"Captain Hamilton," I replied in a dignified tone, forcing her to smile.

"Jesse," she said, then glanced at Savannah and the kids, then at Maddy and DJ. "And *family*. I'm deeply sorry about what happened yesterday. I hope you're feeling better."

"I am," Maddy replied. "Thanks."

"This morning," Maggie began, in a more official tone, "based on evidence obtained while interviewing a suspect, as well as information received from a concerned citizen, warrants were issued and Franklin County deputies, along with officers from Apalach PD, conducted raids on the homes of three suspected co-conspirators in the drug ring, apprehending all three without incident, and seizing nearly two ounces of the same drugs we found at Bishop's house. The lab guys will need a few days to determine if the drugs from all four came from the exact same batch, though."

"Are they still out there?" I asked.

"The ME removed the bodies before sunrise," she replied, pushing a tuft of hair behind her ear, "and the forensic techs finished an hour ago, with their findings supporting the statements of all officers on the scene."

"Then we can shove off?" DJ asked.

"There's no reason for you to stay that I know of," Maggie answered.

"Grab your gear," DJ said to Maddy. "We can have the sails up in ten minutes."

She went over to the cockpit to get her backpacks, and I turned to the others. "Would y'all mind checking to make sure she has everything?"

"Oh... yeah, sure," David said, taking Florence's hand and guiding Alberto toward the steps. Savannah followed them.

"Go get ready to cast off," I said to DJ. "We'll be leaving right behind you."

He grinned. "And behind us is where you'll stay," he said, picking up his small pack and extending a hand. "Thanks for the assist, Gunny."

Once he walked down the dock, I turned to Maggie. "DJ will mark this case closed," I told her.

"Wyatt and I don't keep things from each other, Jesse," she said, searching my eyes. "This morning over coffee, he told me what you said to him about my dad. I never had any idea."

"That's what Gray wanted," I said. "He claims that he's no longer the man I knew back then, but he's wrong. In many ways he's even more."

"When did it happen? Were you there?"

"It was before my time," I replied, shaking my head. "Eleven days before you were born."

She considered it long and hard.

The thoughts that must have gone through Gray's mind, holding a dying girl in his arms who he couldn't save, and knowing his wife was at home about to give birth to his own baby girl, must have been soul-crushing.

"The Marine Corps is no longer a part of Gray's life," I said. "Hasn't been for a long time. Let him hoist a beer with Jim and Cowboy and toast those lives lost in their own way."

"To the grave..." she said.

"Or until *he* wants to tell you," I replied, as Maddy came back down the steps with one of her backpacks.

Alberto followed her, carrying the smaller one.

"Straight there and straight back, Son," I called after him.

"I'll leave you to get ready," Maggie said, then hugged me. "I think 'semper fi' is what Daddy would say."

"Always faithful," I answered.

See You

AFTERWORD

What a great time I had writing this story. And what a joy it was to research! Dawn Lee McKenna and I had talked often about sharing characters or cowriting something, but cancer took her too early for us to accomplish what we'd discussed.

A year ago, Dawn's daughter Kat Scheideler came to me for advice on how to keep Dawn's legacy alive, and her request ignited my imagination about what her characters might have been up to over the years since Dawn passed. Kat finally regained control of Dawn's books and business and is now adding to her legacy.

So I decided I wanted to know what Maggie, Wyatt, and the others were up to, and I went to Apalach to spend a week soaking it in as I started writing this book.

Kat, along with Dawn's cousin and editor, Debbie Maxwell Allen, helped me with organizing the facts we knew about the characters, and insights Dawn had shared with each of us, and then we dug into the *Forgotten Coast* books looking for more clues and information.

I had to find a way to connect my characters to Dawn's without it appearing too forced. And the answer was right there at the end of the first book in the *Forgotten Coast Series, Low Tide*.

Although we never collaborated or shared our characters, we did appear as ourselves in one another's books, *Low Tide* and *Fallen Honor*.

In *Fallen Honor*, Dawn was Coral La Roc's aunt, a Key West fortune teller, who actually saved Jesse with a shotgun. And in *Low Tide*, Maggie's dad, Gray Redmond, served in the Marine Corps with a crusty old oysterman named Wayne Stinnett, who witnessed a young girl jump to her death at the end of the book.

Those who know me from my time in the Corps know that when I was an active-duty Marine, my nickname was Cowboy. So in this book, Wayne Stinnett is Cowboy, though the first name is only mentioned three times. Those who know me best, know that Jesse McDermitt is *not* modeled on me, but his good friend Rusty Thurman is. Rusty and I even have the same birthday.

So, if Gray Redmond served with Cowboy, and I am actually Rusty, and Rusty and Jesse served together, then Grey also served with Jesse McDermitt.

It ain't rocket surgery.

Sergeant Gray Redmond was first introduced in *Bad Blood*, my second in the *Jesse McDermitt Tropical Adventure Series*, which was released in March 2024. That was the beginning of the connection that was extended in this story.

It's kind of important, but not necessary, to read *Low Tide* and *Bad Blood* before *Apalach Affair*. You'll find a ton of little Easter eggs in this story by doing so. Or read them after and have that "Aha!" moment.

We dug further into Dawn's books, and discovered Maggie's birthday, which was important in establishing a timeline and age difference between Jesse and Gray.

More revelations appeared pointing to Maggie's mother, Georgia, becoming pregnant while still in high school, so we determined that she, and thus Gray, were only a few years older than Jesse. My fictional connection in *Bad Blood* worked, with Jesse being new in the Corps and Gray, the wise and caring sergeant nearing the end of his tour.

In fact, it worked so well, I had the distinct impression all through the writing process that Dawn had intentionally set this whole thing up, starting back in 2015.

Thanks, Dawn Lee, for allowing me to play with your tribe, if only for a little while. And thanks, Kat and Debbie, for the immeasurable help in finding all the clues and connections she left us.

And also, thanks to Dawn's audience for indulging me with this, I hope I did her proud.

Then there's Apalach.

As I was writing this story, my family and I spent nine days on St. George Island, one of the barrier islands around Apalachicola Bay. We visited the town, where I met Kirk and bought the T-shirt from him that Maddy gave to Jesse in this story.

I walked the same beach where Maggie began her investigation in *Low Tide*, examining the body of the man who'd raped her as a teen. I got a bird's-eye view of the landscape from the top of the lighthouse, walked down the street where Maggie lived, and drank coffee in her favorite haunts. I even indulged in a cold bottle of Mountain Dew on the dock, while looking out over the bay.

And I visited Tate's Hell.

This story was obviously more about the relationship between Jesse and Gray, as well as Gray's relationship with his son-in-law, Wyatt. I couldn't begin to emulate Dawn's style with Maggie, so she became more of a secondary character, and I let Dawn's secondary characters take the lead.

If this is the first time you've met Maggie, Wyatt, Gray, Georgia, Dwight, Miss Evangeline, and Boudreaux, I urge you to pick up *Low Tide*. You won't be sorry.

We took our new pup, Milli, to Apalach with us. She's now a year old and the emotional model for Tank, though she could walk under him and not touch his belly.

Greta and I strolled the beach every morning with Milli, usually in the fog, and once in a light rain. It was March, and the changing of the season, so Greta suggested the fog would be a good character, since I tend to give my settings a personality.

Many thanks to my technical advisors, Dana Vihlen, Alan Fader, Mike Ramsey, Katy McKnight, Deg Priest, and Ron Ramey, who provided valuable feedback on the early manuscript.

Thanks also to my editor, Marsha Zinberg, my proofreader, Donna Rich, and my narrator, Nick Sullivan, who provided the final touches and tweaks the story needed.

This is the twenty-fifth of my stories that Marsha has edited, and Donna's been my proofreader for more than thirty. And Nick's been my *only* narrator since book one.

My dad always told me a man didn't need to be overly smart to be successful; he just needed to surround himself with smart people.

So I did.

A note about Tank for all the dog lovers out there. The breed is properly called the Tibetan mastiff. I know two people who own these gentle giants and both use the term Tibet mountain dog. When I asked them why, both gave nearly the same answer. Basically, they didn't like the word mastiff, and mountain dog seemed to fit their four-legged companions' personalities better. Either way, Jesse will still refer to Tank as being part mountain dog. Keep in mind, he's the same guy who uses such idioms as rocket surgeon, smug druggler, and piece of pie.

Don't forget to visit my Ship's Store, www.gaspars-revenge.com, established in 2015 by my daughter, Jordan. She has links to all the stores that sell my eBooks, audiobooks, and signed paperbacks, as well as T-shirts, coffee mugs, stickers, and other swag related to my stories, including a new T-shirt design featuring *Taranis*.

I'm currently working on *Dominica Blue*, the twenty-ninth book in the Jesse saga, which will be released on December 1 as my fourth solo project of 2024. Then I think I'll take the rest of the year off before starting again in 2025.

Wayne

Made in the USA
Columbia, SC
24 September 2024

42841184R00163